Chase Me

By Tessa Bailey

Chase Me

A Broke and Beautiful Novel

TESSA BAILEY

AVON

An Imprint of HarperCollinsPublishers

CHASE ME. Copyright © 2015 by Tessa Bailey. Excerpt from WRECK THE HALLS © 2023 by Tessa Bailey. All rights reserved. Printed in the United States of America. No part of this book may be used or reproduced in any manner whatsoever without written permission except in the case of brief quotations embodied in critical articles and reviews. For information, address HarperCollins Publishers, 195 Broadway, New York, NY 10007.

HarperCollins books may be purchased for educational, business, or sales promotional use. For information, please email the Special Markets Department at SPsales@harpercollins.com.

FIRST AVON IMPULSE MASS MARKET PUBLISHED IN 2015.

Designed by Diahann Sturge

New York City illustration © wanpatsorn/Shutterstock
Title page illustration © Tatiana Garanina/Shutterstock

Library of Congress Cataloging-in-Publication Data has been applied for.

ISBN 978-0-06-332934-8

23 24 25 26 27 LBC 5 4 3 2 1

*For K-Dee's, the place that got me
through those early NYC days.*

Acknowledgments

*T*o my husband and daughter, for supporting me and believing in me a hundred percent of the time, thank you.

To my fabulous editor, Nicole Fischer, for being excited about these books and loving the characters almost as much as I do. Working together is fun and easy (for me, at least!). Thank you.

To my agent, Laura Bradford, for her valuable guidance and dealing with me when I'm wearing my tin foil hat and strung out from too many hours in front of my laptop. Thank you.

To Sophie Jordan for her amazing encouragement and being an all-around good friend. Thank you.

To Edie Harris for being a ball-breaker and super bossy right when I need her to be. Thank you.

To all my friends who knew me in my early twenties, like Roxy, Abby, and Honey, and still decided they liked me. You guys know who you are. Love you.

Chase Me

Chapter 1

Today's weather forecast: imminent shitstorms across the Tri-State area.

Roxy Cumberland's footsteps echoed off the smooth, cream-colored walls of the hallway, high heels clicking along the polished marble. When she caught her reflection in the pristine window overlooking Stanton Street, she winced. This pink bunny costume wasn't doing shit for her skin tone. A withering sigh escaped her as she tugged the plastic mask back into place.

Singing telegrams still existed. Who knew? She'd actually laughed upon seeing the tiny advertisement in the *Village Voice*'s Help Wanted section, but curiosity had led her to dial the number. Her laughter had stopped abruptly when she'd heard exactly how much people were willing to pay in exchange for her humiliation. So here she was, one day later, preparing to sing in front of a perfect stranger for a cut of sixty bucks.

Sixty bucks might not sound like much, but when your roommate has just booted you out onto your ass for failure to come through on rent—again—leaving you no place to live, and your checking account is gasping for oxygen, pink bunnies do what pink bunnies must. At least her round, fluffy tail would cushion her fall when her ass hit the sidewalk.

See? She'd already found a silver lining. Maybe the shitstorm would hold.

Or not. Over the last week, she'd been on thirteen auditions, trudging on blistered feet between callbacks and will-definitely-never-call-backs, smiling and reciting lines for bored production executives. Toothpaste commercials, walk-on roles for daytime soaps . . . hell, she'd even auditioned to play a mother in a diaper rash ad. They'd all but laughed her twenty-one-year-old ass out of the building.

Too bad they couldn't touch her. Nothing and nobody could. She was from New fucking Jersey.

While Roxy usually kept that fact to herself, she couldn't help but admit that Jersey had prepared her for this constant rejection. It had given her the brass balls to say "their loss" every single time someone in a business suit decided her acting skills weren't good enough. That *she* wasn't good enough. One word kept her going, kept her boarding the subway to another audition. *Someday*. Someday she would look back at this pre-stardom experience and be grateful for it. She'd cozy up to Ryan Seacrest on the red carpet and have a damn good story to tell. Although she might just leave out the pink bunny suit.

Unfortunately, on days like today, when a shitstorm cloud was riding low above her head, following her everywhere she went, *someday* seemed a long way off. Sixty dollars couldn't plug the hole in the shitcloud, it could only keep her eating properly for the next week. As far as her living situation went, she'd figure something out. If it meant taking the bus to Jersey and sneaking into her old bedroom for the night, she'd bite the bullet. The next morning, she'd slip her feet back into her heels and get back to pounding the pavement, her parents never being the wiser.

Through the eyeholes of the bunny mask, Roxy glanced down at the piece of paper in her hand. Apartment 4D. Based on the song she'd memorized on the way here and the swank interior of the building, she knew the type who would answer the door. Some too-rich, middle-aged douchebag who was so bored with his life that he needed to be entertained with novelties like singing bunny rabbits. He'd close the door when she finished, text his main squeeze some emoticon-heavy thank-you, and forget all about this little diversion on his way to play indoor tennis.

Roxy's gaze tracked down lower on the note in her hand, and she felt an uncomfortable kick of unease in her belly. She'd met her new boss at a tiny office in Alphabet City, surprised to find a dude only slightly older than herself running the operation. Always suspicious, she'd asked him how he kept the place afloat. There couldn't be *that* high a demand for singing telegrams, right? He'd laughed, explaining that singing bunnies only accounted for a tenth of their income. The rest came in the form of *strip-o-grams*. She'd done her best to appear flattered when he'd told her she'd be perfect for it.

Would she go that far? Taking her clothes off for strangers paid a damn sight more than sixty bucks. It would be so easy for her to take that leap. As an actress, she had the ability to detach herself and become someone else. Being the object of attention didn't bother her; it was what she'd trained herself for. That kind of income would guarantee her a place to live, allow her to continue auditioning without worrying about her next meal. So why the hesitation?

She ran a thumb over the rates young-dude-boss had jotted down on the slip of paper. Two hundred dollars for each ten-minute performance. God, the *security* she would feel with that kind of money. And yet, something told her that once she took that step, once she started taking off her clothes, she would never stop. It would become a necessity instead of a temporary patch-up of her shitstorm cloud.

Think about it later. When you're not dressed like the fucking Trix Rabbit. Roxy took a deep, fortifying breath, the same one she took before every audition. She wrapped her steady fingers around the brass door knocker and rapped it against the wood twice. A frown marred her forehead when she heard a miserable groan come from inside the apartment. It sounded like a *young* groan. Maybe the douchebag had a son? Oh, *cool*. She definitely wanted to do this in front of someone in her age group. Perfect.

Her sarcastic thought bubble burst over her head when the door swung open, revealing a guy. A hot-as-hell guy. A naked-except-for-unbuttoned-jeans guy. Being the shameless hussy she was, her gaze immediately dipped to his happy trail, although, on this guy, it really should have been called a rapture path. It started just beneath his belly button, which sat at the bottom of beautifully defined ab muscles. But they weren't the kind of abs honed from hours in the gym. No, they were natural, I-do-sit-ups-when-I-damn-well-feel-like-it abs. Approachable abs. The kind you could either lick or snuggle up against, depending on your mood.

Roxy lassoed her rapidly dwindling focus and yanked it higher until she met his eyes. Big mistake. The abs were child's play compared to the face. Stubbled jaw. Bed head. Big, Hershey-colored eyes outlined by dark, black lashes. His fists were planted on either side of the door frame, giving her a front-row seat to watch his chest and arms flex. A lesser woman would have applauded. As it was, Roxy was painfully aware of her bunny-costumed status, and even *that* came in second place to the fact that Approachable Abs was so stinking rich that he could afford to be nursing a hangover at eleven in the morning. On a Thursday.

He dragged a hand through his unkempt black hair. "Am I still drunk, or are you dressed like a rabbit?"

His voice was rough from sleep. Probably not his usual voice. That had to be the reason her tummy did a backflip. "I'm dressed like a rabbit."

"Okay." He tilted his head. "*Should* I be drunk for this?"

"If anyone should be drunk for this, it's me."

"Good point." He jerked his thumb back toward his dark apartment. "I think there's some tequila left—"

"You know what?" *This is my life right now. How did I get here?* "I think I'm all set."

He nodded once, as if out of respect for her decision. "So what now?"

"Are you . . ." She consulted her slip of paper through the round eyeholes. "Louis McNally?"

"Yeah." He leaned against the doorjamb and considered her. "I was named after my grandfather. So, technically, I'm Louis McNally the Second. How's that for fancy?"

"Why are you telling me this?"

"Just making small talk."

"Is this a typical Thursday exploit for you? Get a lot of forest creatures on your doorstep?"

"You'd be the first."

"Well, then. Call me Pink Bunny the First. How's that for fancy?" When he laughed, she was grateful for the mask that hid her unexpected smile. Honestly, this situation was getting more ridiculous by the minute. She definitely didn't have time for this. At one o'clock she was auditioning for a small theater company's ironic production of *Lassie*. Priorities, Roxy.

"You sound cute." He squinted at her, as if attempting to see through the plastic mask. "You cute under there, bunny?"

"Being that your one-night stand from last night sent me here to sing for you, I don't know if that matters," she answered sweetly.

"Cute girls trump all." One dark eyebrow rose. "What was that about singing?"

Roxy cleared her throat, letting the horrifically stupid lyrics imprint on her brain. Lyrics she hadn't written, thanks God. The sooner she got this over with, the sooner she could get out of the suffocating costume and forget this ever happened. Until tomorrow. When she was scheduled to dress like a giant bumble bee. For fuck's sake.

Make every performance count. Channeling Liza Minnelli, she cocked one hip and raised the opposite hand.

To my hot shot honey bunny
Last night we went places and had some fun-ny

You brought me home and we skipped the small talk
Now I'm daydreaming about your perfect—

"Stop." Louis shook his head slowly. "Jesus, please, make it stop."

Roxy let her hand drop to her side. "You better be complaining about the lyrics and not my singing."

"I—sure." He scanned the hallway, looking relieved when he saw that none of his neighbors had overheard. "Who did you say sent you?"

She stared back at him, dumbfounded. Not that he could tell with the mask hiding her face. "You had more than one girl over last night?"

"I was celebrating," he said defensively. "Don't be a judgmental rabbit. They're the worst."

"O-kay, my work is done here." She turned tail—*literally*—and started walking back toward the elevator. Over her shoulder, she called, "Zoe sent me. You might want to write that down."

"Is she the redhead?" Louis called back. When Roxy stopped in her tracks, he smiled to let her know he'd been kidding. Maybe. "Hold up. Can you just wait here a second? I should give you a tip."

As he fumbled in his jeans pocket, Roxy smirked. "Which tip are we referring to here? I *did* just sing an ode to your penis."

"Please don't remind me." He drew a twenty-dollar bill out of his wallet, pinching it between his fingers. "Just one request, though. I want to see your face first."

Roxy felt a stab of irritation. What the hell did it matter what she looked like? Everywhere she went, every part she read for, critical eyes poked and prodded her. Too thin. Too curvy. Too tall. Too short. *Never* what they wanted. And just this morning, she'd been told she had a stripper's body. The fact that this wealthy party guy was holding money over her head in order to judge her appearance only tripled her annoyance. "Why? If you like what you see, will you invite me inside? You haven't even showered off the last girl yet."

He actually had the grace to look a little ashamed. "I—"

Roxy didn't give a shit about his answer. "Would you expect me to be flattered?" She clutched her chest dramatically. "Please, oh keeper of the golden penis, let me worship at your flawless phallus."

"Careful." His shame morphed into irritation. "You're starting to sound a little jealous to me."

"*Jealous?*" Oh, that did it. The shitstorm cloud above her head darkened, lightning bolts shooting through its sides. Kicked out of her apartment, not a single callback in weeks, and leaning toward stripping. He'd caught her on a bad fucking day. Honestly, good days were getting harder to come by, and right now, she could think of only one thing that would help. Wiping the smug superiority off the Penis Prince's face.

She bit down on her lips to plump them up, then reached up and removed the mask. Satisfaction danced in her bloodstream when his jaw went slack, brown eyes melting into a deeper shade. *That's right, buddy. I ain't half bad.* As she strode toward him, he straightened from the doorjamb, a groan working its way free of his throat. He saw the intention in her expression, knew what was coming. It didn't escape her that even though she wore a thick pink bunny suit, he was looking at her like she wore a string bikini. Louis McNally the Second was an interesting character, she'd give him that.

"Jealous?" she repeated before shoving him into the apartment, bringing his back up against the inside wall just beside the door. "Sweetheart, I would rock your world."

Not giving him a chance to respond, she surged up on her toes and melded their mouths together. *Ohhh, snap.* There was zero hesitation on his part, just a long, expert pull of her lips. As if she'd let go of a trapeze and he'd caught her in midair. The kiss hit the ground running, mouths opening, tongues fighting to take the lead. One strong hand found her chin and pulled it down further, allowing him to slant his head and deepen the kiss even further. Shock exploded behind her eyes, and she swayed a little under the wave of heat. *Affected.* He was affecting her in a way she wasn't familiar with. She'd kissed a lot of guys, but she'd never felt dread over the idea of stopping. Louis pushed his tongue deeper, making a hungry sound and sending it vibrating into her mouth. She echoed it. Louder. Her head fell back and he moved with her, keeping their lips locked together, as if he couldn't allow her to get away. What was happening here? She was losing control of the situation. *Get it back.*

Roxy pulled back and sucked in a deep breath. His mouth was damp and parted as he tried to draw in his own oxygen, his face a mask of stunned disbelief. "Who the hell *are* you?"

Swallowing the odd feeling in her throat, she plucked the twenty-dollar bill out of his fingers. "I'm gone."

She blew into the hallway, sensing him staring after her. With as much dignity as one could muster while dressed like a pink bunny, she bypassed the elevator and took the stairs, two at a time.

Chapter 2

Louis split a look between his two best friends over the rim of his beer. Russell looked impressed by his story. Ben, as usual, looked as if he had just short of *one hundred* follow-up questions. None of which Louis had any desire to answer. He wanted to piggyback his hangover with a newer, fresher one and attempt to forget the kiss that had launched a thousand boners, thank you very much. Which is how he found himself in the Longshoreman less than twenty-four hours after tying one on within its four ancient walls. What was that saying about returning to the scene of the crime? Never do it? Well, too late.

"Wait . . . I'm confused. How did she grab the twenty with a big, furry paw?"

Russell groaned. "Leave it to you to get stuck on logistics, Ben. Louis made out with a rabbit. Just appreciate that for what it is."

"It wasn't a make-out," Louis lamented. "It was like a . . . *ha ha* you *wish* this was a make-out, dickhead."

"Bring her home to Mom. She's a keeper."

Ben leaned back in his chair. "How did she get past your doorman?"

Russell's forehead hit the wobbly pub table, rattling the empty pint glasses. "Next he'll point out that it's not even Easter."

Louis ignored them both. Kind of rude of him, really, considering they were both nursing their own hangovers and were still here keeping him company. "Look, she caught me at a bad time. One minute I'm sleeping under my coffee table with a coaster stuck to my forehead, the next I'm talking to a life-sized rabbit." He massaged the bridge of his nose. "I didn't even find out her name."

"Trixie."

"Jessica."

"You two are a couple of gems." He drummed his fingers on the table. "She seemed more like a Denise. Or a Janet. The kind of name a girl has when you can already sense she's your future ex-girlfriend."

Russell nodded his shaved head. "If you had ex-girlfriends. Which you don't."

"Right."

It was true. He didn't usually date girls exclusively. Or ever. Not because he had some kind of rule against it, but he'd been an unwilling witness to his parents using their extramarital relationships against each other, and he'd just been soured on the whole idea from a young age. As long as he remained accountable only to himself, he couldn't hurt anyone. Turn bitter and vindictive. Unfortunately, that unspoken policy had left him feeling kind of . . . lousy lately. All right, just since this morning. When he'd delivered the worst first impression in history.

"Are you saying you're in the market for an ex-girlfriend?" Ben asked, pausing in the act of cleaning his glasses. "You realize the present tense of *ex-girlfriend* is *girlfriend*."

Louis crossed his arms impatiently. "I didn't realize I'd enrolled in one of your English classes, Professor Ben. Should I grab a number two pencil?"

His friends exchanged a look. "So testy tonight, our boy," Russell said. "And over a girl, no less. I might have to track this girl down and buy her a carrot cake."

"Listen, I don't want a girlfriend. Or an ex-girlfriend, for that matter." Louis downed the last of his pint. "But if you figure out a way to track her down, I'm open to suggestions. She and I aren't done."

Ben sighed toward the ceiling, but there was an eagerness to it. He'd gone into teaching for a reason. He loved having all the answers. "This is easily solvable. Ask the girl who sent you the telegram which agency she used. There can't be that many. I didn't even know singing telegrams were still a thing."

"Yeah, how's that conversation going to go?" Russell laughed. "Oh, I know. 'Hey, girl who wrote a song about my dick? I'd like to introduce that dick to another girl. Show a dude some love?'"

"You are an actual idiot."

"Both of you, please. Shut up." Louis rubbed a hand over his unshaven jaw, considering his friends a moment. So different from him. Different from each other. How had they ever become friends, again? Ah, yes. Through the power of beer. Its magical qualities really knew no bounds. Ben, the newly minted college professor at twenty-five, and Russell, the construction worker, oldest among them at twenty-seven, but far from the most mature. Louis, the . . . asshole. *Jesus,* he'd actually tried to bribe the girl with twenty dollars when she was clearly hard up for cash. She must have written him off as a self-entitled prick before she'd even made it down the stairs. He'd just been so desperate to see her face. Associate it with that husky voice, that sharp sense of humor. So he'd momentarily morphed into his father. All in a day's work. He quickly shook off the disturbing thought. "Hang onto your seats, because I have another, equally pressing problem."

"I'm all bunny ears," Russell deadpanned.

"Funny you should say that." Louis lowered his voice. "After she left, I started, you know, *thinking* about her in that bunny costume. Getting her out of it, mostly. I couldn't *stop* thinking about it, actually. And I might have—"

"You didn't."

"Oh, God. You went on the Internet."

Louis squeezed his eyes shut. "So much bad porn, guys. People with cotton tails. Carrots going places they should never, *ever* go. I'm pretty sure I'll die with these images tattooed on my brain."

"Happens to the best of us." Russell leaned forward. "All you need is a good porn cleanse. Replace the bad with good. Do it soon, though. Bad porn festers if left out too long."

Ben gave them both a disgusted look. "Do you two really need porn to get off? How about you try using your imaginations?"

Russell and Louis stared at him blankly before Russell finally broke the silence. "Porn. Cleanse."

Louis nodded. "On it." Even as he spoke the words, he knew nothing would help until he saw her *out* of the bunny costume.

He'd put everything he'd had into that kiss, and she'd walked. It was fucking with his head. Making him jumpy. Where was she now? Why had this talented knockout been reduced to singing shitty telegrams for a living? And dammit, wasn't showing up on the doors of complete strangers a dangerous job? He'd been able to make out her slim form even through the furry costume. If someone wanted to drag her inside their apartment, stopping them would be impossible.

The memory of her shoving him up against the wall blew through his mind. Okay, so she wasn't completely helpless. And shit, now he was back to being turned on with no way of satisfying the craving. There had to be an explanation for this. Girls came and went for him. He appreciated them, treated them well, then he got the hell out. A system that never failed him. Afterward, he spent zero time dwelling or rehashing. None. Yet he'd only shared a ten-second kiss with this girl and he suddenly felt restless. Anxious.

Truth be told, he'd liked her *before* she'd even taken off the stupid mask. She'd had this mixture of confidence and vulnerability that had arrested him the second she'd started speaking. Even with his shittastic hangover, he'd wanted to keep talking to her all day. Figure her out. Then she'd taken off the mask and he'd been screwed. Not in the way he usually preferred.

Big green eyes flecked with gold. Lips that looked like she'd just sucked a cherry Popsicle. Good Lord, he got hard thinking about the way those lips had felt moving with his. The way she'd kissed him until he'd gotten worked up, then pulled back, leaving him dangling over the side of a cliff. He'd been so stunned by his own reaction that he'd let her take off without a word. A rarity for him. He always, *always* had something to say. He was a goddamn lawyer. A framed piece of paper on his office wall said so.

Of course, she didn't *know* that he was gainfully employed. He'd been shirtless and unshaven at eleven in the morning on a fucking Thursday. He'd offered her tequila before asking her name. If she *hadn't* written him off as a clown, he'd be disappointed. In his defense, he'd been celebrating a victory for his firm the night before. One of his pro bono clients, a small business owner from Queens, had lost his family-owned convenience store in the recent hurricane. He'd been unable to get assistance to rebuild, financial or otherwise, thanks to the uncooperative insurance company and a landlord who wanted to lease the space out to a more lucrative business. Louis had worked on the case for weeks, in between the paying clients he was required to take on. As of yesterday, the man had the funds he needed to rebuild, his family's livelihood intact.

Okay, so he'd gone a little overboard last night and slept late this morning. He didn't make a habit of it. Much. Dammit, if for no other reason, he wanted to track the girl down just to correct her misconception of him. All right, maybe he wanted to kiss her again, too. A lot.

He could accomplish it with a couple of phone calls.

"He's considering it," Russell said, breaking into his thoughts.

"I'm considering what?"

"Calling the girl who sent you the telegram to get the name of the agency," Ben explained.

"No. I can't do that. Zoe was a nice girl." Louis racked his brain for a single memory of her. "I think."

Russell shrugged. "Tell her you thought it was an amazing gift and want to send one to your mom."

"To my mom. In the south of France."

"She doesn't know your mother's geographical location." Russell set his empty pint glass down with a *thunk*. "Come on, man. Desperate times. Save the bunny, save the world."

"You're a jackass." Louis signaled the waitress for another round. "And speaking of your donkey brethren, I'm a little too well acquainted with them after I clicked the wrong link this afternoon."

Ben and Russell shivered.

Chapter 3

Holy flying shit monkeys. No fuckin' way.

Roxy's paper coffee cup paused halfway to her mouth. She leaned closer to the computer screen, positive she'd read the Craigslist advertisement wrong. When someone cleared their throat beside her, she realized she'd cursed out loud. Apparently profanity was frowned upon in this Internet café. She'd spent the last few hours here after bouncing around all night between different coffee shops and twenty-four-hour diners, not having an apartment to go to and reluctant to wave the white flag by returning to Jersey. Sleep deprivation must have taken its toll, because she had to be seeing things.

One bedroom available in a three-bedroom apartment. Chelsea. Girls only, please. I'm not sexist or anything. It's just that I don't want to be self-conscious in my own apartment. You know? If you're a man and still reading this ad, it's nothing personal. I just want to hang my bra in the shower without worrying about you judging my cup size. I'm a 32B, so I pad liberally. Well. This has all been very therapeutic. I'm taking applications for the next hour. My address is 110 Ninth Avenue, Apartment 4D. $200/month.

The last part. The price. That's where Roxy kept getting tangled up. In Chelsea, that rent was completely unheard of. A thing of fairy tales whispered about in bars late at night, only among the closest of friends. The unicorn of living spaces. Even a closet-sized bedroom with bars on the window went for upwards of seven hundred dollars per month in Chelsea. It had to be a typo. Or she'd stumbled across the holy grail of rent-controlled apartments, which were usually only advertised by word of mouth. Never on Craigslist. Based on the rambling nature of the ad, she supposed the renter could just be too crazy to attract a well-paying tenant. If so, it was Crazy Pants's lucky day, because Roxy was desperate. She'd consider living with a family of circus performers at this point, convincing herself it would be a good character study.

Her first week in the Big Apple had been a dream come true. She'd nailed her first audition and starred in a national television commercial for SunChips. They'd been going for a youthful angle, calling for her to crunch into a chip as she flopped onto her college dorm bed, then sighing in contentment into the camera. The kind of money it had brought in had allowed her to live comfortably. For a while. It would only be a matter of time before she got her next gig, right? Wrong. No one appeared impressed with her debut as SunChip princess, especially when her competition had resumes that made hers look like a grocery list. They'd pulled the ad after a short run, leaving her without a royalty check.

Her current problem, though? She was *far* from the only desperate, aspiring actress in this town. A fact she knew all too well from the droves of eager girls who showed up to read for the same parts as herself. Tired girls dressed in thrift-shop glamour. At that very moment, she was willing to bet there were hundreds—nay, thousands—of starving artists stampeding their way toward 110 Ninth Avenue. A sense of urgency blooming through her veins, Roxy quickly closed out the Internet screen and yanked her backpack over her shoulders. She was ten blocks away, and the ad had been posted three minutes ago. If she hustled her ass off, she *might* have a slim chance of making it. As she tossed her coffee cup in the nearest trash can, a girl with a pink bandana wrapped around her forehead stood up at the computer beside her. They locked eyes.

"You saw it, too?" Roxy asked casually.

"Maybe."

They both sprinted for the door, ignoring the outraged clerk. Apparently not paying for your web surfing time was frowned upon in this Internet café. Roxy didn't have time for rules, though. Not with the mother of all bargains on the line. With her new semi-dependable job humiliating herself, she could easily afford this place. Screw that, she'd have cash to *spare*, for the first time, well, ever. Acting classes would stop being an unreachable dream and become a reality.

Roxy zigzagged between a crew of delivery men unloading crates from a truck, then leapt over a poodle doing its business. Beside her, pink bandana huffed and puffed. "It's probably already gone by now," she said. "We'll never make it."

"Speak for yourself." With that, Roxy hip-checked her competitor into a group of bushes. "Nothing personal!"

"*Bitch!*"

Comfortable with the insult, Roxy merely picked up her pace, ever-present heels striking the pavement with a succession of *clicks*. Three more blocks. She ran one block, then skidded to a halt at the stoplight. *No.* Cameras, white trailers, and giant spotlights everywhere. A quick glance up the block told her a movie was being filmed. The familiar scene of production assistants talking into earpieces usually comforted her, but today it was only thwarting her chances of landing a cheap place to lay her head. By tonight, she could be homeless, and the only thing standing between her and 110 Ninth Avenue was this movie shoot with . . . was that Liam Neeson? *Huh. He's actually pretty tall.*

A group of extras caught her eye. They were being held back by a PA with a walkie-talkie up to his mouth. Roxy could tell from the group's body language that they were getting ready to enter the shot. Just waiting for the signal. She flipped her hair once, then slipped across the intersection. When the PA turned his back, she inserted herself into the group of extras, smiling brightly when one of them gave her a curious look.

"When's lunch, right?" she whispered. "I'm starving."

"Uh, yeah. We just *had* lunch."

"Oh, shut it."

The PA waved his hand at them. "Action."

At once, the extras started screaming and ducking as they moved along the sidewalk. Jesus, she should have known it was a fucking action movie with Liam Neeson involved. With a lack of hesitation worthy of an advanced improv group, Roxy let out a shrill scream and tore at her hair, moving as one with the rest of the actors, even tripping once for added effect. Unlike them, however, when they reached the end of the shot, she kept running, right off the movie set. Straight toward 110 Ninth Avenue.

Another block of sprinting and she could see it. The building was located on a corner, increasing the likelihood that the bedroom had a window. Blisters be damned, she kicked her sprint into high gear. Three college-age girls reached the steps of the building at the same time as her. Briefly, she considered going with another hip-check to knock them out of the running, but she decided physical assault was only acceptable once per day.

Instead, she blocked their progress on the steps and pointed across the street with a gasp. "Oh, my God! Look! It's James Franco."

God bless them, they all looked. Roxy didn't waste a second laughing, though, instead trucking her way up the final steps and hitting the buzzer for apartment 4D. A tinny noise filled the vestibule a moment later, and she pushed open the door with a cry of victory. One James Franco enthusiast tried to catch the door before it closed, but Roxy pulled it shut just in time.

"*Bitch!*"

"Yeah, I'm getting that more than usual today," she called back through the glass, turning toward the stairs. "Hopefully I'll be a bitch with a two-hundred-dollar rent, though. Wish me luck."

When she reached the fourth floor, she saw that the door leading to apartment 4D was slightly ajar. A sinking feeling hit her in the stomach when she heard female voices coming from within.

Too late. She was too late. Unless she could convince Crazy Pants she was the better candidate than the person who'd beat her to the punch. Fat chance, especially if she required a credit check. Or a deposit. *Shit*, she hadn't really thought past getting here, had she? The twenty she'd snaked from Louis McNally the Second yesterday was all she had in her pocket. All she had to her *name*, actually. Ignoring the sliver of warmth in her belly at the thought of the shirtless kisser-of-the-century, Roxy entered the apartment sporting the biggest smile she could muster.

Two girls turned to look at her, their conversation grinding to a halt. A pretty blonde in Converse and a ratty jean skirt stood on one side of an antique dining room table. On the other side stood a brunette with a deer-in-the-headlights look. She wore a navy pantsuit that probably cost more than Roxy's entire wardrobe. It had to be Crazy Pants. Roxy would bet . . . twenty bucks on it.

"Afternoon, ladies."

"Hey," said Converse, with a distinct Southern twang.

"Good afternoon," Crazy Pants answered. "I assume you're here about one of the rooms."

"Rooms?" Roxy's eyebrows hit her hairline. "Plural?"

"Two. There's two." CP crossed the room to look out a massive window overlooking Ninth Avenue. She started wringing her hands, possibly because she'd spotted the gathering mob outside the building. As if on cue, the apartment's buzzer went off three quick times. "In retrospect, I probably shouldn't have included my address in the ad. There should have been some kind of pre-screening involved. I've just . . . I've never done this kind of thing."

Roxy let her gaze run discreetly through the apartment. Good

God, the place was a veritable palace by Manhattan standards. Massive common area, renovated kitchen complete with stainless steel appliances. The décor was modern industrial with a homey twist. She'd bet . . . twenty bucks that it had been decorated by a professional. Exactly zero IKEA furniture assembly had taken place here. At least until *she'd* move in with her ragtag possessions. What would these girls think when they saw how few items she called her own? She pushed that worrisome thought aside and decided she would do whatever it took to call this place home. It *felt* like a home. Not just some place to crash, like she'd been doing off and on for the last two years.

"Well." She reached into her backpack's front pocket and pulled out her checkbook. "No need to search any further. Two girls here, two rooms. I'm shitty at math, but it seems like a good fit."

When Converse took her cue, Roxy decided she liked the blonde already. "Do you take cash? I got a whole heap of it."

Then again, maybe not. "The first order of business might be to delete the ad," Roxy suggested. "Before the police arrive in riot gear."

"I already did that," CP burst out. "It was only up for five minutes. They just keep coming."

Roxy strode toward the window, winking at the polished brunette as she passed. "Let me take care of that for you." She yanked open the window and stuck her head out. Christ, it looked like an episode of *The Walking Dead* out there. Accurately enough, she had a feeling some of them would chew off another person's arm for a chance at the ridiculously low rent. "*Hey,*" she shouted. "*You weren't fast enough, shitheads. Room's gone. Beat it.*"

She closed the window on a chorus of B-words screeched in her honor. Honestly, if one more person called her a bitch today, she might take it to heart. Maybe, but not likely.

"Thank you," CP sighed, wilting down onto a dining room chair. "The super already hates me because I called him the wrong name for two weeks."

"What's his name?" Converse asked.

"Rodrigo."

"What were you calling him?"

"Mark."

Converse made a sympathetic noise. "Easy mistake."

Oh, boy. There might be two pairs of crazy pants being worn in this room. Hoping to restore some sense of sanity, Roxy held out a hand toward the brunette. "Well, I'm Roxy Cumberland. If you call me the wrong name, I promise I won't wait two weeks to let you know about it."

"I'm Abigail. Abby for short." They shook hands. "I live here."

"I put that together." Roxy raised an eyebrow at the blonde. "And you are?"

The teeth that were revealed by her smile might have been the whitest pair Roxy had ever seen. That was saying something, considering actresses whitened their teeth regularly. "Honey Perribow. Pleasure."

"Same," Roxy murmured before turning back to Abby. "If you don't mind me asking, what happened to your last roommates?"

"I've never had any." Abby looked around the apartment as if seeing it through fresh eyes. "I've been here by myself for five months."

She's effing loaded. "Really."

"Yes. Except for the ghost."

"Ghost?" Honey squeaked.

Abby grinned. "Just kidding."

Roxy actually found herself laughing under her breath. Maybe this wouldn't be so bad after all. She just needed to guarantee her spot in the apartment, then she'd figure out the money situation. In her pocket, the slip of paper with the *strip-o-gram* rates glowed hot.

Before she could say a word, Honey put a hand over her heart, Pledge of Allegiance–style, and spoke up. "You know, I feel honor bound to inform you that these rooms could be rented out for a heck of a lot more than two hundred dollars."

Roxy shot the blonde a look. "Can't put a price on good company."

Abby held up a hand. "I'm aware of what the rooms could go for. I work in finance. Also, duh."

"So what's the deal?" Roxy asked, genuinely curious. And a little suspicious. "Is there something wrong with the place? Rats . . . bad plumbing . . . neighbors with rifles and a grudge against the youth of America?"

"No, none of that." Abby raised an eyebrow. "Where have *you* been living?"

"It's a jungle out there."

"Amen to that," Honey piped up. "I've been to three apartment showings this morning. One was a dirty old man who offered free rent in exchange for naked maid service. I barely fit into the other two rooms. I'm pretty sure one of them was a broom closet."

Abby stood up and started to pace across the Persian rug–covered floor. Based on the worn-out section down the center, Roxy decided this chick must pace a lot. "I could have offered the rooms to some of my colleagues. Or listed them at a higher price. But my colleagues are, well, they're assholes. I get enough of them at the office." She blew out a heavy breath. "I'm bored, okay? I'm bored and lonely and I have no friends."

Roxy rocked back on her heels, finally seeing the big picture. "So you thought you'd buy a couple friends to entertain you?"

"And yet still not the weirdest thing that happened to me today," Honey muttered.

"When you say it like that, it sounds horrible." Abby shrugged. "Okay, it's a little horrible. But mostly, it's a cry for help. I'm starting to talk to myself. I'm talking two-sided conversations, here. It would be nice to say 'pass the orange juice' to someone other than the ghost."

Honey shifted on her feet. "I'm going to need the ghost jokes to stop here."

Abby's mouth tugged at the corner. "So? In or out? I'm throwing caution to the wind. I'm not going to do credit checks because, honestly, I don't need the money bad enough to care. You both seem relatively normal in a way that tells me I won't be fearing for my life. Move in today?"

Roxy tapped the checkbook against her thigh. A minute ago, she'd been ready to do whatever it took to live in this apartment. Now she wasn't so sure. Abby had thrown down the one requirement Roxy didn't feel comfortable offering. Friendship. Not that she didn't have friends, per se, but they were mostly girls she ran into at auditions who only had five minutes for conversation before they took off on their next theatrical quest. What passed as communication with her old roommates had consisted of a palm being held out on the first of the month, looking for that elusive rent check. But this? This would be different. She'd be expected to interact. Drop character. She hadn't done that in a while. Especially since she'd been on her own. In high school, she'd brought antisocial to a whole new level, and after facing so many setbacks in New York, she'd grown even more comfortable in her me-against-the-world cocoon.

Despite Abby's assurances to the contrary, Roxy could see this for what it was. A rich girl looking to rebel. She wanted companionship, someone to talk to and possibly confide in. Roxy had never been anyone's confidante save her own. Against her will, she felt a spark of sympathy for Abby. In the brief moments since entering the apartment, she'd kind of started to like her. But she wasn't what Abby was looking for. She didn't do girly chats. She didn't share giant bowls of popcorn while a *New Girl* marathon played in the background. For two years now, she'd been on her own. Something told her that if she wrote this check—this *bad* check—that would change. Was she ready?

Screw it. What choice did she have? She took a pen out of her backpack, wrote a check for two hundred dollars, then handed it to Abby. "Can you, uh, wait a couple of days to cash that?"

Abby watched her closely, too closely, before nodding. "Sure."

To her left, Honey approached with a fist full of twenties. "I'm in, too."

"Well." Abby shoved the cash and check into the front pocket of her blazer. "Shall I cook dinner for us tonight?"

"Don't push it," Roxy said, just as Honey answered, "I'll make the salad."

Roxy headed toward the front door, shaking her head. "Catch you girls later. Don't wait up."

When she closed the door behind her, she stood in the silent hallway for a beat before grabbing her cell phone from the side pocket of her backpack. Cursing once under her breath, she dialed the number on the slip of paper, just beneath the strip-o-gram rates. No other way she'd be able to bank two hundred dollars in time for Abby to cash the check. She supposed she could scramble and try to find a waitressing job, but she knew from experience that restaurants usually required at least a full shift of training without pay before they let you take home tips. She'd never been trained in bartending. No, on short notice, this was all she could come up with.

Looked like she'd be using Louis McNally the Second's twenty-buck tip to get a cheap wax.

Chapter 4

*L*ouis tapped the pencil against his desk in rapid succession. He should be working. A stack of legal briefs on his desk were calling his name, taunting him, whispering about his slacker nature. Unfortunately, he only had eyes for the digital clock on his computer screen. Six minutes past ten in the morning. If he could've placed a bet on rabbit girl being the type to run late, he would have made it without hesitation. She seemed like the type to make a man suffer before gracing him with her presence. Applying that last stroke of lip gloss and missing the train in the process. Every minute that passed was torture. A delay of the inevitable explosion that would happen when she walked into his office dressed as Lady Liberty and realized he'd ordered her from the agency to sing "New York, New York" bright and early on a Monday morning.

In his humble defense, he'd been given no choice in the matter. The smug prick who'd answered the phone at Singaholix Anonymous had refused to pass on her contact information. Wouldn't even tell Louis her *name*. Instead, his response had been, "There's only one surefire way to see her again, isn't there, buddy?" Realizing the move would almost completely screw his chances with rabbit girl, Louis had nonetheless found himself reciting his credit card information into the phone, giving a phony name so she wouldn't blow him off completely. And this came on the heels of calling Zoe, his one-night stand, to get the agency's number, earning him an affronted screech and an aching eardrum.

Yeah, he was *that* desperate to see rabbit girl again. Desperate enough to risk having his eyeballs clawed out before he ate the peanut butter and banana sandwich he'd brought for lunch. But the weekend had done nothing to dull the memory of her from his mind. If anything, it had grown stronger. There had been one weak moment in the shower this morning when he'd considered trying to recreate the kiss with the back of his hand. It had been a damn close call.

He leaned back in his chair and did a quick scan of his cluttered office. What would she think of him when she walked in here? Most girls were impressed by his law degree, his securing a position at the prestigious Winston and Doubleday law firm at the young age of twenty-six. He usually left out the part about his father being Doubleday's golf partner since the late eighties. Yeah, his boss had seen him in diapers. How many people could claim that? Thankfully, Doubleday had retired to an estate in Palm Beach with his ex-secretary, making it possible for Louis to walk into the office every morning without a brown paper bag over his head.

If he hadn't been fascinated by law, he never would have let his father get him the job. Fact is, he *loved* the intricacies of the justice system. He'd wanted to be a lawyer since Take Your Daughter to Work Day 2001. It had been his sisters' gig, but they'd dragged him along to act as entertainment. True to form, his father had left them in the conference room under the supervision of an intern while he'd left to do something *important*. The intern had promptly fallen asleep, and Louis had seen his Sister Escape Hatch. He'd crawled under the table and slipped out the door. While they'd carved their initials into the conference table with letter openers, he'd found himself fascinated by a meeting taking place two doors down. A woman had quietly explained to the suited man behind the desk that she couldn't afford to pay him his entire fee up front. The man had been . . . unaffected. Cold. He'd apologized that he couldn't do more for her and shown her the door. So while Louis had always let his father think he'd become a lawyer to be just like dear old dad, it really came down to the fact that he'd hated seeing that woman cry.

In the hopes of becoming the kind of lawyer that did *good* for people and didn't just chase his next fat paycheck, he'd made his father a deal. He would take the position at Winston and Doubleday if his contract required him to perform one hundred hours of pro bono work for the entire length of his employment. Louis was all too aware of how easily a lawyer could lose sight of why he'd wanted to practice law, as his father had. He was counting on the clause in his contract to keep him honest. To remind him why he'd worked his ass off to pass the bar.

Unfortunately that part of his contract had been fulfilled, faster than he'd ever thought possible, and now the agreement was up for review. He'd asked that another one hundred hours be added to his new contract with the firm, and it was currently "under advisement" with Doubleday. That worried him like hell. His boss tended to make snap decisions, usually so he could get back on the green. This postponement of any real decision had been out of character, leaving Louis in limbo. He *liked* the pro bono work. More than the paid work, actually. Helping someone who didn't have unlimited cash to throw at a problem was infinitely more satisfying.

Rabbit girl would be aware of exactly none of his honest intentions, however. She would see his ordering her services as a power play, something to amuse him while he lounged around in his cushy, air-conditioned office. Louis estimated he'd have about three seconds from the time she walked in to convince her not to flip him the bird and dive straight back down the rabbit hole. It had been a pretty bold move, bringing her to his place of work, but most of the office spent Monday mornings in court or at client meetings, so he'd taken a gamble. He knew for a fact she wouldn't return to his apartment, so he'd been left little choice.

When he heard the unmistakable sound of high heels clicking down the hallway toward his office, Louis shot to his feet, abandoning the pencil on his desk, where it rolled to the floor. Jesus, the receptionist hadn't even buzzed him. She was probably too busy laughing. At his rabbit girl. That thought caused a pit to form in his stomach. Shit, this had been a really bad idea. Possibly his worst idea of all time. If his intention had been to charm her, he was off to a piss-poor start.

The door swung open. For one brief, shining moment, his gaze was locked with hers. The girl he'd been dreaming about. The girl who had exiled him to the land of disturbing Internet porn. For just an instant, he saw hurt cloud her features.

With a lift of her chin, it transformed into outrage. He admired her for it, in a way. Her ability to rein in her pride when she was dressed in a sparkly green Lady Liberty costume. "You're one slimy motherfucker, you know that?" She tested the weight of the torch in her hand. "A tourist outside tried to take a picture with me."

She hurled the torch at his head.

As he ducked under his desk to avoid impact, Louis acknowledged his error in picking a costume that included a prop. His own fault, really. Behind him, the glass frame holding his law degree shattered and crashed to the ground. He ignored it, launching himself toward the door before she could escape.

"Hear me out." Taking his life in his hands, he grabbed onto her by the shoulders, preventing her from charging back out into the hallway. When she didn't protest as he anticipated, he watched her cast a reluctant glance toward the reception area, where he could now hear his colleagues' amused voices. Of course. *This is the morning they would pick to return to the office early. She's deciding between the lesser of two evils. I'm one of those evils.* Louis hated himself in that moment. Whatever it took to make this right, he would do it.

"You have thirty seconds," she said finally.

He blew out a relieved breath. "Thank you. I—"

She yanked the green robe over her head and tossed it onto the floor. The spiky crown came next, sending auburn hair tumbling down around her bare shoulders, curling around the sexy, handful-sized breasts pressing against her white tank top. Her trim stomach peeked out from underneath the hem, just above skintight jeans. Louis's mouth went dry. His train of thought seeped out through his ears.

"What are you doing?" Louis managed.

She looked at him as though he'd sprouted a third eye. "I'm not going back out there dressed like a fucking statue. They're not going to laugh when they see what these jeans do for my ass, now, are they?"

"No." *Don't look. Don't look.* "I seriously doubt it."

"You have twenty seconds to tell me why I rode the subway dressed like an asshole."

"Right." *Jesus, man. Eyes up. Focus. You've seen a hot girl before.* "Not this hot."

"What?"

"Did I just say that out loud?"

"Fifteen seconds."

Louis ran an impatient hand through his hair. "I wanted to see you again, all right? The guy who answered the phone wouldn't give me your number, so this was my only option. I don't even know your name, and honestly, it pisses me off. It pisses me the hell off because you kiss like a fucking dream and I can't think of anything else." Taking advantage of her openmouthed shock, he pushed the door shut behind her, hopefully buying himself a few more seconds. "You can walk out of here hating me if you want, but I need to know your name so I can track you down the normal way next time. Stalking you on social media." He stepped closer. "Because I'm going to kiss you again. I have to."

She laid a hand on his chest, stopping his forward progress. For the first time since arriving in his office, she didn't look seconds from beating him to a pulp with his own unattached arms. Those smoky green eyes had turned thoughtful, if still slightly suspicious. "I'm Roxy," she said slowly.

Roxy. Of course her name is Roxy. "That might be the only name I didn't guess." He licked his lips, hoping to taste some of the cherry blossom scent she'd brought in with her. "I'd settled on Denise."

Her nose wrinkled. "Why?"

Ben and Russell had decided it sounded like the name most likely to belong to a future ex-girlfriend. "You don't want to know."

"Yeah?" She pushed him back a step. "Denise is my mom's name, so you're probably right."

If he'd had a wood chipper in his office at that moment, Louis would have seriously considered jumping into it feetfirst. "Jesus. I'm not exactly knocking this out of the park, am I?"

She didn't answer, sidestepping him instead to circle his office. "A lawyer, huh? Yikes."

"Try not to sound so enthused." When she hopped up onto the edge of his desk and leaned back, exposing more of that smooth midriff, Louis barely resisted the urge to adjust himself in his pants. Why did this particular girl get him so worked up? "Everyone hates lawyers until they need one."

"Why did you bring me here?"

God, she didn't waste time. He liked that. "I want to take you out. On a date."

She laughed, but sobered when she realized he wasn't joking. "You're not exactly my type, Louis McNally the Second."

He shrugged, not even close to throwing in the towel. She had no idea who she was dealing with. Every time she told him no, he would only grow that much more determined. "Give me a date to convince you otherwise. Most dates are classified as bad. What's the difference if you have a bad date with me or some other jerk who I suddenly want to kill?"

Those Popsicle lips twitched. "Only a lawyer would make that argument."

"Is that a yes?" She still looked dubious, giving him the feeling he'd run up against a commitment-phobe. Maybe if he gave her the impression that his intentions were only casual, she'd agree to see him. He'd work on the commitment thing later. If it was a little too early to be thinking in the long term, he gave himself a pass. His reaction to her didn't fall within the bounds of normal. "I'm not asking for a relationship. I don't do them either," he said, telling the truth. Or what the truth had been before she'd rung his bell. *Door*bell, that is. "Just a date."

Her legs swung back and forth, a good foot and a half from the ground. "Why don't you make up for dragging me down here dressed as the symbol of freedom? Before I'd even eaten breakfast, no less."

Louis was surprised to find how much he hated the idea of her sitting there hungry. Before she'd even finished speaking, he was crossing to his suit jacket hanging on the wall. He reached into his pocket and took out the peanut butter and banana sandwich, placing it in her lap. As when he'd made his speech to keep her from leaving, she looked taken aback by the kind gesture. It made him want to bury her in an avalanche of sandwiches.

He watched as she unwrapped the foil with delicate fingers tipped with chipping red nail polish. "Okay, that's a pretty good start."

"What's next?"

"Tell me something embarrassing that happened to you. It's the only way to get us back on equal footing."

Louis couldn't contain his burst of laughter.

"What?"

"Nothing. Just that . . . *even footing* made me think of a rabbit's foot . . ."

She paused in the act of taking her first bite. "That seriously isn't helping your cause."

"Right. Something embarrassing." He blew a breath toward the ceiling, silently calling himself every name in the book. She threw him so far off his game that he wasn't even on the playing field anymore. "Junior year in college, my friend Russell shaved off my eyebrows when I was passed out. They took six months to grow back."

"Ooh." She winced. "Did you pencil them in with makeup while you waited?"

"Of course not," he said defensively.

"Too bad, then. Not embarrassing enough." She waved her hand. "Next story, please."

Louis smothered a smile. "I have two older sisters. They're twins and they're terrifying." He shifted, hoping he wasn't shooting himself in the foot with this next story. "When I was in fifth grade, they were crazy into the Backstreet Boys. They played the album so many times, I . . . kind of started to like it."

"Getting warmer."

"Oh come on. That's pretty bad."

"Remember the tourist that wanted a picture with me outside?" She waited for his nod. "He suggested a more *creative* use for my torch."

"Point taken." Louis racked his brain, but all he could think about was how good she looked sitting on his desk. How badly he wanted to step between those thighs and relive the kiss heard round the world. He'd hook his hands under her knees and scoot her to the edge. Grind against her until she begged him to rip those jeans off and give her the real thing. And he would. He'd give it to her as long as she needed. *Your dick is getting hard. Stop thinking about it. Stop thinking about it.*

"Are you thinking about me naked, Louis?"

"Yep."

"Hmm." She took the final bite of his sandwich. "I'm owed a properly embarrassing story, and I don't have a lot of time. I have an audition this afternoon."

"Audition?"

She nodded. "This might come as a shock to you, but I don't do this full time."

"You're an actress."

"I'm trying to be." She gestured to the costume on the floor. "Obviously it's not going well. Yet."

Even though he had more questions, she seemed disinclined to discuss it anymore. Plus he was running out of time. *Find out more about her later.* "Okay. At my high school graduation, I tripped on the way to accept my diploma. My foot caught on the robe and I just"—he slashed his hand in the air—"ate shit."

"Ouch."

"I'm not finished." He moved closer to her as subtly as he could, stopping when her eyes narrowed. "When I fell, I knocked my front tooth out. I sat there bleeding while everyone searched for the missing tooth so they could rush it, and me, to the dentist. But they never found it." He tapped his front tooth with the tip of his finger. "This one's fake."

Only this girl would look delighted over his worst moment. Her smile sent something winging through his chest. "I can't even tell. It looks just like its neighbor."

Louis resisted the urge to hide the tooth by closing his mouth. "Did I pass?"

Roxy grabbed a pen off his desk and put it between her lips. Watching him under hooded eyes, she took his arm and rolled up his sleeve. When her fingertips made contact with the sensitive underside of his arm, there was no way of preventing The Reckoning any longer. His pants felt so tight all of a sudden that he had to work to keep his breathing even. She knew it, too. He could tell by the way her mouth curved around the pen. Torture, perfection. If this girl could get him hard merely from touching his arm, he was in bigger trouble than he thought.

After finishing the task of rolling up his sleeve, she plucked the pen from her mouth and started writing on his skin. "Okay, Louis McNally the Second. You've got my number. Don't blow it."

"Thank you." Taking a risk, he planted a hand on his desk and leaned in. "But I want a date. I want to look at you when I'm talking to you. Not an iPhone screen."

Hell if it didn't make his entire morning to see her affected by his closeness. "I'm a busy girl."

"Make time."

Her pupils expanded just slightly, letting him know she'd liked that. Liked being ordered around, even if he suspected she'd rather eat nails than admit it. He filed that away for future use.

"I'm not free until Saturday."

The perks of being a lawyer gave him a pretty good idea when people were lying. Briefly, he debated calling her on the fib but decided to let her play hard to get. As long as he got her in the end. "Saturday, then." He pulled his phone out of his pocket and dialed the number on his arm, not taking any chances that the number was fake. She laughed under her breath when it became clear what he was doing. When her ring tone went off—"Money Maker," by the Black Keys—he could feel the stupid grin on his face and couldn't do a single thing about it.

Roxy slid off his desk, brushing against him. Just enough to ensure he'd need to go home on his lunch break and work off some steam. Solo-style. Louis watched transfixed as she took his phone and opened the camera application. She snapped a quick picture and handed him back the phone. "There. Now you can look at me when we talk."

"You're trying to make me crazy, aren't you?"

She winked at him as she bent over to retrieve her costume. "Count on it."

Christ. It was usually breasts that did him in. With Roxy, he didn't know where the hell to look. *So much fucking trouble headed my way.* He joined her at the door. "Good luck at your audition."

"Thank you." She started to leave but turned back. "You're not the only one who's been thinking about that kiss, you know."

He trapped a groan in his throat. "I'm standing right here, beautiful. Come get another."

Again, the green in her eyes disappeared momentarily. "I think you know I'm going to make you work harder than that for it."

"I'm counting on it."

She squared her shoulders and faced the reception area. "Bye, Louis."

"Bye, Roxy."

He waited until he heard the front door of the office close before going back to work. No one laughed. Especially him, thanks to his new position as Mayor of Bonerville.

Chapter 5

Roxy stared, dumbfounded, at the eighteen-year-old film student.

"You called me back here to reread for the role of Lassie? As in, the dog."

"You were great in the first audition." He consulted his clipboard, thick-rimmed glasses slipping down his nose. "So good, we thought you might be right for the title character."

"*Might* be?" She must still be asleep and dreaming this whole scenario. Or she'd fallen into a bizzaro-world vortex on her walk from the train. A world where prepubescent children had more professional success than herself. If he didn't look so earnest, she might have clotheslined him by now. "Ashton. Can I call you Ashton?" She pasted on her best smile when he nodded. "This is where I'm getting stuck. Lassie has no lines. He's a fucking dog."

"He speaks with his eyes."

"Okay." Roxy laughed a little hysterically, yucky embarrassment finally breaching her inner wall. This was definitely the bottom. She really resented these kids for making her feel stupid, so she tried to deflect, even though her cheeks felt like they were on fire. "Let me ask you a question. What is written on that clipboard? Anything? Or is it just the note your mother sent in your lunchbox this morning?"

He flushed red, not that you could see much of his face, obscured as it was by a struggling beard. "We're practically the same age. And anyway, Lassie is timeless."

She crammed her fist against her mouth. "Oh my God. I can't even tell if you're making fun of me anymore. I've lost my grip on irony."

"Me, too," he whispered. "Don't tell anyone, but I've never even seen *Lassie*."

"You need to be deprogrammed." She snatched her purse off the stage and turned in a circle, splitting a glance between two other student filmmakers dressed like beat poets. "You all do. Go home to your parents and start from scratch. Before you suffocate yourself in summer scarves."

Ashton tapped her on the shoulder. "Does this mean you don't want to be Lassie?"

"Yes, dipshit. *Yes*."

His brow wrinkled. "Yes, like you do? Or yes, like you don't?"

"Oh, *God*. Where is the closest bar?" Her question directed at no one echoed through the performance area as she stomped toward the exit. This morning, a typical Wednesday, had started out marginally decent. She'd woken up on her futon in Chelsea, greeted by the smell of bacon. *Bacon*. She'd practically floated on the aroma toward the kitchen, where she'd found an apron-wearing Honey making cheese grits. Without even asking, the smiling Southerner had heaped a pile of food onto a plate and slid it across the counter in her direction. Roxy had walked to this audition with a belly full of food and a positive outlook, something she hadn't done in months.

They'd called her back to play a Border collie. It seemed humiliation was now part of her everyday agenda. In the two years since she'd dropped out of Rutgers University's acting program to pursue an actual career instead of performing for a half-empty theater in Jersey, she'd never been brought as low as she had this morning. That was saying something, since she'd once read for a feminine itch cream commercial. Worse, tonight was her first and hopefully *last* foray into stripping. She'd been stopped by Abby on her way out the door this morning. Her new roommate had haltingly informed her she would be cashing the two-hundred-dollar check tomorrow. Roxy only had half that amount in the bank. No more singing telegram work had come her way since Louis's appointment on Monday, and now she was left with few options. Strip or lose the apartment dreams were made of. Lose bacon. Lose cheese grits. Lose a kind of security she'd never really experienced.

So in a matter of eight hours, she would get naked in a room full of strangers. Her boss at Singaholix had assured her this particular bachelor party would be low key. The groom didn't want strippers or a big deal made, but the best man and organizer had convinced him to allow a ten-minute show. Namely, *her*. Dressed as a cheerleader.

She was doing her best to keep a good mental attitude about it, even though part of her was scared. Being scared didn't happen to her often, nor did it sit well, churning around in her stomach like a cake mixer. No, this would be a *good* experience, one she might be able to utilize for future roles. Hadn't Marisa Tomei played a stripper? Jennifer Aniston, too? She could do this. Ten minutes of taking her clothes off couldn't be worse than dressing like a dog and expressing doggie thoughts with her eyes. Those men would all just be faceless audience members to her. Nothing more.

A brief scenario in which her parents found out flashed in her head. It wouldn't be the typical parental reaction. Horror, denial. No, they would probably be delighted. *How the mighty have fallen.* Her ambition to become an actress, become *anything*, had always been viewed as a negative by her parents. When they bothered to weigh in. They hadn't said so in as many words, but she'd always thought her inability to be content . . . offended them somehow. As a result, she almost got the feeling they hoped she *didn't* make it. Hoped she came crawling home, begging for her old room back and a job hookup at the local mall.

As Roxy flopped back against the outside of the building, the weight of those dark thoughts had her wishing she still smoked. In her purse, her phone signaled an incoming text message. She didn't recognize the number, but based on the message, she knew who it was.

Is it Saturday yet? I'm starting to talk to your selfie.

Unbelievable. He'd made her smile. After a Lassie callback. Quickly, she saved the number under his name, *Louis McNally the Second*, and responded.

Is she saying anything back?

She's telling me she wants to move the date to tonight. And that Louis looks lonely.

Oh, it was so tempting after the way her shitstorm cloud had rained on her parade this morning. She'd thought about him a lot since Monday. A lot. Weirdly, although they'd only met twice, she found herself kind of . . . missing him. Shaking her head at her dopey thoughts, she set off in the direction of Chelsea. This Collie needed to regroup.

I have plans.

So do I. But they involve us being in the same room.

You thinking about me naked again, Louis?

It's becoming a habit. Come meet me for lunch.

No. Do you always pack your own?

Almost always. Today I brought cold pizza. Jealous?

> Careful. Remember the last time you accused me of being jealous?

> Why do you think I said it?

> Where are you taking me Saturday?

> Don't be nosy. How did your audition go?

> If anyone you know needs a singing telegram, send them my way.

> Sorry, beautiful. Their loss.

A warm flutter in her throat had her pressing a hand to the spot, pausing on the sidewalk. Oh boy, there was so much trouble headed her way. Too bad she wanted to cannonball right into the center of it. She needed to keep her head above water with Louis, though. Jesus, he hadn't even remembered the first name of his one-night stand. For all she knew, she was one of several girls getting sexy/sweet texts at that very moment. She'd *been* there before. Dated college guys, other actors. They all started out promising her an eternity of sunshine and roses. As soon as they got what they wanted, it was like flipping a switch, turning them from charming to disinterested. Smitten to . . . gettin' . . . away. As fast as possible. In her experience, guys were always looking for what was next.

Her mother hadn't exactly been brimming with helpful advice

when it came to boys. Once, after a few too many Budweisers, she'd told Roxy that girls like them "settled." They didn't wait for some knight to come sweep them off their feet and gallop them out of the Tri-State area. At the time, Roxy hadn't known what to make of that, but now, with some perspective, she wondered if her mother simply wanted her to fit into a pattern. If she managed to do some good with her life or find a decent guy, maybe it would remind her mother she'd only gotten married because she'd had the misfortune of being knocked up with her first and last child. A child who had the nerve to want more. To *be* more.

They never wanted me.

Roxy shook off the dark thoughts and glanced back down at her phone. At Louis's message. Without any real guidance from her parents, she'd learned the hard way throughout high school and college that all men want only one thing. Sex. As long as she reminded herself as often as possible that Louis would be no different, she could enjoy him while . . . whatever this was . . . lasted.

You there?

See you Saturday xo

LOUIS TUGGED AT the collar of his dress shirt, wishing he were anywhere but at his future brother-in-law, Fletcher's, bachelor party. This had to be every dude's version of hell. Not that he didn't like a decent bachelor party as much as the next guy. Beer, bullshit . . . the occasional boobs. But he wasn't exactly thrilled

TESSA BAILEY

about watching Fletcher get shit-faced for the final time before surrendering his "freedom." Especially when the "old ball and chain" Fletcher's friends kept referring to happened to be his sister. Their relationship might be the kind that would eventually land him in a straightjacket, but he still felt a strong sense of sibling loyalty.

For the tenth time in less than an hour, he slipped his cell phone out of his pocket with the urge to text Roxy. Was she actually busy? Maybe he'd read her wrong and playing hard to get wasn't her intention. As the week wore on, it became increasingly obvious she *was* hard to get. No playing involved. Saturday could not get here fast enough. He wanted to see her face, talk to her. Figure her the hell out. Even if her lack of enthusiasm in regards to going out with him was less than satisfying. It didn't hurt his pride at all. Really, it didn't.

Work hadn't exactly been great today, either. In between meetings, he'd called his boss in Florida to get an update on his request to extend the pro bono work in his contract. Doubleday still hadn't had an answer for him, leaving him more than a little frustrated. What would he do if the answer was no?

He went to the fridge and pulled out a fresh beer. The plan for the night was to meet at Fletcher's Upper West Side apartment before heading out to dinner. First, though, the group of ten guys was apparently waiting for some live entertainment to arrive. Fletcher made a big show of protesting the stripper, but Louis had seen him glance toward the door on more than one occasion. Louis couldn't help but think the protesting had been for his benefit, in case tonight's events ever got back to his sister.

Yeah, right. As if he would tell her about her fiancé getting a lap dance. Knowing his sister, her reaction to that news would spur the apocalypse.

A chorus of half-tipsy cheers went up in the living room when the door buzzed, signaling someone's arrival downstairs. Louis leaned against the kitchen counter and sipped his beer. He'd stay right here, thank you very much. What he *didn't* see might end up saving his and Fletcher's lives if there was ever an interrogation. *What stripper? I never once saw a stripper.* Another skill he'd learned being a lawyer was to make sure you were able to tell the truth and mean it.

He heard the apartment's front door open and close, and the silent anticipation from men who'd been shooting their mouths off moments ago was almost comical. Then the husky voice he'd been hearing in his fantasies reached him.

"I heard there's an ex-quarterback in the house. Think maybe he needs a cheerleader?"

Louis's beer hit the ground, splattering everywhere, but he barely saw it. *No way. Not happening.* He shot forward from his position at the counter and strode toward the living room with a knot in his throat. He felt sluggish and ill at the same time, dread settling over him like a fog blanket. Just before he reached the living room, slow, pumping music started to play.

Roxy. His rabbit girl. Dressed like a cheerleader. Hips swaying, hands clutching her own hair and piling it on her head sexily. He couldn't stop himself from acknowledging how truly fucking hot she looked, skirt so short he could see the tops of her toned thighs. It rode low on her waist, exposing her stomach. Against his will, his body reacted. Fast and painful. Probably just like every other asshole in the room. She had a smile on her face as she moved slowly toward a seated Fletcher, body undulating, but he saw the strain around her green eyes. The trapped-animal vibe she was giving off was amazingly potent. How could none of them feel it? He wanted to shout and rage and break things. Then she saw him. And froze.

It was the worst moment of his life. Hands down. Even losing his tooth in front of three hundred high school seniors didn't compare. Her face fell, arms dropping to her sides. Pain slashed across her features and straight into his chest.

She thinks I did this. She thinks I ordered her. Again.

"Roxy."

"You dickhead."

"*Roxy.*" He weaved through the group of guys ogling her, grabbing her hand before she could spin for the door. With a tug, he brought her back against his chest. "I didn't. I didn't know."

Louis racked his brain, trying to figure out how a massive coincidence like this could have happened. He hadn't even *known* Roxy was a stripper, so ordering her here would have been impossible. Deductive thinking wasn't an easy feat when he was more concerned with shielding her from everyone's view. The answer finally struck him: Zoe, his one-night stand, worked with Fletcher's best man. She must have shared the details of the agency with the guy. *Ah, fuck.* After *he'd* called Zoe asking for the agency's phone number. So he could get in touch with Roxy. This is what he got for doing something he knew was screwed up. Zoe had obviously done this out of spite, sending the girl he was interested in to strip for his brother-in-law's friends. And him. To shame her? Make him sorry?

His head dropped on her shoulder. "Goddammit, Roxy. I'm so sorry."

She went very still, the tension slowly seeping from her body. He didn't understand the change. Any minute now, she would turn around and deck him, right? A part of him couldn't wait for it. Instead, she turned in his arms, a slow smile playing around her lips. It stopped at her eyes, though. They were glassy, far-off. Slightly unfocused.

"You ordered a stripper, Louis. Didn't you?" She shoved at his chest unexpectedly, knocking him back a step. Sauntering toward him, she did it again, his confusion sending him falling back into an empty chair. "Then it's only polite to watch me do my job."

To his horror, the men around him started whistling, excited by what was taking place. No. *No.* He couldn't let this happen. Not only did the idea of these guys seeing her naked make him livid but she didn't *want* to do it. He could see that. This was her attempt to maintain her pride, thinking he'd been the one to take it away. In a sickening twist, he inadvertently had. A fact he had a feeling would haunt him for a very long time.

Someone turned up the music until it pounded in his ears, mimicking the race of his blood. Because despite the wrongness of it, Roxy was coming closer in a barely-there pleated skirt, little white panties peeking out to weaken his conscience. Getting her out of this room required him to turn down a lap dance from the girl he wanted to take to bed so badly that he'd been aching for a week. But while his brain might only be registering *her* in the room, they weren't alone. *Wake up, asshole.* "No, I won't let you do this. You're going to come with me and let me explain."

"What's to explain, baby?" She gripped his shoulders and straddled his thighs. Then, oh sweet Jesus, she slid down onto his lap, settling her weight on his hard dick before working her hips in a circle. *Fuck.* Stars winked behind his eyes. He started to sweat, fingers itching to smooth up her thighs and cup her ass, jerk her closer. Those pouty lips grazed his neck just before she spoke. "You wanted your fun, now you're going to have it. Just sit back and enjoy the show."

His hand shot out to stop her from removing her top. "No. You're not doing this. I'll carry you out of here if I have to, but it's not happening."

She ripped her hand free of his, leaning forward to whisper in his ear. "Hoping if you take me somewhere private, I'll do more than just strip for a twenty?" Temporarily distracted by sickening shock, he didn't manage to stop her this time from peeling the shirt over her head. The bra she wore was little more than sheer, black material. He could see right through it to her mouthwatering breasts beneath. Which meant everyone else could, too. A growl ripped from his throat as he surged to his feet, taking her with him. Their position left her legs looped around his hips as he stormed past the crowd of jackasses and into the nearest bedroom, leaving catcalls in his wake.

As soon as Louis kicked the door shut behind him, she started fighting to get free. He had no choice but to let her, even though he wanted to gather her close and squeeze as hard as he could. He'd have to settle for blocking the door. Until she heard him out.

"Get out of the way," she grated.

"No," he returned, shaking his head.

Her chest heaved. "Is this how you get off? Embarrassing girls by sending them around in costumes when you have a fucking whim? Pretending to like them, then revealing that you're actually some kind of sick jerk?"

"I didn't know you were coming here tonight, Roxy." He reached a hand toward her, but she flinched back. "I didn't even know you were a stripper."

"Oh, bullshit. Then what were you apologizing for out there?" She cursed under her breath. "What about your text message today about wanting to switch our date to tonight? There was never going to be a date. I'm such an *idiot*."

Seeming to remember then that she wasn't wearing a shirt, her hands flew up to cover her breasts. She looked so exposed, so fragile suddenly. A state he'd never thought to associate with her. He couldn't take another second of it, so he went toward her. She backed away and he kept going. As he'd anticipated, she struck out at him, pummeling his chest with her fists. His arms wrapped around her in an attempt to prevent her, but she kept thrashing. All Louis could do was hang on tight until she stopped, which she finally did with a sob.

"I'm not a stripper." Her voice was toneless against his chest. "I know you won't believe me or care, but I'm not. I needed some quick cash for rent on my new place. This was my first time."

"Why wouldn't I believe you?" he asked into her hair.

"Liars always assume everyone else is lying, too." She sniffed. "Was the tooth story even real?"

"Afraid so. You thinking of knocking it out again?"

"In vivid detail."

"Fair enough." He tried not to be obvious about inhaling her scent. What if this was the last chance he got? The pit in his stomach yawned wide. "One of the guys out there is Zoe's coworker. You know, the, uh—"

"Girl who penned an ode to your dong?"

"Yes. That one." He cleared his throat, praying like *hell* his one-night stand never came up again in conversation. "She might have been a little on the upset side when I called her to get the agency's number. So I could find you."

"You didn't *tell* her that, did you?"

"Ah, but I did. I thought being up-front was the adult thing to do. Would a liar do that?" No response. His long exhale of breath ruffled the hair at her temple, fascinating him. He wanted to brush it back with his fingers but didn't want to risk her pulling away. It felt so fucking great to hold her. "She gave her coworker the agency name. I had no idea you'd walk through that door. Christ, the last thing I want is other men to see you naked. I haven't even had a chance to yet."

His attempt to make her laugh didn't work. "Your chances are slim to none at the moment, dude."

"That appears to be the sad reality." He gave in to the desire to touch her hair, releasing his breath slowly when she stayed put. Time to take one more leap. "I guess I'll have to start convincing you all over again on Saturday."

She jerked her head up. "You're joking, right?"

"Nope. I made reservations and everything."

Her eyes were twin mirrors of confusion. "Even if I forgave you long enough to break bread with you in some snobby restaurant . . ."

"What?" he prompted when she didn't continue.

She pushed away from him, continuing to watch him closely. A hint of insecurity showed through her questioning look before she hid it. "Even then, you really want to bring out the girl who . . ." She swept a hand down her body, clad in only a see-through bra and cheerleader skirt. A sight that he felt slightly ashamed to be storing in his spank bank. In a safety-deposit box all its own, sealed with a triple lock so it couldn't get out. *Pay attention.* " . . . the girl who showed up to get naked for your friends? I get the feeling you don't date a lot of strippers."

"But you're not a stripper. This is your first time."

"What if I do it again?" She lifted one shoulder and let it drop, but he could tell her casualness was feigned. "What then?"

Honestly, he didn't like it. No, he fucking *hated* the idea of her walking into a room full of douchebags with singles in their fists and no clue about the awesome girl she was. Those faceless men were his worst enemies. Above all, they could be *dangerous* to her. When Louis felt his hands clench and shake, he breathed deeply through his nose. While he might feel this way, something told him that if he was honest about it with Roxy, she'd walk. She would see this as temporary before it even got started.

So he proved her right and made himself a liar.

"What you do for a living makes no difference to me." The lie tasted bitter in his mouth, so he tempered it with the truth. "I want to take you out. I want to know you." *Better than anyone else does.*

She cast a glance toward the door. "I can't go back out there."

Louis unbuttoned his shirt and draped it across her shoulders, watching as she did the buttons with trembling fingers. "See? Now I'm the shirtless one. They'll all be too busy staring at my rippling muscles to notice anything else."

Her soft laugh puffed warm air against his neck. "That's the second time you've made me laugh today under impossible circumstances."

Oh man, that made him feel good. Really good. Ten-feet-tall good. "That's something, isn't it?"

As they walked back out into the living room, a plan began to form in Louis's mind. A bad plan. The perfect plan. He wasn't sure. If he offered to loan her money until she got back on her feet, he risked his nut sack being torn clean off his body. But he would do what was necessary to keep Roxy out of another dangerous situation. If there were selfish reasons involved, too, such as wanting her to himself, he couldn't help that.

No one was going to make her feel vulnerable again.

Chapter 6

*R*oxy's junior year in high school, she registered late for classes and got stuck with theater as an elective. Emoting in front of strangers sounded about as appealing as a full body cavity search, especially when her modus operandi included hiding in the back of lectures to sleep, then copying her friends' notes the day before a test. Until the fateful day she was stuck with the dreaded elective, the sum total of her high school education had consisted of how to smoke cigarettes in the girl's bathroom without getting caught. She'd seen the theater kids around campus before. They ate lunch on the grass outside the auditorium in a big circle, making jackasses out of themselves. As if they were on stage at all times. Throwing themselves into fits of dramatic laughter, twirling around like hippies after a B12 shot.

The theater coach took one look at her this-is-my-personal-hell expression and made her a prop designer, which suited her down to the ground. She sat backstage and painted trees while the geeks worked themselves into states of euphoria doing readings on stage for each other. When they settled on *The Chocolate*

Affair for their spring production, Roxy was beyond indifferent. Just give her a paintbrush and fuck off until the bell rings, please. One afternoon she got a little cocky about breaking the rules, and the theater coach caught her smoking in the bathroom. Her punishment was to sit in on student auditions for various parts in the play. She sunk down in the back row, intending to text throughout the whole ordeal, when a monologue caught her attention. Really, that was an understatement. The monologue, given by the character Beverly, grabbed her by the throat and shook her like a bottle of salad dressing.

When it ended, she was shocked to find tears rolling down her cheeks. Those words—words about monotony and self-loathing—had woken something dormant inside her. Something she normally kept at bay by acting out. Showing she didn't care. Not about her parents' lack of interest in her life. Her own void of talent, direction, or purpose. The continuous way she fell into bad relationships with guys, only to have her heart trampled on. No. *Those* words understood her and she understood them. They took away her permission to be indifferent, because now she was aware of other people experiencing the same feelings. She suddenly couldn't wait for an outlet to express herself. The use of other people's words made it easier for someone with the emotional maturity of a kindergartner.

The next afternoon, the theater coach allowed her to audition after everyone left, understanding her need to test herself without anyone bearing witness to it. What if she failed? What if the twirling hippies laughed at her? At least this way, she would only have to blind one man if she blew chunks. Miraculously, she didn't. Those long hours she'd spent rehearsing her monologue the night before paid off. She was finally *good* at something.

He'd already cast the play, but the coach named her understudy for Beverly, much to the astonishment of every geek in the vicinity. Funny enough, as she learned over the next few weeks of rehearsals, those geeks turned out to be kind of fun. They lived life like no one and everyone was watching at the same time. They lived for life *after* high school.

Her moment came one week into the play's run. The lead actress broke her leg while horseback riding and Roxy had to step in. As she stood at the edge of the stage, waiting for the lights to go on, she debated running. Just running away and never coming back. There would be an auditorium full of pissed-off folks, but who cared, when her spleen wanted to jump out of her throat? So she'd channeled Marisa Tomei. Marisa didn't take no shit from anyone. She was a badass from Brooklyn who owned the screen whenever she was on it. That was the push Roxy needed to climb out on stage, but as soon as she got there, she became the character, Beverly. The play passed in the blink of an eye, as if it had been performed in under a minute. She wanted to do it again. And again. An addiction of sorts.

Now, as she walked back toward the living room, back toward a room full of men she'd disappointed by not getting naked for their enjoyment, she called on Marisa once more. Louis's reassuring arm around her was just a crutch, and a confusing one at that. She needed to face this herself and walk out of here with her chin up. Otherwise it would become a recurring nightmare that played whenever she closed her eyes. No way in hell were these fuckers going to feel bad for her or make her feel guilty. If she tried hard enough, she could own this moment and then file it away like it never happened.

The group of men came into view, quieting when they saw her. Not surprisingly, the groom she'd been sent to undress for looked more than slightly disappointed. Like he'd paid for a show and hadn't gotten one. It gave her an idea.

She shrugged off Louis's arm. After a tiny struggle, he let her go, even though, based on his scowl directed at the other men in the room, he wanted to hustle her out of there under a blanket. "Listen, gentlemen. I apologize. I'm officially the worst stripper ever, right? Don't recommend me to your friends all at once." They laughed uncomfortably. *Deep breath. You got this.* She held eye contact with the groom, not caving in to the urge to look away. "Well. I guess congratulations are in order for your upcoming nuptials. She's certainly a lucky lady."

He drained his beer, choking a little on the last gulp. "Thanks."

"Look, I clearly didn't earn my fee here tonight, but I'm hoping you'll let me make it up to you in a more fully clothed type way." She could feel Louis's body heat behind her, giving her a little kick of confidence. "What's your favorite movie?"

The groom looked thrown by the question, but he finally answered. "I don't know. *Wall Street,* I guess."

Shocker. She should have known, based on the expensive suits in the room. "Why don't we pretend your favorite movie is, I don't know, *Pulp Fiction.* Every man loves a little Quentin Tarantino, right?"

"Great flick," someone chimed in. A few suits agreed.

"All right," the groom agreed with a shrug.

Roxy hid her immense relief. Using Louis's shoulder for balance, she climbed up on the ottoman wedged up against the couch, confident that the long dress shirt hid almost her entire thighs from their view. With a deep breath through her nose, she thanked Marisa Tomei one final time for her assistance, then swapped her for Samuel L. Jackson. As the room full of marginally drunk bachelor party attendees watched in astonishment, she performed Jackson's famous monologue from *Pulp Fiction*. The one in which he quotes Ezekiel 25:17 before explaining that his 9mm is the "shepherd protecting his righteous ass in the valley of darkness." It was a wickedly awesome monologue. One that she'd used to land the SunChips ad two years ago. It had been unexpected. And a risk. Still, she'd felt true to herself performing it. As if deep down, she was meant to be a gangster instead of a struggling actress. It made her feel untouchable. A feeling she desperately needed right now.

About halfway through, the moment became hers. Not only did she have the rhythm of these words down by heart, but she'd also forced these men to pay attention. Sure, they were probably just amused, maybe a little impressed that she'd memorized this profanity-heavy speech about violence, but for her own satisfaction, she would take their smiling nods as a sign of respect. Whatever it took to walk out of here with that part of herself she'd checked at the door. Toward the end, she made the mistake of looking at Louis. Shirtless and gorgeous, the pride radiating from him almost caused her to fumble the lines, but she pushed through, finishing with a flourish of her hand.

She took an exaggerated bow as they applauded, just before Louis plucked her off the ottoman and set her on her feet. He didn't let her go, though, holding her hand in a tight grip as he led her toward the door. Louis picked her purse and trench coat up off the floor where she'd left them upon entering and handed both to her before pulling her into the hallway.

He cupped her cheeks, tilting her face up. "Hey. You're fucking amazing, you know that?"

"Yeah? Sometimes I'm not so sure," she answered, shocking herself with total honesty. Crazy how people she knew well couldn't get an honest reaction out of here, while this guy who'd put her through the ringer did it with so little effort. She didn't want to ponder that realization for too long, so she did what came naturally. She avoided it. With steady fingers, she started to unbutton his shirt, which she still wore, intending to give it back to him so he didn't have to face the evening shirtless, even if the female population of Manhattan would go mental over his approachable abs. God, he was sexy. And she really shouldn't be thinking about that right now.

Before she reached the second button, he stopped her with a hand on her wrist. "What are you doing?"

"Giving you back your shirt."

He shook his head vigorously. "Keep it."

She pointed at the trench coat resting on top of her purse. "I have my coat. I'll be fine."

"Yeah, but in order for this transfer of clothing to take place, I'll still have to see you in that cheerleader uniform. And I do not want to be turned on by it."

The corner of her mouth tugged. "You don't *want* to be. But you are?"

"To an appalling degree."

Why am I giving this guy the time of day? Any other human being who'd seen her fall this far not once but *three* excruciating times would be banished to the furthest recesses of her mind, never to be resurrected unless she drank too much wine. When she'd accused him of being a liar in the bedroom, she'd meant it, but he'd slowly wedged his way back under her skin. She actually believed that he'd been just as blindsided by her presence at the party as she'd been by his. Why? Not a clue. She only knew he felt more like an ally than a foe. It didn't hurt that he'd turned down a killer lap dance.

"How do you feel about kissing me right now, Louis?"

His answering groan didn't end when their mouths met, it only got louder. Or maybe that was her own groan joining forces with his. Roxy couldn't form a decent thought besides *More* and *Closer* as Louis slanted his lips over hers and obliterated what she knew about kissing. His lips pushed hers apart, and for a moment, they just inhaled against each other's partially open mouths, savoring the moment. The pulse-pounding rush of sensation. When his tongue traced her lips, then dove in to tangle with hers, she swayed a little under the gust of heat. She wrapped her arms around his neck to steady herself, aligning their bodies. Which reminded her he wasn't wearing a shirt. With no choice but to act on her desperate impulse, she dragged her fingernails lightly down his chest, giving an extra scratch over those abs, ending just above his belt buckle.

"Please, baby. Go lower." His voice sounded like gravel. "One squeeze so I can finally know what it feels like to have your hands on me."

Oh, she liked that. Liked hearing that hot thread of desperation in his voice. Desperation for her. *Willpower, thou hath no place here.* Slowing the kiss so she could look into his eyes, Roxy let her palm smooth over the bulging fly of his dress pants. *Oh shit. A two-hander.* When Louis gave a pained laugh, she realized she'd delivered the sentiment out loud.

"Get to it then, Rox." He bit her bottom lip and dragged it between his teeth. "Let me feel them both."

"Keep your shirt on," she murmured before sinking back into the kiss. When she took his full length in her hands, squeezed and dragged upward, his growl sent warmth pooling at the juncture of her thighs. As if he sensed that chemical reaction from her, he reversed their positions, pressing her back up against the wall. Rough hands dragged up the sides of her thighs to clutch her hips. Hard.

Her head fell back on a gasp, giving him the room he needed to trail his lips down her neck. Lost to the moment, Roxy fisted two handfuls of his hair and arched her back. His breathing growing harsher by the moment, Louis licked across the swells of her cleavage, letting his tongue dip down into the valley between, before licking all the way back up her throat.

A little cry of shock burst past her lips. "Oh, wow. I like that."

"You'll like everything I do to you." Louis took her ear between his teeth. "You going to let me show you how much, Roxy?"

"I don't know yet." She hooked a leg around his waist. "More convincing, please."

Louis gripped her knee. "Fair warning, Rox. If you wrap the other leg around me, I'm taking you home to my bed, where I can get you off properly." His hand flexed. "If that's what you want, hop on up. Otherwise . . ."

"*Don't* wrap my legs around you?" she panted.

He grazed her lips with his. "I couldn't say it out loud. It's too sad."

Did she want to go home with him? *Hell* yes. In her current worked-up state, she'd probably let him carry her fireman-style down West Broadway, ass in the air. So much *confidence* radiated from him. Not the overinflated-ego kind of confidence she'd experienced in guys before. No, his confidence came from a place of maturity. While he obviously knew his way around women, he wasn't smug about it. He just wore that self-assurance like a second skin. She wanted it directed at her. Instinctively she knew that being naked and sweaty with Louis would be unbelievable.

After the night she'd had, though, she didn't want a hero. That's exactly what Louis would be if he took her from this place and gave her a mind-bending orgasm across town before she even took off the cheerleader uniform. No matter how she'd ended up here tonight, he'd gotten her out of a *strippy* situation and now he was making her feel needed, desirable. Okay, *hot*. But she wanted to be her *own* hero tonight. She wanted to leave on her own merit, remembering the way she'd walked back into that living room and faced her fears. He could be her hero a different night. Tonight was hers.

Dammit. I pick now *to start making good decisions?*

He cursed on an exhale. "You're not coming, are you?"

"Looks like neither one of us will be coming tonight."

Already regretting her decision to leave, Roxy let her leg drop and began to back away from the magnetic pull buzzing between them.

"Oh no." His brown eyes went dark. "Before you leave, I'm going to give you something to think about, beautiful."

Her stomach bottomed out. "You haven't done that already?"

A gravelly laugh. "While you're lying in bed tonight, think about this." Big hands slipped down and around from her waist to cup her mostly bare backside. She had no time to enjoy the kick of lust in her belly before he seized her flesh tightly and hauled her onto her toes.

"*Oh.*"

Louis placed his mouth directly over hers, as if to absorb her gasp of shock. "The first time you ride me, I'm going to grip your ass just like this. I'm going to move you where I want you. How fast. How slow. It'll all be up to me and this grip."

Oh, God. Oh, *God.* His promise had a kick of lust whipping into a frenzy. *Breathe through it.* "S-sounds like a solid plan."

"Not a plan. A promise." He licked into her mouth, kissing her in a way that promised . . . *everything*. More. "Good night, Rox."

When he set her back on her feet, it was incredibly difficult to move away from him. "When did we graduate to nicknames?"

He planted his hands on the wall and dropped his head forward, still facing away from her. "Since you started turning me inside out. Is that a fair enough reason?"

She was grateful he couldn't see her expression. Hell, she was grateful *she* couldn't see it. Knowing what it looked like would make it too real. His words punched an uncomfortable hole in her chest. One she couldn't spackle over as quickly as usual. Licking her kiss-sensitive lips, she quickly unbuttoned his shirt and drew on her coat. He still hadn't moved, so she laid the borrowed shirt over his shoulder. "Hey, put this on. I don't think you're what this bachelor party had in mind when they requested topless entertainment."

Slowly, he turned to face her, replacing his shirt with movements that spoke of leashed restraint. "Excuse me for not laughing."

"If I can laugh about it, so can you," she said seriously.

He considered her a moment, then nodded stiffly.

She couldn't leave things awkward. It would bother her until she saw him again. Why? Why did he drag these foreign reactions from her? Any other day, she'd have already blown this joint and grabbed a falafel from the food cart she'd seen outside. Giving in to her urge, she leaned in and kissed the underside of his chin. "See you Saturday, Louis. Think about me."

"Try and stop me."

Somehow she managed to hide her smile until the elevator doors slid shut.

Chapter 7

*E*at. *Eat!*"

Louis felt his stomach pitch as Mrs. Ravanides dropped a third portion of spinach pie onto his plate. Like most guys in their midtwenties, he ate food like it might disappear, but if he packed away one more bite of Greek cuisine, he would keel over. If it incurred the wrath of his spatula-wielding dinner host, so be it. He wanted to live to see Saturday, dammit.

The reminder of Saturday led to a memory of Roxy sitting on his desk, hungry because she'd skipped breakfast.

With an inward curse, he picked up his fork and took another bite.

Roxy. He couldn't keep her in one place longer than ten minutes, yet she'd become his biggest distraction. If her strategy was to drive him crazy so he'd be a more entertaining date tomorrow night, it was working. At this rate, he'd probably try everything from balloon animals to poetry readings to get her to sit still for an hour. He wanted to look at her face. Wanted to make her laugh. And for chrisssakes, he wanted to take her home.

What they'd done in the hallway outside his future brother-in-law's apartment . . . even with two helpings of spanakopita in his stomach, he still felt a wave of need. Pulse-pounding, sweaty, unquenchable need to have her underneath him. Not a comfortable feeling when two elderly faces were smiling back at you from across the table, remarking on what a good eater you are.

He'd accepted his pro bono client's dinner invitation in hopes of taking his mind off the elusive Roxy for a few hours. Not to mention the fact that the man's wife had come to his office and refused to take no for an answer, practically dragging him out the door by his tie. At first, he'd enjoyed himself. He'd sat on their plastic-covered couch and looked at old photos of their kids. Listened to them tell the story of their emigration to America thirty years earlier, the way their convenience store had played such a huge part in their success in New York City. They didn't take what they had for granted, and Louis was fascinated by that. He'd come from a world where taking what you had for granted was a given. The norm. His father probably wouldn't even step foot in their tiny shop for fear he'd get dust on his wingtips, but to them, it meant the world.

Louis had always wished for something like that. Something that didn't come easy. Something that required work as opposed to money. When you had everything handed to you from such a young age—summer vacations, clothes, sailing lessons—your idea of value got skewed. Was the free work he was doing enough to earn everything he'd been given? He hoped so. But he couldn't shake the feeling he needed to do more.

In an attempt to clear his head of those thoughts, he'd summoned Roxy to block them out. Her mix of confidence and insecurities, as well hidden as she could get them. The way she'd looked up at him, green eyes shining, and said, *Think about me.* Ah, it all made sense now. She'd cursed him.

It figured that the first girl to make him *want* to work this hard—*hard* being the operative word—acted like she could take him or leave him. This was his punishment for never pursuing a relationship that took place outside his bedroom. As a result, he didn't know how. He sucked at it.

And he really sucked at sucking at things.

As a result, he'd spent today trying to convince himself he didn't *want* a relationship with Roxy. Or anyone. Oh, and he'd been *really* convincing, too, checking his phone for a text from her before he'd even finished his thought. Of course she hadn't texted him. Pathetic.

All right, that's it. He'd held out for two days. Giving Mr. and Mrs. Ravanides his best smile, he pushed back from the table. "Would you excuse me for a minute? I just need a little air."

"Sure, sure." Mrs. Ravanides, very businesslike, cleared his plate. "I'll wrap this up for you."

"If you didn't, I was going to." He winked at her. "That's my lunch tomorrow."

Her cheeks turned pink. "As it should be. I'll just throw in some more lamb and pita."

Louis walked out onto the front porch and collapsed onto their stoop. Thank God he'd planned on an Italian restaurant tomorrow night. If he ever saw another piece of feta cheese again, he'd probably run away screaming. He reached into his pocket and took out his cell phone, pulling up Roxy's picture. Immediately, his annoyance with her dulled to a whisper, and all he wanted to do was hear from her.

Help me.

What appears to be the problem, sir?

Great. He was already smiling. Why couldn't everything with her be this easy?

Ate too much. Need someone to roll me back from Queens. A crane might work, too.

What kind of food was it?

Greek.

Worth it.

Tell that to my belt buckle.

A long pause that had him feeling restless. Had he caught her in the middle of something? It was a Friday night. Did she have a date? Oh, man. He really didn't like thinking about her out with another guy. It made him go a little insane, actually. Finally, his phone buzzed.

> If I get that close to your belt buckle, are you
> sure you want me talking?

Jesus H. Christ. That comment had taken his current state of sexually frustrated and turned up the volume to deafening. Even without seeing her in person, he knew that comment had been meant to keep him off balance. It had worked.

> Good point. But not cool when you're not
> within reaching distance.

> Will it help if I tell you I'm looking forward to
> tomorrow night?

Before that last comment, maybe. Now? Definitely not.

> No. Distract me.

> I'm at an audition right now for a hair color
> commercial. The call was for twentysomething girls
> with a beachy, windswept look. One girl brought
> her own fan. Another is dressed like a mermaid.

> I don't believe you.

A picture hit his phone a minute later.

> Okay, I believe you.

While they might be making light of the situation, knowing what she subjected herself to every day only justified the phone call he'd made last night. Even the short performance she'd given at Fletcher's bachelor party, *after* they'd returned from the bedroom, had proven how much talent she had. It was such an easy fix. All she needed was a shot. Soon she wouldn't have to face the constant rejection anymore. Wouldn't have to take her clothes off to get her by until the next audition that very likely wouldn't pan out. No more living day to day. Paycheck to paycheck. But would *she* see it that way?

> I'm up next. Wish me luck.

> Give me your address, Rox. I want to pick you up tomorrow night.

So much time passed that he thought she'd blown him off. That he'd pushed too far, too quickly. His frustrated curse was interrupted by the buzzing of his phone. She'd texted him her address, apartment number, and everything. A slow smile spread across his face. Progress. Finally.

"What's her name?"

Louis turned to find Mr. Ravanides standing behind him, leaning against the house. Jesus. How long had he been there? See, this is what happened when five feet five inches of beautiful, complicated girl crowded everything else out of your mind. You risked being crept up on by hairy, foreign men. And the knowing look in the other man's eye told Louis he wouldn't accept any bullshit answers. "Roxy. Just Roxy. I don't even know her last name."

"Have you gone to meet her father yet? Asked for permission?"

"Permission for what?"

His thick eyebrows slashed down. "To see the girl."

Louis laughed. "I'm having a hard enough time getting *her* permission."

"Ah." Mr. Ravanides nodded sagely. "She's one of those."

"I don't know what you mean by that." Louis turned and stared back out at the street. "But I'm guessing you're right. She covers all the bases."

"Just as long as *you're* not covering bases," the other man said sternly. "Not until you shake the father's hand. Look him in the eye."

Louis nodded to appease him. "Is that what you did with Mrs. Ravanides?"

"Hell, no. We eloped."

With all the food in his stomach, it hurt to laugh, but Louis couldn't help it. Damn, he really liked the guy. His whole family, really. The easy bond between them. It made him wish for the same thing. It made him wonder what Roxy's relationship with her family was like. God, he didn't know a damn thing about her. That would change starting tomorrow. Everything would.

"Let me ask you something," Louis said as he shifted uncomfortably. "Back when you met Mrs. Ravanides, if you had a way to make her life easier, would you have done it? Even if it meant leaving out the truth?"

"My lawyer is asking *me* for advice now?" He pushed off the wall and joined Louis on the top step. "Don't worry. I'll do it pro bono."

Louis's laugh turned into a groan when the spanakopita used his arteries as a water slide. "Thanks."

Mr. Ravanides handed him a roll of Tums he'd kept hidden in his hand until now. "I tell all my children that honesty is the best policy. Always. But sometimes people are too proud to ask for help when they need it. Those people need a gentle push." He clapped a hand onto Louis's shoulder. "I know the kind of man you are. If you're leaving out the truth, you have a good reason."

Louis popped the antacid into his mouth. For the hundredth time since last night, he wondered if his selfish reasons for wanting Roxy to have some security outweighed his good intentions. No time for regrets now, though. The deed was done. "Let's hope you're right."

"I'm usually right. Unless the argument is with my Ms. Ravanides." The older man stood. "Now. Come inside. My wife baked two pans of baklava, and they're getting cold."

Sweet Jesus.

BISCUITS. THE MOUTHWATERING smell catapulted Roxy up the stairs toward the apartment. She swore she could actually feel herself gain three pounds from the aroma alone. If Honey had anything to say about it, she'd *never* get hired in this town. Not because she couldn't afford the extra weight, but because she'd spend all her time in food comas, butter and icing smeared on her face. *What audition? Pass the sticky buns, fool.*

Unfortunately, turning down free food was sacrilege in her

personal religion. Free food was to be cherished and treated with respect. Every morsel savored. She'd eaten too many meals involving ramen noodles and stale Wonder Bread to forgo the opportunity to try out her roommate's latest creation. She'd been caught a little off guard by Honey's willingness to share, as if it were a foregone conclusion. With her Southern accent and constant presence in the kitchen, she reminded Roxy of those women in old-timey cartoons who left apple pies cooling on the windowsill. A nurturer.

She shook off those bizarre thoughts. At least *this* time she'd come prepared with a bottle of tequila to contribute. Honey and Abby seemed determined to create some kind of evening meal ritual. Apparently Roxy had gotten shacked up with a couple of functional human beings. That shit should have been in the ad, really.

The first two nights, she'd taken a plate and slunk off to her room, feeling like a moocher. She'd listened to them discuss their day through her cracked bedroom door, wanting to know more about them against her will. Honey came home and cooked between classes at Columbia. Abby, true to her word, didn't have any friends, so she'd taken to the friendly, guileless Honey like, well, a fly to honey. But where did Roxy fit in? Her conversational comfort zone started and ended with a snappy greeting and an exit strategy. Not a play-by-play of her day.

Oddly, she found herself feeling kind of left out as her roommates bonded a little more each day. Which made no sense, since her exile was self-imposed. Still, the sticky feeling remained. Why couldn't they just avoid each other like typical New York

City roommates and communicate via a dry-erase board in the kitchen?

Tonight, she intended to keep alive her streak of dining and dashing, but at least she'd come bearing a gift this time to alleviate her increasing guilt. Booze for biscuits. A fair trade if she'd ever heard one. Hopefully it would distract her roommates long enough to make off with her dinner to the safety of her room. Maybe she didn't have a bosom buddy, but at least she had her view. Last night, she'd found herself staring out over Ninth Avenue, taking comfort in the wave of cabs that came with each cycle of green lights, people dipping out of their apartment buildings long enough to grab something from the corner bodega.

Okay, so she'd *pretended* to be fascinated by the creature habits of her new Chelsea neighbors, but her mind had actually been on the Lower East Side with a certain physically blessed lawyer. She'd debated with herself, one half determined to stay away from him until Saturday, one half dying to jump on the train, travel downtown, and knock on his door. Images had tangoed behind her eyelids as she'd tried to sleep. Images of what Louis would do if he found her on his doorstep at midnight, obviously there for one shameless reason. Would they even make it to the bedroom, or would she end up flat on her back in the entryway? Or maybe she'd be on top . . .

The first time you ride me, I'm going to grip your ass just like this.

Roxy's neck flushed hot. Tomorrow night felt ten years away. With a deep breath, she took out her key and opened the door. "Honey, I'm home!"

Honey squeaked.

Biscuits went flying everywhere.

It happened in slow motion, like something out of a bad dream. A terrible event was occurring, but Roxy's feet wouldn't move. Standing in the doorway with her mouth dropped open, she was totally useless. Not that she could prevent the tragedy, but if she'd been quicker to the punch, she might have caught at least a *couple* of them midair, like tiny Frisbees of goodness. One by one, the little handfuls of doughy perfection hit the hardwood floor, the subtle *poff* sounds they made a taunting proof of their fluffiness.

Honey stood in the kitchen, baking pan in hand, looking like she was in denial. Abby walked out from her bedroom and stared at the mess for a moment before shrugging and walking purposefully toward the broom closet. Did she actually intend to sweep those suckers up?

"Oh no, you don't." Roxy let the door slam behind her. "Ten second rule."

She lunged for the floor. At the same time, Honey tossed the pan onto the counter with a clatter and joined her on hands and knees. When Roxy picked up the first biscuit, she realized she hadn't thought this genius plan all the way through. Fresh from the oven, biscuits were hot as hell. Still, no way was she letting them go to waste. Not going to happen. Tossing the first flaky casualty between her hands like a hot potato, she huffed and puffed her way to the counter, dropped it, and went back for more. After a few trips, she noticed that Abby had joined them, too, transporting biscuits from floor to counter as if they were wounded soldiers on a battlefield. Their concentrated, semi-pained expressions were what finally did it. The situation was just too absurd. Roxy plopped down cross-legged on her butt and started to laugh.

"What are you doing?" Honey demanded. "You're the one who called ten second rule."

Roxy laughed harder. "I know, it's just . . . no biscuit left behind . . . give me biscuits or give me death . . . ?"

It was a disjointed ramble, but Honey seemed to interpret her military comparison. She dropped the biscuit being passed between her hands and giggled under her breath.

Abby stood and grabbed an oven mitt off the counter, carrying the remains of the baked goods to the counter with casual grace. "I might have spoken too soon the other day when I called you both relatively normal."

"It took you this long to realize that?" Roxy reached back toward the door and retrieved the bottle of tequila she'd set on the ground to participate in Operation Biscuit Salvage. "Can I interest anyone in a drink?"

Honey jumped to her feet. "I'll get glasses."

Abby sat down beside Roxy in a series of awkward movements, as if she'd never sat on the floor before in her life. Maybe she hadn't. "I guess one drink won't hurt."

"Never does." Roxy took a glass from Honey and poured. This didn't feel as uncomfortable as she'd anticipated. Possibly because she'd taken them out of their comfort zone and stuck them in hers. Drinking tequila on the floor. "So, what's up with that guy on the third floor? Every time I pass his door, he clears his throat. Super loud, like he wants me to know he's spying through the peephole."

"I thought I was the only one." Honey took a healthy sip without wincing, going up a notch in Roxy's book. "Have you ever seen him, Abby?"

"Nope." She eyed the drink in her hand warily. "I've only seen one person since moving in. There's an older gentleman who wears a captain's hat and smokes cigars on the first floor. He always tells me my shoe is untied, even when it's not. Thinks it's hysterical."

"We should bring him dirty floor biscuits," Honey said. "He'd never know. But we would."

"Oh, you're bad."

The blonde smoothed her hair. "It's been said."

"So." Abby found yet another sitting position. "How has everyone's week been so far?"

Roxy sipped her tequila, assuming they would start their usual chatter and leave her out of it. When the silence lengthened, however, she realized they were both looking at her expectantly. It quickly became obvious to her that they'd talked *enough* to each other lately. Now they wanted to know about their wayward third roommate who'd spent the first week of their acquaintance hibernating. Had she unintentionally staged her own friendship intervention? Crap. The girls might be smiling, but they looked ready to spring and handcuff her to the radiator if she tried to vamoose. Even in the midst of her nerves at being the center of attention— being *herself*, not a character she was pretending to be—she felt a sense of gratefulness. There hadn't been many times in the past when she'd sensed people had been truly interested in what she had to say. In *her*.

She had a choice to make. Either she would be honest and tell this corporate debutante and this bubbly scholar what her week had actually entailed. Or she could lie and make something up. Apart from her vague explanation that she was an actress, they knew nothing about her. It would be so easy to give them a lie to buy herself more time. More time to become something worth telling. If she did that, though, would she be admitting that she was currently . . . nothing?

Fuck that.

She threw back the remaining inch of her tequila. "I met a guy."

Honey brightened. "Ooh. Tell us."

"What does he do?" Abby asked.

"He's a lawyer." She cleared her throat into the silence. "I was sent to his door to perform a singing telegram while wearing a giant pink bunny suit. We kissed. We texted. Then I showed up to a bachelor party where he was one of the guests. I was there as a stripper. We kissed some more. We texted some more. I'm seeing him tomorrow night." The two girls were silent a moment. Very slowly, Honey reached for the bottle of tequila and refilled her glass. Something about that gesture eased the pressure in Roxy's chest, but not completely. "Also, I got called back to read for the part of Lassie by a couple of hipster film students in scarves."

Abby frowned. "Dogs don't talk."

"I know."

Silence reigned in the apartment. Just as Roxy got ready to gain her feet and make toward her room, Honey blurted, "I'm going to seduce my English professor."

Abby's mouth dropped open. "We've been having dinner together for days. You never said anything. I *earned* this knowledge."

"It's not polite dinner conversation." Honey reached up and
grabbed a biscuit off the kitchen counter, biting into it with a
grin. "He's going to be a challenge. I can tell."

Roxy couldn't hide her amusement. "That doesn't appear to be
a concern for you."

"Concern?" She popped a bite into her mouth. "It's a requirement."

Abby looked at a loss. Not judgmental, as Roxy had predicted,
although both roommates did appear to be looking at Roxy dif-
ferently. As one *would* after having an information bomb dropped
on them. Based on their curious expressions, the questions weren't
over, either. But they weren't pressing for now, and Roxy appreciated that. What had she expected from these girls? For them to
throw her out? Obviously, she hadn't given them enough credit.

"Come on, Abby." Roxy tipped her chin at the brunette. "You
must have a skeleton hiding in one of the eight closets in this
apartment."

"Nope."

"Give us something," Honey begged. "It can't be as bad as
Roxy's."

"Thanks, roomie."

"All right, fine." Abby choked on a slug of tequila. "I've only
kissed two guys. One was my stepbrother."

A beat of shocked silence passed.

"Okay, then." Roxy nodded. "Pass me a fucking biscuit."

Chapter 8

*L*ouis knocked on Roxy's apartment door and waited. The light filtering through the peephole darkened, then brightened again a second later. He heard a shuffling sound from inside the apartment, but still the door remained closed. Whoever had buzzed him into the building knew he would eventually make it up the stairs, right? Getting into the apartment was a two-step process.

"He's hot," a muffled female voice said from the other side. Not Roxy. Maybe a roommate? "He's at least a nine."

Nine? He fought the urge to look himself over and figure out where a point had been deducted. Maybe he should have brought flowers. It would have at least bumped him to a nine point five. "Hey, I can hear you in there. You want to open the door?"

"Yes, but I'm wearing a kimono."

Too bad it wasn't Roxy wearing it. He wouldn't have minded seeing her in a short silk robe. Although at this point, he wouldn't mind seeing her in a burlap sack. "Do you want to go change?"

"Yes, but I'm afraid if I go change, I'll miss the date pickup."

At times like these, he was grateful he'd grown up with two

sisters. He spoke fluent female. In most cases, anyway. Apparently Roxy spoke a completely different dialect. "How about you let me in and I'll close my eyes? I promise not to leave with Roxy until you come back from changing."

"Yes. That." The peephole darkened again. "Close your eyes."

Louis obeyed, wondering when exactly weird doorstep introductions had become the norm in his life. He heard two dead bolts being turned before the door creaked open. A hand curled around his elbow and tugged him through the doorway. "Is she here?"

"We're *all* here," another voice said to his right. Still not the girl he was looking for. "For each other. When things go bad." Something that sounded like an oven door slammed. "You catch my drift, lawyer?"

"I'm starting to feel at a major disadvantage without my eyes open."

"Honey, don't scare him off," Kimono Girl said. "I'll be right back. Don't move."

He wanted to open his eyes and take in his surroundings or any potential threats from the evil disembodied voices, but he kept his promise and waited until Kimono Girl's footsteps disappeared before doing so. *Wow.* Louis turned in a circle. Knowing what he did about Roxy's money troubles, he hadn't expected a place this nice. It was bigger than his own apartment. To be fair, it needed to accommodate at least three crazy girls, while his only needed to fit one sexually frustrated lawyer. Still, it relaxed something inside of him, seeing that she lived in a safe building with people who apparently cared enough about her to threaten well-meaning strangers. Speaking of which . . .

A blonde chopped carrots in the kitchen. With a gleaming butcher knife.

"Hey." He grinned. "I'm Louis."

"I know who you are." *Chop. Chop.* "I'm Honey. And this is my knife, Bubba."

Louis nodded once. "Rox?" he called into the giant apartment. "You about ready?"

"Behind you."

Every muscle in his body tightened at the sound of her smoky voice behind him. Finally. He wanted to whirl on her and catch her off guard. Kiss her hard to make up for the last few days of *not* kissing her. But he needed to be careful how fast he moved with this girl, needed to feel her out first. Slowly, he turned to face Roxy. The amusement in her green eyes told him she'd overheard his exchanges with her roommates. Maybe even had a little appreciation for his efforts to meet the crazy halfway. That's all he had time to read on her face before she sauntered toward him and he became aware of her legs. Her breasts. Her hips.

Russell had a theory that every girl owned one perfect dress that could make men do anything they wanted. Louis had always laughed at his friend, smug in his ability to dictate his own actions. Make his own decisions. Especially where girls were concerned. Yet if Roxy told him to leap out the window just then, he'd be a pancake on Ninth Avenue before she finished voicing her request.

More disturbingly, his first coherent thought was not about how the tight material hugged her breasts or how the hem flirted with the middle of her thighs when she walked. Not even how simple it would be to tug the floaty material up around her waist and get at the panties beneath. Nope, it was, *Who the fuck else has seen her in this dress so I can hunt them down like dogs?*

It worried him how intense the thought hurled itself through his head, like it had been fired from a cannon, wrecking everything in its path. He wanted to back her into the bedroom visible behind her and lock them both inside it. Fuck the date he had planned. Why couldn't he be the only one who looked at her? Was that so much to ask?

She stopped in front of him, and her cherry blossom scent went to his head like back-to-back shots of Jägermeister. Oh, Jesus. Fuck. She was so pretty up close. He'd forgotten how much.

"Uh-oh. What's going on in that head of yours, Louis McNally the Second?"

No way could he tell her the truth. She'd lock herself in that room. *Without* him. If that happened, he just might break down and cry. *Casual. Be casual.* "Your roommate brandished a weapon at me."

"She's Southern."

"I want to rip that stupid dress off your body," he murmured for her ears alone. *So much for casual.*

Those sleep-ruining lips spread into a smile. "Then it's doing its job." She sent a look toward the kitchen. "Honey, you mind stowing the knife? Louis is Mama's friend. He's not a threat."

Louis turned just in time for a brunette to charge back into the room, then skid into a casual walk when she saw they hadn't left. She looked somewhat familiar to him, but he couldn't recall where or how he would have met her. The familiarity might have come from the air she gave off, similar to the people he'd grown up with. Old money. It was an invisible cloak that sat on her shoulders.

She came forward with her hand out, obviously comfortable with polite formalities. At least, when fully clothed. "Pleasure to meet you. I'm Abby. Where are you taking our roommate?"

So this is what it's like on the other side of an interrogation. "I'm going to feed her first."

Honey crossed her arms, still holding the knife. "I can feed her right here. What else you got?"

Roxy came up beside him. "O-kay. There's enough crazy in this room to power New York for a week. Let's get out of here before they ask for your medical records."

Abby jogged ahead of them to open the door. "Have a good time. I want to hear all about it when you get back."

Roxy took her light jean jacket off the wooden coatrack and slipped it on, partially covering her breasts. He hadn't noticed the charge at the back of his neck until it disappeared. God, he needed to cool it. Other men might look at her, but she was out with *him*. If he reminded himself of that once in a while, maybe he could prevent a slow descent into lunacy throughout the evening.

"You're not supposed to let the guy know we'll be talking about him, Abby." Roxy smiled as she opened the door. "Better to let him think I have a different date every night."

Abby nodded, as if cataloguing that information for later. "Right. Even though you don't."

"You're terrible at this."

With that slip of reassuring information, Abby became frontrunner for his favorite roommate. He smiled at Honey, and she sniffed. Apparently he had some work to do with his potential murderer. Hopefully he'd get the chance. Taking a gamble, he reached down and clasped Roxy's hand. Her smile slipped, but she didn't pull away. "Ready?"

"Sure."

On the way out the door, he turned and looked back at Abby. "I'm happy with the nine, but just out of curiosity, what did you deduct the point for?"

She winced. "Don't make me say it in front of you."

"Say it," Honey commanded, her head partially inside the oven.

"You didn't even shave."

He ran his free hand over his jaw. "I did this morning. It kind of grew back."

"Well." Abby folded her hands in front of her, looking slightly embarrassed. "Next time, then."

Next time. Yup. Definitely his favorite. "Good night, ladies. I'd promise to bring her back safely, but you should know something up front. I'm going to do everything in my power to get her to my place for the night. I'm actually hoping like hell neither of you sees her until tomorrow." All three of their faces transformed with different expressions. Honey looked disgusted. Abby, scandalized. Roxy appeared impressed. "Just thought I'd give you fair warning."

LOUIS's WARM HAND felt oddly natural in hers as they walked through Eataly, the massive, multi-floored Italian marketplace. She'd heard about the bustling foodie Mecca before but had never been inside. It was actually so freaking huge that every section boasted its own restaurant, with crowds at each one waiting to be seated. Voices bounced off the dome ceilings, combining with opera music to create a whirlwind of sound. On a Saturday night, it was particularly busy, but Louis didn't seem concerned at all about getting a table. He seemed content to stroll through the aisles, occasionally picking up food samples and handing them to her. Tugging her closer when they needed to squeeze though human traffic jams. Brushing against her in a way she suspected was strategic. If so, it was working. Her neck felt sensitive, her lips felt fuller. And he hadn't even kissed her yet. Why hadn't he kissed her yet?

Don't be a head case. "Which restaurant did you make the reservation for?"

He grinned sexily, and her tummy flipped. "All of them."

Roxy stepped closer to him when a woman asked to get by. He didn't follow her lead by moving back; he simply let her bump into his chest and held her there with a strong forearm. She tried not to think about which parts of her body were pressed against certain parts of his. He was standing too close, and he'd see it all over her face. Approachable abs. Approachable abs. *What were we talking about?* "All seven of them?"

He hummed in his throat, and she felt the vibration against her chest. "The only thing I know for certain you like is peanut butter and banana sandwiches. I wanted to give you options."

"You're a little dangerous, aren't you?"

"Depends what you mean."

She wet her lips when his gaze landed on her mouth, but he made no move to kiss her, the prick. "You didn't even bat an eyelash at my nutso roommates. Now you're giving me the feeling of being in charge of this date even though you planned the whole thing. And I'm kind of buying it."

"My evil plan is working." His hold on her tightened. "So, which restaurant? If you leave it up to me, I'm just going to pick whichever one is busiest so there's a chance you'll have to sit on my lap."

"Ah, there's the catch. You made a reservation for one person, didn't you?"

"No." His head fell forward onto her shoulder with a groan. "I didn't think of that. See? I'm not the date mastermind you thought I was. Disappointed?"

She moved free of his grasp, even though he didn't make it easy. *Keep your head, girl. He's way better at this than the guys you're used to, but he's not different. He can't be.* "I'll only be disappointed if we don't check out the brewery on the roof. Come on."

"That's the most beautiful thing I've ever heard."

They took the stairs to Birreria, a glass-enclosed restaurant on Eataly's rooftop. Their table—for two—overlooked the skyline, which had just started to light up with the oncoming darkness. Every table in the place was filled with couples and groups of friends, laughing and tossing back drinks. Waiters moved gracefully through the rows of seated customers, dropping off pints of beer and plated meals. She took a moment to marvel over the way everything moved like clockwork, just like the rest of the city, predictable in its unpredictability. It was nice to have a reminder of how much she loved this city, when lately her experience here had her forgetting why she came in the first place.

She felt Louis watching her, his gaze moving like a rough palm over her skin. In this lighting, his dark eyes were even more shadowed, the scruff on his face more pronounced. Throw in the panty-melting way he perused her and she felt the sudden need to dump ice water over her head.

"I know what you're thinking about," she said.

"You might know the what, but you don't know the how."

Good God. The more time she spent with him, the more she *did* want to know. Badly. "Hmm. Why were you in Queens yesterday eating Greek food?"

His hand went to his stomach, a pained look claiming his expression. "A client of mine . . . he and his wife decided to feed me for a whole year in one sitting. She thinks people are like camels, storing food in their humps until they need it."

"Does she want to adopt me? I earn my keep."

"I'll put in a good word." A waiter approached, and they gave him their drink orders. Roxy returned her attention to Louis to find him considering her. "Where are your parents, Rox?"

She thought the question had come out of the blue until she remembered her remark about being adopted. The last thing she wanted to talk about was her parents, but she supposed she better clear up his misconception that she was an orphan. "New Jersey." And then change the subject as quickly as possible. "What about yours?"

He looked as though he wanted to press for more details, but he relented with a sigh. "Dad is in Manhattan, Mom is living in France with their divorce attorney."

"Whoa."

"Yeah."

They both sipped their recently arrived beers. "What about your sisters, the twin terrors? Are they in the city, too?"

"Oh yes, they're here. I'm surprised you can't feel their gravitational pull of mayhem."

"Is that what I'm feeling? I thought the beer had already gone to my head." His low laugh traveled across the table and settled over her, making her feel as though they were the only people in the room. "Tell me a story about them. The worst one."

He leaned in closer. "I'll tell you a story, but then I get three questions and you have to answer them. No more redirecting."

"You won't impress me with your fancy lawyer talk." When he only waited, she nodded reluctantly. It didn't feel right deflecting his questions anymore. Not when she knew so much more about him, his family. Not when she kind of *wanted* him to know something about her. What would it hurt? "Fair enough. You can have your three questions."

The pleased look on his face made her skin feel hot beneath her dress. He looked like . . . he wanted to reward her for making the concession. Now. In a very specific way. She almost gave in and asked him to describe the thoughts in his head, but the waiter appeared at the table and broke the spell. Not even having looked at the menu, she decided quickly on the fish entrée and handed the menu to the waiter.

"Okay, I'm ready. Horrify me."

Louis propped both elbows on the table and swiped a hand through his hair. His storytelling pose? "Lena was born three minutes before Celeste. It's always been kind of a sore spot, and that's putting it mildly." He picked up his beer and put it back down. "When they were both six years old, Lena hit a growth spurt first and was one inch taller for a single year. *One* inch. The nanny found Lena tied up in her room. Celeste was standing over her, holding a saw. She'd stolen it from the super's supply closet. She was getting ready to saw off the extra inch."

Roxy clapped a hand over her mouth to prevent her sip of beer from escaping. "No way. That didn't happen."

"Fine. It didn't happen." He dodged the napkin she threw at him. "You ready for the real story?"

"It's going to be a letdown after that."

"You think so?" She nodded, which only made him look smug. "When they were ten, my parents sent them to summer camp. It wasn't the kind you're thinking of. They didn't do arts and crafts or go hiking. They basically sunbathed and read magazines for two weeks at a lakeside resort. Anyway, there was a talent show. They lip-synced to 'The Boy Is Mine' . . . Brandy and Monica . . . you know the one?"

"Yes, and it's a classic. Continue."

"Well, the judges gave them second place. I don't even think there was an actual prize for winning, it was just a way to enter-tain the kids for a couple hours." His tone turned serious. "They didn't strike right away. They bided their time. Waited six years, until they got their driver's licenses. Then they drove to the first-place winner's house in the Hamptons and slashed his tires."

Very slowly, she set her drink down. "Please tell me this one is made up, too."

"Nope. I was in the backseat, being scarred for life."

The waiter sidled up to their table holding a tray full of food. Both of them leaned back so he could set down the plates. "Have your sisters found husbands to terrorize yet?"

Louis nodded once. "Lena is getting married next week."

"Poor guy." She picked up her fork. "Is it a blood ceremony?"

"She hasn't involved me in the planning, but I wouldn't discount anything." He stayed silent until the waiter left. "Actually, you met her fiancé last week, Rox."

Confusion had her pausing in the act of taking her first bite, but unwanted recognition finally crept in. She lowered her hand until it rested on the table, her heart beating dully in her chest. "That was your sister's fiancé's bachelor party? I almost . . ." *Took my clothes off for him.*

"Almost." He shook his head. "But you didn't."

Stupid. So stupid that she'd never put it together. Never asked Louis how he knew the guest of honor. Instead, she'd avoided any memory of it, the same way she did with anything else unpleasant. Just pretending it didn't happen. Jesus, what was she doing here with this guy? What could come of it? She could never show her face around his friends or family lest they judge her straight into the ground. Their entire association was doomed.

Louis scrubbed a hand over his face. "I should've waited longer to tell you."

She forced herself to take a bite of fish. "What difference would it have made?"

"Maybe if I'd waited for you to know me better, you wouldn't be looking for the closest exit."

"I wasn't."

"Rox."

"Fine, I was." She took an impatient sip of her beer. "You earned your three questions, Louis. Fire away."

He stared at her hard a moment in a way that suggested he wanted to shake some sense into her. "You're the type who fulfills her end of a deal, aren't you?"

She shrugged, wondering where he was going with this line of questioning. "Yes. I am."

"Good." He dug into his meal. "Then I'll have to make sure I space those three questions out."

Roxy's eyebrows rose. *Well played.*

Chapter 9

*L*ouis watched the breeze lift Roxy's hair off her neck as they walked along East 37th Street. This time, she kept her hands firmly in her pockets, where he couldn't reach them, sending a signal louder than a reversing semitruck. After their speed bump at dinner, she'd rallied, asking him questions about work, telling him funny audition stories. But the sparkle in her eyes had been gone. Or rather, he'd doused it with a bucket of Stupid Juice. If she hadn't given him the perfect opening to tell her whose bachelor party it had been, he would've kept it to himself just a little longer. As it was, he'd already set a plan in motion that required him to omit the truth. The idea of lying to her twice made him feel like the world's biggest asshole, so he'd bit the bullet.

"The truth will set you free"? Apparently that didn't apply to him.

Back at the restaurant, he'd been able to read the thoughts on her face. Horror had turned to resignation, right before his eyes. She thought this date was pointless now. Thought *he* was pointless.

It was fucking awesome.

Because while Roxy probably assumed her shift in attitude would shut him down, it wouldn't. This is where his lawyer mind went into warp speed, examining reactions from every angle, weighing words, actions. It was a knee-jerk quality that usually irritated him outside of work. Tonight, he wanted to buy that quality a car, because it was giving him some much-needed hope. If Roxy felt as though pursuing anything with him was pointless now, it meant she *hadn't* felt it pointless prior to his coming clean about Fletcher. Before he'd revealed his future brother-in-law as the bachelor party's guest of honor, she'd felt something, too. She'd anticipated *more* with him. Or she wouldn't have had any hope to lose in the first place.

Right?

Okay, this explanation was what he was going with. For now. Otherwise, he'd have to face facts that he wouldn't be spending any more time with this girl who made him hot and crazy, yet calm all at the same time. That, he just couldn't allow to happen. Being with her felt right, like this was where he should have been all along but he'd been epically late. Yeah, that scared the shit out of him. He'd never been committed to another person. Hell, he didn't know how. What example did he have to go on? His parents had been more committed to their personal shoppers than to their own marriage. One thing he did know? The possibility of her not feeling the same, or finding him not worth the trouble, scared him even more shitless. Basically, in either scenario, he was flat out of shits.

He just needed more time to figure her out. Needed more time to figure out why he suddenly wanted to spend every night with the same girl, when they hadn't even spent the night together yet. Speaking of which, the night air was picking up that dress of hers and fluttering it around her thighs like a checkered flag at a NASCAR race. Worse, she kept pulling her jean jacket tighter around her, as if she was cold, but her look-but-don't-touch vibe prevented him from warming her up. In his arms, back where she'd been inside Eataly before he'd doused the sparkle.

"We've been walking east awhile." She sent him an absent smile that made him want to kiss it right off her face. "Any further and we'll fall into the river."

"Almost there." He heard the tightness in his voice and tried to clear it. Jokes wouldn't make this go away. His instinct where she was concerned told him that. No, everything had to be out in the open before he could work through it. So he braced himself and asked the question that had been plaguing him for days. "You said Wednesday was your first time stripping. I know you needed quick cash, but wasn't there someone you could have asked for help?"

"Does this count toward your three questions?" She asked the question as if she'd been expecting him to ask, had already loaded her response.

"Yes. If there's no other way to get you talking."

She sent him a wary look, then released a slow breath. "The day I showed up at your apartment, my roommate had just kicked me out. I didn't have anywhere to go that night, so I stayed up in an Internet café looking for an affordable place." Louis's stomach twisted. He'd been out with his friends drinking, and she'd been virtually homeless. He wanted to go back in time and kick himself in the nuts, but she was still talking, so he put his time travel plans on hold. "I saw an ad for the room in Chelsea. It was . . . well. You saw it. I winged it with Abby and wrote her a bad check. I needed it to clear, and I didn't have enough money in the bank, so I took the job. It was only going to be once."

"It *will* only be once," he growled before he could think better of it.

She frowned. "I don't need a hero, Louis. I'm doing just fine on my own."

"I'm getting that loud and clear." It wasn't lost on him that she hadn't fully answered his question. *Did* she have anyone to ask for help? He closed the distance between them and put an arm around her waist. When she stiffened, he only held tighter. "Stop this. I want to see you, Roxy. Why won't you just let me *see* you?"

"Because I *know* what this is now. I see the kind of guy you are." She rounded on him. *Finally.* A reaction. He wanted to shout with relief, but he didn't think she'd appreciate it. "You're decent, Louis . . . maybe you feel a little bad for me after what happened at the bachelor party. Maybe you want to make some kind of point to yourself, or your family, that you can look past money and jobs and things that matter. Make the point with someone else, all right?"

Ouch. He hadn't quite been expecting that. If that's how she saw him, he had more work ahead of him than he thought. "You know what? That's a load of horseshit." *Swing for the fences, why don't you?* "I don't need to make a point to anyone, especially my family. In fact, I make it a point *not* to make points to them."

"What does that even mean?"

"Hang on. I'm going somewhere with this."

"Okay."

He blew out a breath. "The only opinion that matters to me is yours. Yes, you were hired to give my brother-in-law a lap dance. Stranger things have happened."

"What if your sister finds out?"

"Don't joke like that." Laughter bubbled from her throat, but she still looked sad. He brushed her hair back from her face and decided to focus on the laughing part. "Why did your roommate kick you out? Do you have some terrible habit I need to know about?"

"That's question number two. And, no. I was just late with the rent one too many times." She pursed her lips. "I did eat her bag of flaxseed tortilla chips, though. Even though they were clearly labeled with her name. I think it might have been the straw that broke the roommate's back."

"Those chips are horrible."

"I was in a pinch."

God, she was cute. "Still, friends don't just throw each other out onto the street."

"We weren't friends, we were roommates. Just like my roommate before her was *just* a roommate." She looked away. "You're the kind of guy who makes friends easily, aren't you? You probably stop to pet strangers' dogs on the street and talk to them about the weather. I don't do that. We're too different."

Louis stepped closer until she was forced to tilt her head back. Awareness shone in her eyes, and he absorbed it like a drug. It meant he wasn't imagining this draw between them. Gradually, her curves relaxed against his, and a small sigh drifted past her parted lips. "Dammit, Rox. Stop trying to pick a fight to get rid of me. It's not going to work."

"It works with everyone else." Something seized inside of him at the mild panic in her eyes. "Is this what I get for hooking up with a lawyer?"

"Are we hooking up?" He slid his fingers into her hair and let his mouth ghost over hers. God, it felt amazing to have her close. *Oh yeah.* She'd definitely just looked at his mouth. "Come on, beautiful. Put me out of my misery."

"Hmm." She curled her fingers around his collar and tugged him lower. "Why don't we start with a kiss and see how you do?"

Their hips met on a mutual roll and his eyelids lowered like they weighed two tons each. The slide of her body against his sucked the breath out of his lungs and filled them with something else. Need. Determination. Her. They were on a busy street and he couldn't see, couldn't feel anything but Roxy. For just a split second, her playful pretense dropped and he saw what she'd kept hidden until now. The ache he'd been feeling since they'd met was displayed on her features for him to see. To memorize. He only took a moment to savor it before the prevailing urge to satisfy her ache took over. He'd put it there. He'd made her ache, and now he needed to take it away.

"Why haven't you kissed me yet?" she breathed.

"Good question," he managed before—

She vibrated. She . . . *vibrated*?

"Shit." One of her hands left his collar to dig in her jean jacket pocket. "My phone . . . I have to answer. It could be a callback from an audition, or—"

He couldn't form words, so he just nodded woodenly. Close. He'd been so close.

"Hello?" The apologetic look she sent him froze on her face. "Yes, this is Roxy Cumberland. Who d-did you say was calling?" A beat passed. "Wow. I thought I'd heard you wrong."

A feeling of dread took up residence in Louis's stomach. No. It couldn't be.

"But I've never auditioned for Johan Strassberg, how did he . . . ?" Roxy trailed off, nodding a moment later. Jesus, no. Louis wasn't supposed to be with her when she got this call. Who called someone on a Saturday night to schedule an audition, anyway? He hadn't expected Johan to contact her until Monday, when Louis would be safely in work, *thinking* about her but not *looking* right at her. And lying. Pretending he had nothing to do with Johan calling her to read for a part in his upcoming movie.

Now? Now, he'd have to smile and congratulate her. Keep the truth to himself. Again. This is why he hated lying, because one lie almost inevitably led to two. Then three. Until you couldn't see your way clear of it.

Johan Strassberg was a family friend turned wunderkind filmmaker. They'd been brought up in the same circles, attending the same parties, the same private schools. While they'd never been close friends, this was how things worked in their world. Louis's father was one of Johan's parent's legal advisors. Louis had called Johan and asked for the favor because he knew Roxy was talented, knew if he could get her in front of someone with a little influence, it might be the break she needed. But she would never see it that way, however, especially after what she'd said to him moments ago. It would be charity to her. So he had no choice but to suck it up and lie.

Or he risked losing her, right here and now.

When her face broke into the most heart-stopping smile he'd ever seen, Louis decided that maybe, just a little, the deception had been worth it.

For now.

ROXY DISCONNECTED THE call and swore everything around her was sparkling. This couldn't be the same street she'd walked down five minutes ago. That street had seemed like nothing more than a gray pedestrian walkway, but this? It reminded her of that moment in *Wizard of Oz* when everything turns to color. Only this wouldn't turn out to be some elaborate dream. At least she didn't think so.

Louis shoved both hands into his pockets. "Everything okay?"

A laugh shuddered out from somewhere deep down. Like she'd been saving it up for something amazing to happen. And it had. Johan Strassberg, the filmmaker *of the moment*, wanted her to read for a part. Monday afternoon. In less than forty-eight hours, she'd be reciting lines as he watched. Everything she'd worked for, all the miles she'd put on her high heels, would all come down to a handful of minutes.

Yeah, okay, there was a chance she would fail. A big, fat chance. But at least she'd know afterward if she had what it took or if this was just a pipe dream she shared with a million other aspiring actresses. She'd given herself two years to pursue this dream, and the end of that allotted time had come and gone. This was it. Her make-or-break moment.

"Rox." Louis stooped down and looked her in the eye. "You in there?"

"Yeah." She nodded vigorously. "I'm here. I—"

Oh, the hell with it. She clutched two handfuls of Louis's hair and dragged his mouth down to meet hers. Unexpectedly, he hesitated, even though she could feel his breathing go shallow the second their lips touched. She didn't let it stop her, though. Kissing Louis was her only way of knowing she hadn't hit her head and imagined the phone call.

A throaty groan signaled the change in him. His arms banded around her like steel, yanking her up against him as he sunk into the kiss. He met her mouth with such force that she had no choice but to arch her back or lose balance. She could feel his belt buckle, the muscles hidden underneath his clothes, pressing and moving over the light material of her dress. Rubbing, chafing her skin until she got hot. So hot. It had started as long, indulgent pulls from each other's mouths, but it graduated to something more. Louis licked inside her mouth and drew his tongue out slowly, all the while squeezing handfuls of her dress's material. As if he wanted to rip it off her body. She kind of wanted him to. *Kind of?*

One of her knees inched up the outside of his thigh without any conscious thought on her part. She only knew she wanted to get closer, wanted to feel him move against her in the best way possible. The way she was suddenly craving, as if his mouth were an aphrodisiac.

Louis made a tortured noise and shoved her leg back down. "Next time you wrap even one of those legs around me, I swear I'm going to fuck you like a madman." He pressed their foreheads together. "Unless you want what I've got right now, on this street, keep your thighs under that dress."

Roxy's knees threatened to give out. This wasn't the first time she'd experienced this aggressive side of Louis. Hot *damn*, she liked it. Liked being the person making his teeth clench, making his usual cool-guy façade desert him. She wanted more of it, but reality started to reintroduce itself around her. People whispered as they passed, laughing when they thought they were out of earshot. She needed to stop acting like a hormonal high school sophomore. Kick it up to at least junior year, bare minimum.

"I got carried away." She forced her lungs to accept a slow breath. "Sue me."

When his hand released the material of her dress, she realized he'd still been clutching it hard. "I did, too. I shouldn't have said that."

"No, it was good stuff. I liked it."

He dropped his head onto her shoulder with a groan. "You're trying to kill me, huh?"

"That would suck. I kind of like having you around." It was the simple truth. After dinner, she'd avoided the reason for her bad mood, but the phone call had jolted her into remembering them for what they were. She'd thought about Louis's friends and family knowing her identity, what she'd nearly done, and she'd felt momentarily embarrassed, which had royally pissed her off. She resented that feeling. Didn't want it. Unfortunately, she wanted

Louis. For more than just his apparent penchant for manhandling her. She enjoyed being with him, talking to him, listening to him. Kissing him. Oh yeah, she liked that, too.

"A few minutes ago, you were trying to get rid of me," he said, staring just over her shoulder. "Did something change?"

"No. I just decided to admit it."

"Okay." The poor guy looked like he was silently praying for patience. "You, uh . . . sure it had nothing to do with that phone call?"

"*Phone call.*" God, she'd been more wrapped up in him than she thought. "You're not going to believe this. That was Johan Strassberg's assistant. The indie filmmaker who wrote *Bangkok Boogie*? He wants me to read for a part on Monday." Excitement fizzed like champagne in her chest, mixing with the warm sensations left over from their kiss. At this rate, she *would* need that dip into the river to cool off. Followed by an ice bath. "Some casting director I auditioned for recommended me, sent him my headshot . . . I can't believe it. This kind of thing never happens. At least, not to me."

His smile looked strained. Sexual frustration? Had to be. She hadn't known him long, but she already knew he was the kind of guy who would be happy for her to have this opportunity. He'd literally growled at her on the way here for inferring she might strip again.

He tucked a stray hair behind her ear. "That's great. You're going to knock them dead."

"You really think it's my goal to kill people, don't you?"

"I'm living proof."

"Not for long." She gave an evil cackle, which eased some of the tension around his eyes. "So am I ever going to see the rest of this date?"

"Yes, if we're not too late." Louis grabbed her hand and took off heading east again, pulling her along behind him. She had to speed walk to keep up with his long strides, but she decided not to comment on his suddenly weird behavior. As soon as they crossed Second Avenue, she saw a crowd gathered near the Queens Midtown Tunnel entrance, snapping pictures. They seemed to be looking over the wall at something below . . . something that was illuminated by several giant spotlights. A film shoot?

A loud animal noise had her stumbling. "Was that an elephant?"

He sent her a grin over his shoulder as they reached the crowd. "Yup." All she could do was stare at his broad back as he bypassed the crowd and led her to a bench area that was recessed in from the sidewalk. She didn't understand why he was leading her away from the action until he boosted her up onto the bench. From her vantage point, she could see over the retaining wall to the tunnel entrance beneath. It took her a few seconds to believe what she was seeing. Elephants, walking in a line, out of the tunnel. At least ten of them had already exited, and they kept coming, one after another. Each one held the preceding animal's tail with its trunk, making a big elephant daisy chain.

"What is this?"

Roxy didn't realize Louis had gotten onto the bench behind her until he spoke against her ear. "They walk through the tunnel once a year when the circus comes to town. It's tradition."

"I can't believe I never knew about it," she murmured.

He slid an arm around her waist, pulling her back against him. "I'm glad you didn't, or it would have been a lame surprise."

"It's the opposite of lame. It's un-lame."

They stayed silent for a while, watching as the procession of elephants finished passing through the tunnel. She let herself relax against Louis's reassuring chest, stopped thinking about what it meant to stand there with him holding her, as if they were a couple. Or why it felt so good and natural. Once the last elephant came out of the tunnel, the bright spotlights began going out one at a time, the crowd dispersing and heading in all different directions. In a matter of minutes, Roxy and Louis were bathed in darkness, mostly alone on the street. Tucked away from the sidewalk as they were, the way he held her from behind went from comforting and sweet to something else entirely.

His breath on her neck started coming a little faster. The arm around her waist dipped lower to her hips, pulling her back until her ass met his lap. A tiny gasp slipped past her lips when she felt his hardness, and she barely checked the urge to grind against him. With a curse, he pulled away. She started to voice her protest, but he climbed down from the bench and plucked her off before she had the chance, keeping her facing forward. His hard chest met her back again, his hot mouth finding her neck as he walked her farther into the dark alcove. When they reached the stone wall, she had no choice but to brace her hands against it or run into it face-first. The position felt perfect and indecent all at the same time. Palms flat on the wall as Louis kissed her neck, as his hands roamed over her hips. They were mostly hidden in the darkness, but they were still in public. At the moment, she was too hot to care.

"I'm going to finger you, Roxy. Tell me you want it."

The roughly delivered words sent an electric current zapping along her skin. "I want it." Acting on impulse, she took his hand and guided it under her skirt. She left it resting high on her thigh, hoping he would make the next move. To touch her where she was dying to be touched.

His teeth grazed her ear. "No, you're going to put my hand where it's *supposed* to go."

Heat rushed between her thighs, made more intense by the challenge. Should she be worried about the difference in him when they were touching? She wasn't. She wanted more. Finished with savoring the anticipation, she took his hand again and guided it between her legs, sucking in a breath as her discomfort eased and grew at the same time.

Louis groaned into her hair. "You hot and wet under these panties?" He squeezed her covered flesh with just enough pressure to make her eyes roll back in her head.

"It's safe to say I am now," she breathed.

"I can't even keep my fucking hands off you long enough to bring you home." His lips traced up the side of her neck, ending at the sensitive flesh behind her ear. "*Will* I get you home tonight, Rox?"

"Yes." She hadn't made a conscious decision, but the inevitability had been there. Long before the date had started. "I'm going home with you. And that was your third and final question."

"*Good.*" She felt a breeze as he lifted her dress, but warmth replaced it immediately. He pushed his hips against her mostly bare bottom, pinning her to the wall. "Feel what you did, you sexy-as-fuck girl. I need you to take care of it."

"I'm going to take care of it so good." Her head spun a little when she heard herself. She never said things like this. Never sounded like this. It was exciting. It was disconcerting as hell.

Her scattered thoughts imploded as he yanked her panties aside and pushed his middle finger inside her. The sudden fullness was so unexpected that she barely managed to trap the scream inside her throat. Her fingers curled on the wall, scraping for purchase and finding none. As if sensing her lack of balance, Louis held her tighter with his other arm, keeping her locked against his body.

"I've got you." He leaned back a little, taking her with him. "You just tell me what you like and I'll make sure you get it. That's how this is going to work."

When he began worrying her clit with his thumb, her head dropped back onto his shoulder. "Oh, God. More of that. Faster."

Slowly, he licked up the side of her neck. "You'll want my tongue fast, too, won't you?"

Oh, God. "Yes."

His hips circled against her bottom, smooth dress pants the only barrier between them. He pushed a second finger inside her without letting up on his perfect torture of her sensitive flesh. The ache inside her moved and expanded, encompassing her. She wanted to writhe against him but didn't want to move for fear the quickening feeling would go away. An anchor. She needed an anchor, so she turned her head and found his mouth, moaning when he gave her exactly what she needed. Hot, furious kissing.

When he finally pulled away, his eyes were so dark they looked as if they belonged to somebody else. "Come on my fingers now, Roxy. I need to get you somewhere I can be inside you."

His final two words were accompanied by hard thrusts of his fingers, propelling her across the finish line. She bit her lip to keep from crying out as she shook against his hand. Louis's hold on her was the only thing keeping her from falling into a heap on the sidewalk, her body felt so limbless. Between her legs, he continued to stroke her, but his touch had turned soothing, gentle. Experienced. Good Lord, he'd accomplished in two minutes what usually took her ten minutes, a bottle of wine, and a Jason Statham movie. It threw her a little, exactly how good he was at this.

The stroking between her legs stilled before his touch left her altogether. "What's going on inside your head?"

Stop being ridiculous. You performed a singing telegram about his penis on day one. This isn't news to you. Nothing has changed. You're not his girlfriend.

Roxy turned and looked into two questioning eyes. "Nothing." She went up on her toes and kissed his chin. "Take me home."

Chapter 10

Congratulations, you're a depraved asshole.

Louis nodded at the doorman as he walked into his building. Roxy walked beside him, her hand tucked inside his. It made him feel a little sick, knowing the doorman probably wanted to high-five him for bringing home yet another girl, but he couldn't exactly stop and explain to the guy how she was different. How he hoped she'd be walking through the door a hell of a lot more than once. No, he couldn't do that, because she'd gone somewhere inside that head of hers, and he didn't know how to get her back. He shouldn't be focused on getting her naked, he should be *talking* to her.

This is where he became a depraved asshole, however.

If he could just get her into bed, he could *make* her accept this connection between them. This was his genius plan. He didn't know if the assurance came from an arrogant place, only knew it was battering around inside him, making a friendly heart-to-heart seem like a distinctly unviable option. This feeling, this need to be as close to her as humanly possible, was completely foreign. Yes, he'd been around a little. Okay, maybe a lot. He didn't lack for confidence when it came to sex. Right now, when he sensed her slipping away, it felt like all he had left.

Back on that street, when he was touching her, everything came together for a while. She was trusting him, letting herself go and being honest with him. He just wanted to get back to that place so he could . . . what? Get a promise out of her that she wouldn't go away? Make her pinkie swear that she wouldn't make him wait another week to see her again?

Yeah, that pretty much summed it up.

Since she'd gradually clammed up on the ride home after he'd gone all sex maniac on her, it might not even work. It could drive her away more. *Why?* The single word raced from one end of his mind to the other. She'd liked what he'd done to her. No way to fake that kind of reaction. So why wouldn't she look at him as they boarded the elevator? He thought back to the dark street, the things he'd said to her. Maybe he'd come on too strong, but there hadn't been any help for it. When they were touching, he lost control of his mouth. Lost the ability to run words past his brain and make a mutual decision if they should be set loose. These . . . feelings for her spent so much time being locked away that maybe his subconscious had just disguised themselves as something else.

All right, so he'd found a twisted way to excuse his plan of screwing her into staying with him. What about the rest? What about the fact that he'd looked right into her excited green eyes and lied? Even if she never found out about the favor he'd called in, it would always be there, reminding him he'd deceived her to get what he wanted. What he wanted was her. And in order to *have* her and maintain his sanity, taking her clothes off in a stranger's apartment couldn't be on the agenda.

This business of keeping her around was going to be complicated, but not having her around would be worse. For now, he would focus on that and worry about the axe hanging over his head later.

"You've gone quiet on me."

Roxy shifted and tucked a stray hair behind her ear. "Yeah? Well, last time I was in this elevator, I was dressed in a bunny costume."

He sighed. "I thought we agreed not to talk about that anymore."

"We agreed not to talk about the *song*," she corrected him, finally giving him a smile.

"And yet you just did."

"Well, since I already broke the agreement. . . ." She cleared her throat and started to sing. "To my hotshot honey bunny—"

He lunged toward her side of the elevator and cut her off with a hand over her mouth. "Not cool." His body registered her closeness on impact and began to tighten. *Christ.* Just like that. When the laughter in her gaze lessened and those pupils started to dilate, he knew she felt it, too. That response, so in time with his own, gave him that final push. Taking her home and getting her underneath him was the right thing to do. Being with her in any way couldn't be wrong. Not when she made him feel like this. Maybe his reasons weren't as honorable as they should be, and yeah, he'd lied to her. But this, *this,* was the most honest fucking thing in the world. So were the words that followed. "Roxy, even in that costume, you were so goddamn beautiful, I don't think I've taken a decent breath since."

She made a small noise behind his hand, reminding him he still had her mouth covered. The second he removed it, she threw her arms around his neck and plastered her sexy little body against his. He only had a split second to savor the fact that he'd distracted her from whatever thoughts she'd been having, before their mouths were moving together. Licking, nipping, then devouring. Somewhere in the distance, he heard a ping and the elevator doors roll open. *Get her to your bed, depraved asshole. Now.*

Breaking away with a groan, he gripped her tight, sweet ass and boosted her up so she could lock her legs around his waist. She completed the move with such hungry desperation that his thoughts momentarily blurred and he stumbled from the elevator, still carrying her. They crashed into the opposite wall of his hallway, their mouths meeting once more in a hot tangle of tongues and lips. The heat between her thighs sat directly on top of his hard dick, giving him no choice but to thrust up against her. *Fuuuuuck.* Knowing all she wore under that dress was a thin pair of panties made him crazy to rip them off. Crazy to unzip his pants and sink into her. If the fingers tearing at his hair were any indication, she wanted it.

"Hold on, baby. Just let me get you inside." She locked eyes with him and moaned, working her hips in a circle and sending him closer to the edge. *Unbelievable. I might not even make it to the fucking door.* "My fingers weren't enough?" He drove her higher on the wall with a hard thrust. "You want this, don't you? You want it all?"

"Yes." Her breasts swelled over the top of her dress with every panting breath. "Please, Louis."

"Oh *fuck,* I like you saying my name." With the remaining willpower left inside him, he pulled her off the wall and walked them toward his apartment. He used one hand to fish the keys out of his pocket, not an easy feat when her breath was racing against his ear, her body bouncing up and down on his with every step. Finally, *finally,* he got his key in the door. "Roxy, I'm going to make you feel so good—"

His apartment lights were on. What the hell?

"Lou-*is*!" The familiar, whiny voice hit him with the impact of a sledgehammer. No, no, no. This couldn't be happening. No way could life be this cruel. Roxy was definitely not climbing off him with an alarmed squeak and ducking behind his back. Definitely not. If he just stood here without speaking, the waking nightmare would dissipate and he could go back to kissing Roxy. Please. Please. Please?

In one final attempt to banish the scene in front of him, he squeezed his eyes shut and opened them slowly. Nope, his sister Lena was still there, sitting on his couch.

In full meltdown mode.

Black mascara was caked on her cheeks, dark hair a mess on top of her head. His eyes quickly scanned the room for clues. Shit, she'd found his tequila. This wasn't going to be pretty.

He turned his head slightly so he could speak to Roxy without taking his eyes off Lena. "Don't make any sudden movements."

"Who is that?"

The hint of jealousy in her voice surprised him. It shouldn't, he realized. What conclusions would he jump to if he found a man in *her* apartment if she was supposed to live alone? It also relieved him a little to know she felt at least some kind of claim on him. Apparently he'd managed to make some kind of progress tonight. "My sisters."

Her body relaxed slightly against his back. "Sisters . . . plural?"

"Where one goes, the other usually—"

"Lou-*is*!"

"Follows."

Celeste stumbled out of his bathroom, lighting a cigarette. "Where were you? We're starving. The only thing you have in your freezer is microwave lasagna and Kraft singles, you loser." She fell onto the couch beside Lena, who stared straight at the wall, as if in a trance. "Who's the girl? I can see you, girl. I hope he took you to dinner, because there is fuck-all available at this shit show."

He heard Roxy take a deep breath behind him before she moved to stand at his side. God, he wanted nothing more than to smuggle her out of there and never come back. "Hey, I'm Roxy. We had Italian food, so it's all good."

Celeste gestured wildly with her cigarette. "Well, lucky you. I'll just sit here and die of starvation, everyone! Grab a seat and watch my ribs grow more pronounced."

Louis pinched the bridge of his nose. "Why didn't you order takeout?"

"Lena threw our cell phones into the toilet."

"Both of them?"

Lena shot to her feet. "Yeah. *Both* of them. You want to know why?"

Roxy patted him on the shoulder. "You know what? I think I'm going to go."

"*No.*" He moved in front of the door. Awesome. Barring her exit for the third time since they'd met. Fuck it. He'd worry about himself growing increasingly pathetic later. If he let her leave now, he might lose his chance. And *God*, he wanted her so bad it hurt. "I'll get rid of them. You're staying."

"You know why I threw our cell phones in the toilet, Louis?" Lena's words slurred behind him. "So my bastard fiancé would stop trying to get in touch with me. A stripper! He had a *stripper* at his bachelor party."

He turned to Roxy. "Hey, maybe you should go."

Louis reached behind her to open the door, but Lena moved in front of him. "*Look*! I found her shirt under his couch."

His sister dangled a familiar white T-shirt in front of his face. It smelled like cherry blossoms. A vision flashed in his head of Roxy putting on his button-down shirt over her bra and skirt. No T-shirt. It was definitely hers. Very subtly, he moved in front of a wide-eyed Roxy.

"I knew something was up, so I asked all his dumbass friends."

Celeste positioned herself just behind Lena. "*Dumb. Ass. Friends,*" she repeated like some sort of psychotic hype girl.

"Not one will tell me the truth." Lena pulled an object out of her pocket. A yellow Bic lighter.

And then she set the T-shirt on fire.

"You'll tell me the truth, won't you, Louis? You were there." The flames moved up the T-shirt, turning it to charred, black rags. Lena seemed perfectly content to get burned if it came to that. Might even enjoy it. "I can always count on my brother, can't I?"

"Can she?" Celeste echoed. "*Can* she, Louis?"

"Should I make my peace with God?" Roxy whispered behind him.

"Lena, look at me." Keeping a close eye on the progress of the flames, he put out both of his hands in a calming gesture. "Remember that vacation where you backed Dad's new Mercedes into the lake?" She nodded, and the knot in his chest eased a little. "Who took the fall for you?"

"You did," she said grudgingly.

"Who told you when your perm in ninth grade looked like a dead poodle?"

She swiped at the mascara tracks on her cheek. "You did."

"Right. So you can trust me when I say not one stripper walked through Fletcher's door that night. Not a single one." As far as he was concerned, Roxy was an actress. He'd told enough lies for the night. He wouldn't add another one to the list. Especially when his sister might burn down the apartment if she sensed he wasn't telling the truth. "Your future husband made it through the night lap dance free. You have my word on that, as your brother."

Lena narrowed her eyes at him.

He unearthed his guileless little brother smile and pasted it on.

"I guess I believe you." She jerked her chin toward Roxy. "Are you going to introduce me?"

"Why don't we put out the flaming T-shirt first?" Having no choice but to leave Roxy standing toe to toe with his sister lest they all die in an epic blaze, he plucked the T-shirt out of her hand and strode to the kitchen sink. After turning on the water to douse the fire, he moved back quickly toward the girls. "Listen, I'm going to see you guys for Sunday lunch tomorrow at Dad's place, right? Do you mind—"

"You're not kicking us out, are you?" Celeste plopped back down on the couch. "We just got here."

"Yeah, come on, bro." Stripper drama swiped from her memory, Lena grabbed his hand and dragged him toward the couch. He barely reined in the impulse to hang on to Roxy, whose fear had turned into what looked like amusement. *Oh, nice.* "Don't send us away. We need a Louis night."

"I brought popcorn," Celeste piped up.

"Why didn't you eat *that* if you're so hungry?" His voice had risen to a near shout, much louder than he typically used with his sisters. Could he help it? No. The girl he wanted more than oxygen already had one hand on the doorknob. *They need a Louis night,* Roxy mouthed at him silently.

"We wanted to wait for you," Lena explained.

Both of his sisters' faces had fallen, like a couple of scolded toddlers. He heaved out a frustrated breath toward the ceiling and threw his arms around their shoulders. On cue, they both snuggled into his sides and let out feline purrs. He had cats for sisters. Two bat-shit crazy cats with anger issues.

He knew it was useless, but he implored Roxy with a look. "Stay?"

She was halfway out the door before he'd even gotten the word out.

Apparently the chase would have to wait until tomorrow.

Chapter 11

*R*ussell almost knocked over his sixth beer in an attempt to grab Louis's phone. "Do *not* call her, man. If you do, I swear to God, I will dropkick that iPhone straight into New Jersey."

Louis dodged his friend's hands. "I'm checking my email." He stared down at his phone. Or phones. How did he get two phones? He closed one eye. *Ah, there we go.* Back to one. "Relax, will you?"

"You're doing a lot of email checking for a Sunday night," Russell said. "Also, you're a shit liar, McNally. If she hasn't called you by now, she's not going to."

"Ignore him," Ben interjected loudly, setting another round of beers on the table and stumbling back a step. "Whatever he's saying is wrong. This is the same guy who told us women who eat salad on first dates will eventually kill you in your sleep."

Russell shrugged and sipped his fresh beer. "I stand by that."

"Where are your statistics?" It took Ben three times to say *statistics* correctly. "You have none. Because it's ramblings of a crazy person."

"I don't know, Ben." Louis shoved his phone into his pocket, although he felt more like launching it across the bar. "His dress theory proved correct."

"Dress theory?" Russell sat up straighter in his chair. "She broke out *the dress* on date number one?"

Louis dropped his head onto the table with a thud in an attempt to block out the image of Roxy's figure wrapped in soft, flowery material. How it had felt in his hands. "Yup."

"She's evil," Russell enunciated. "You need to run like a pack of the Real Housewives are chasing you."

Ben and Louis exchanged a glance. "What have you been watching, bro?"

"I put it on in the background when I'm ironing. Don't try and change the subject." Russell rolled his shoulders. "A girl who wears *the dress* on date one either has a blood vendetta against your family that you're not aware of." He ticked off his fingers. "Or she has more than one *dress*. I don't even want to imagine what she'd have in store for date number two."

"I do." Louis nodded vigorously. "I want to know."

"No," Russell insisted, slamming his beer down. "You don't. Look at you, man. You didn't even shave this morning. And what is that? A Hawaiian shirt?"

"It's laundry day," Louis mumbled. "Have I mentioned what a fucking windfall our friendship has been for me?"

"You'll get around to it."

Ben sent Russell a look of disgust before turning to Louis. "Listen, you can't exactly blame the girl for taking off when your sisters showed up. I've met them. They're not exactly the ideal welcoming committee."

"Are you sure?" Louis hiccupped. "Lena set her T-shirt on fire with a Bic. That has to count for a 'welcome to the family' in some culture, right?"

Ben and Russell leaned forward slowly. "She did what?"

"It's a long story." No way in hell was he telling his best friends *why* said T-shirt had been set ablaze. Not because what Roxy had done embarrassed him, just because he didn't want them thinking about her naked. Which made no sense, since they didn't even know what she looked like, but he didn't even want them *imagining* what she looked like, then picturing imaginary Roxy naked. Okay, he appeared to be drunker than he thought.

Today had been shitty for two reasons. One, he'd woken up to his sisters snoring on the floor of his bedroom, instead of Roxy in bed next to him. Two, his request to add more required pro bono time to his contract with Winston and Doubleday had been reeeee-jected. On a Sunday. Via email. There was something just a little *more* insulting about your hopes being dashed when it was followed by the *Sent from my iPhone* sign-off message.

Where did that leave him? Did he keep the cush job his father had landed him, living up to a reputation he'd never wanted to fulfill? If he didn't have the pro bono work to keep him grounded, he'd be like everyone else at his office, chasing a paycheck, forgetting why they'd gotten into law in the first place. He didn't want to forget. Didn't want to start blurring the lines until the job became all about winning and nothing else. But what choice did he have? Jesus, his father would have a coronary if he knew Louis hadn't given Doubleday a direct answer yet. Louis could hear his father now. *Who in their right mind would give up a job like this?* Who, indeed.

Ben looked as if he wanted to press for the full story, but thankfully he didn't. "I vote for calling her. It sounds like she might be traumatized."

"No. *No* calls on my watch."

Louis ignored Russell. "Traumatized? She walked out smiling."

"Evil."

Ben didn't acknowledge Russell, either. "Hey, that's a good thing. Not many girls come into contact with the Twin Terrors and live to tell the tale, let alone laugh about it."

"Yeah. I know." Something pulled in his chest. Dammit, he should call her. Maybe she'd answer on the third ring and call him by his full name. *Hey, Louis McNally the Second.* At this time of night, she might even be in bed, so he could picture her with damp hair and pajamas, snuggled up into a pillow as they spoke. Her voice would be all soft and sleepy.

Jesus. He was turning into a sap. Something needed to give. He wanted to be able to pick up the phone and call Roxy whenever the hell he felt like it, knowing she'd be happy to hear from him. This second-guessing bullshit was starting to get old. Maybe he'd never pursued a girl like this before, but he thought he'd done a decent job of it so far. Apart from their make-out session being interrupted by a life-threatening situation, that is.

Ben was right, though. Roxy might have been a little thrown off by his sisters' untimely arrival, but she'd looked more amused than anything. She rolled with the punches. God, he liked that about her. It was a skill he'd needed to acquire not only for his profession but also because his family brought drama wherever they went. *That's* where he and Roxy would have a problem. He'd seen the wariness in her eyes when Lena had asked him to introduce her. She hadn't run out of his apartment because she'd been afraid of Lena and Celeste. She'd been afraid of getting to know them. Something a girlfriend might do.

Roxy seemed determined to keep things light and casual between them. Any other time, he would be counting his luck that a girl didn't want a concise verbal commitment. An assigned status, complete with promise ring and parental introduction. A fucking weekend trip to Vermont they could brag to their friends about over brunch. He and Roxy hadn't known each other long, so he knew this irrational need for her to make promises wasn't realistic. It didn't change the fact that he wanted to wrap her up in his arms and demand she agree to see him without this big, fat expiration date hovering over his head. It was there, too. He could feel it every time they were together.

When Russell punched him in the shoulder, Louis realized he'd actually been staring at the ceiling. "What?"

"I draw the line at your unshaven tourist look. Talking to the ceiling is entering scary new territory."

Ben tapped a cardboard coaster on the table. "Just call her. What's the worst that could happen?"

Russell's booming laugh turned heads. "Famous last words. I can't believe you're in charge of educating our youth." He gave Louis a pointed look. "The worst that could happen? As soon as she knows you're on the chase, she'll have your balls in a vise."

"Oh, it's safe to say she knows I'm chasing her."

"It's never too late, man. You can turn this circus train around." Russell pushed some empty pint glasses aside and leaned in. "It's like you're the lion and she's a gazelle. Only right now, sorry, you're kind of being the gazelle—"

"I'm too drunk for metaphors."

"I'm *never* too drunk for metaphors." Ben shook his head at Russell. "Just ridiculous ones."

"All I'm saying is, give it a couple days." Russell crossed his arms over his chest. "You'll thank me, my friend."

Louis took a pull from his beer. "Did I mention she has two cute roommates?"

Without missing a beat, Russell tossed his phone onto the table. "Fuck it. Call her now."

LOUIS HADN'T CALLED her.

Not that she'd necessarily expected a call. Or even *needed* one. She'd just really, really thought he'd call. Up until they'd arrived in Sister Hell on Saturday night, things had been going pretty well. If they'd shown up to an empty apartment, she was pretty sure they'd have eaten diner pancakes together the next morning. So. What the fuck? Should she have stayed and waited for one of his sisters to start asking questions? No, thank you. She liked her eyeballs *inside* her head. If he was mad at her for leaving, well, so be it. She didn't need his stupid, Prince Charming, perfect-date-planning ass.

Only she wanted to hear his voice. Kind of *craved* the sound of it. In five minutes, she would leave her apartment and ride the subway to the audition of a lifetime. Her palms were sweating, her outfit was all wrong, and somehow she knew Louis would say the exact right thing to calm her down. How did she know that? No clue. A week ago, she would have been pep-talking herself, and she didn't like this sudden reliance on him to feel confident. Scratch that, she *had* confidence. She just needed the extra kind right now. A shitload of it.

Had he already moved on? Even without the sex first? That would definitely be a new one. Unless he'd decided she wasn't worth the trouble. She cast a look at herself in the mirror across the room and wondered what he saw. If maybe . . . he'd found her lacking. Less sophisticated than the girls he typically dated. The hurt that thought caused her told her she'd already let herself fall maybe just a little too far.

A knock at the apartment door jolted her back to the present. When she started to call out for Honey to answer it, she remembered her roommate had already left for her afternoon physics class. With a sigh, she tossed her mascara down onto her secondhand dresser and clicked through the apartment on her high heels.

"Who is it?"

"Delivery man."

Louis. A feather-winged creature took flight in her stomach. She started to open the door but decided not to appear overeager. "How did you get in?"

"Some guy with a captain's hat downstairs."

She shook her head even though he couldn't see her. "So much for security."

"I'm persuasive." A long pause. "You realize you haven't opened the door yet, right?"

"Maybe I'm wearing a towel."

"I'll be right back."

She lunged for the peephole to look out at him. "Where are you going?"

He looked straight at her. "To get a battering ram."

Her lips spread into a smile, but she quickly turned down the wattage and opened the door. "Hey," she said casually, trying not to stare at the shopping bag in his hand.

"'Hey'?" He laughed under his breath. "That's all I get, huh?"

"I was just about to leave for the audition." Wow, she was pettier than she thought. Giving the guy a hard time for not calling on a Sunday. Who was she turning into? "What's in the bag?"

Louis came toward her, until she had no choice but to move and let him into the apartment, or let him walk straight into her. Tempting, but she had a feeling that if he got that close, she'd be late for the biggest opportunity of her professional life. She closed the door behind her and turned, ready to explain that she only had two minutes and not to get any ideas.

He immediately backed her up against the door, his muscular body aligning with hers. Pressing, pressing, until she had to suck in her stomach to let him closer.

His breath fanned her ear, sending her pulse into hyperdrive. "Mad at me for not calling?"

"Nope," she said too quickly.

"Yes, you are." He dropped the bag with a thud beside her, then lifted his hand to curl it around the back of her neck. "Good."

"Good?" Irritation prickled along her skin. Irritation. *Not* awareness. Right. "Are you playing games with me now, Louis? I thought that was my job."

"It is. And you're good at it." He pulled back to stare at her mouth, but he didn't kiss her. "I don't play games. But I'm also not going to be the guy who you keep blowing off."

Her throat felt tight. "I didn't blow you off."

He ignored her, massaging the back of her neck with his thumb. Holy hell, it felt great. Everything about this felt great. Having him close. Breathing in his scent. She wanted to sink into him and never come up for air. "I want to know that you're not going to disappear every time we have a bad moment or my sisters show up looking like something out of a haunted house. I need you to stick. The fuck. Around." Their thighs melded together, his belt buckle nudging her stomach. "You've been keeping me awake at night since we met, and until now, I honestly didn't know if you felt anything for me. So, yeah. If you're mad at me for not calling? Good."

Holy wow. She'd never been more turned on in her life. Everything he'd said had been fair. He'd accurately called her on her bullshit, and she liked that. A lot. There might even be a small part of her that got a thrill over keeping him up when he should be sleeping. "Are you finished?"

His minty breath warmed her lips. "Why?"

"So I can kiss you."

He sucked his bottom lip through his teeth as she watched in shameful fascination. God, he really did have the most amazing mouth. "No kissing this morning." *What? Had she heard him right?* "You want to be kissed, you come and find me later. *You* come to *me*."

"That definitely sounds like a game," she said sharply.

"Maybe. But it's a game we can both win if you're not stubborn." Before she could deliver a response, his mouth moved away from hers. Bracing himself with his hands on the doorjamb, he very slowly lowered himself toward the ground in front of her. On the way into a kneeling position, he dragged his partially open mouth between her breasts and over her belly, deep groaning noises vibrating through every spot he trailed over. When he landed on his knees, he gripped her hips and pressed his mouth between her legs, sending her falling back against the door in a rush of sensation. She only had mere seconds to feel the heat of his mouth through her dress before he took it away.

"What are you doing?" she asked in a rush of breath.

He reached for the shopping bag. "Wishing you luck at your audition." As she watched through hooded eyes, he lifted a shoe box out of the bag and set it on the ground. With a flick of his wrist, he lifted the top and revealed a pair of black leather pumps. Angels sang in the distance. They were the most beautiful shoes she'd ever seen in her life. Without even trying them on, she knew they were her size, too. "I had to go shoe shopping with my sisters yesterday to get these. Now that you've met them, you know what kind of a hell it was."

She couldn't take the shoes. Could she? Her own pair were so worn out, but at least they were *hers*. At least she'd paid for them herself. No, she couldn't accept this from him. Especially after she'd run him in circles. "Louis, I can't—"

"Oh, yes. After four hours in Bloomingdale's on a Sunday afternoon, you're going to keep them." He wrapped a hand around her ankle and removed her shoe before slipping the new one on. Good Lord, it felt like a cloud molding itself around her tired, blistered foot. She had no choice but to let him repeat the process with her other one. She had to know what it felt like to have them both on. Louis's big hands holding her foot so carefully might have had something to do with her reluctance to pull away, too. Seeing him kneel down in front of her, frustration evident in every line of his body, sparked an ache deep inside her. If she joined him on the floor now, she could make him cave on the no kissing rule, easy peasy. But it would be a hollow victory. For some annoying reason, she wanted to give him the win he needed, so she would wait until later. Tough as it would be.

"How did you know my size?"

He rested his hands on his bent knees, surveying the shoes on her feet. "My sisters are good for some things. They took one look at you and knew your measurements."

She refused to be hurt over his clipped tone. "You sound really pissed at me."

"I'm looking at your bare legs from an advantageous position and there's nothing I can do about it right now or we'll both be late." He pushed a hand through his hair. "Ah, fuck it. I need *something*." Without warning, he leaned in and kissed the inside of her knee, as if he couldn't stand staying away another second.

His breath huffed out against her sensitive skin as his lips stroked higher, to the inside of her thigh. A wave of heat hit her so hard that she had to steady herself with both hands on his strong shoulders to keep from toppling over. His mouth moved to the opposite leg, using his tongue this time to tease her flesh, giving her small bites in between licks. She heard a loud noise and realized her breath had started to rasp in and out. Louis squeezed the backs of her thighs and released an irritated growl before rising to his feet. Her new heels put her eye level with his mouth, and she wanted to kiss him more than anything. So badly her hands shook. His throaty sigh told her he knew how she felt, but his chin was set with resolve. *Now who's stubborn?* she wanted to ask. "I have to be downtown in court all afternoon, starting about ten minutes ago. But I want to see you tonight, Rox. Come over."

A command, not a request. Part of her was annoyed by that. *She* decided where and with whom she spent her time. Oh, but then there was the other, more significant half of her that appreciated him taking the decision out of her hands. Kind of loved it. It might have been the hot tinge of need in his voice that did her in, too. He needed her. She needed him. Really, there was no decision to make. "See you tonight, Louis."

He tried to hide his relief, but she glimpsed it anyway. "You all set for your audition?"

"With these fancy new kicks? I'm a *shoe*-in."

His face transformed with a reluctant grin. "Stop being so damn cute or I'll break my no-kissing rule."

"We can't have that," she breathed dramatically, pulling open the door for him.

On his way out the door, he raked her with a hot glance. "Wear the shoes for me tonight."

She ran her fingernails down his chest. "Only if you wear the tie."

When she closed the door behind Louis, she heard him groan a curse loud enough to echo through the hallway. She couldn't take the time to laugh, though. She was officially running late.

Chapter 12

I must be in the wrong place.

Two sets of critical eyes swung toward Roxy as she opened the entrance door, giving her the obligatory scrutiny every actress gives her competition. Oddly, it unnerved Roxy more than usual. Most auditions she walked into, she was greeted by forty, sometimes fifty, sets of eyes. Never, *ever* a measly two. The lack of competition somehow made the upcoming read that more worrisome. When you had no chance in hell, you lacked for pressure. With only two girls to beat out, the pressure increased like a vise around her neck. Especially when both of the girls looked like they'd stepped off the pages of *Entertainment Weekly*. Hadn't the blonde been in that sitcom with Neil Patrick Harris? *How I Met Your Brother* or something?

She resisted the compulsion to smooth her hair and instead made her way to a chair in the waiting area, where she sat and immediately withdrew the script from her purse. To her left, the office door she'd be walking through in mere minutes sat closed, not a sound coming from the other side.

She'd been emailed the "sides" yesterday afternoon and had spent most of the night rehearsing the script excerpt in front of the bathroom mirror. Johan Strassberg's newest film centered on a young woman who'd been forced to leave college in New York to care for her ailing mother in the Midwest. While she'd only been given a small section of the script, she was already intrigued with the character of Missy Devlin. There was such resentment, vulnerability, and yearning in the small section of text alone that she was eager to see the rest. Eager to immerse herself in the role if she just got the chance. *Please let them give me the chance.*

A fresh-faced redhead in a headset exited the inner office, holding a clipboard. Roxy sucked in a breath, praying they would call someone else first. She needed a minute to gather her thoughts, especially after the pulse-scrambling scene with Louis earlier. Thankfully, headset girl called a different name, and the blonde stood to follow her into the office.

Roxy sucked in a deep breath. *Okay. Okay, you can do this. You are Missy. You've just been yanked out of your dream school, away from your boyfriend and best friends, to care for your mother. You should be eager to get to her side. Should be eager to be with your mother in her final moments. But you're not. Not at all. You've never understood each other. She pawned you off onto strangers in your youth so she could shack up with the latest flavor of the week . . . and you're angry. You're so fucking angry that caring for her is hard. Even if you know it's your duty, you can't let go of the shitty past. You're guilty. You're helpless. You're mad.*

A voice intruded on Roxy's consciousness, snapping her head up and shooting her back into reality. The redhead stood at the office door, radiating impatience. "Yeah. Roxy Cumberland? We're ready now."

"Great." Roxy uttered the word tightly, the way Missy would. In this moment, she could feel the necessary emotions bubbling around inside her. If she could just walk into that office and let these emotions loose, they would *see* her. See Missy inside her, dying to get out. Roxy shoved her script back inside the purse. She didn't need it anymore. *This is just like any other audition. You've walked into hundreds of rooms just like this. Take the fear and make it Missy's, not your own. For the next five minutes, live inside the part.*

She passed through the door at an efficient pace and found herself staring at a familiar sight. Three bored expressions with notes on the table in front of them. A handheld camera held aloft by a tripod, pointed in her direction. The only *un*familiar sight was seeing famous filmmaker Johan Strassberg sprawled out on a bean bag chair in the corner of the room. He held a laser pointer in his hand, flashing it in quick succession at the redheaded production assistant's head, laughing as he did so. His feet were bare. Giant, noise-canceling headphones hugged his neck. He wasn't so much handsome as he was adorable. That wide, boyish grin and those sparkling eyes had won him a lot of hearts among the public. If this wasn't exactly how she'd pictured the brilliant filmmaker's behavior, maybe it was just part of his process. He could afford to be a little offbeat.

"Which one is this?" Johan singsonged without even looking at her.

A bearded man in a *Book of Mormon* baseball cap consulted his notebook. "This is . . . Roxy Cumberland."

"Never heard of her," the frazzled blonde to his right mumbled into her Diet Coke.

Johan straightened from his casual position, eyeing her curiously. "Ah, Roxy Cumberland. I've heard so many good things." He pointed his laser onto the ground and raised a dark eyebrow. "Are you here to dazzle us?"

"That's the plan."

Bearded Dude snorted.

Good. This is exactly what she needed. She needed them to underestimate her. It would leave her with nothing left to lose, just like the character she needed to portray. They were prepared to be underwhelmed? Well, it was time to wake these motherfuckers up.

The blonde picked up a sheet of paper. "I'll be reading with you today," she droned. "Say your name into the camera and start when you're ready."

Roxy breathed deeply, taking a moment to put herself in Missy's shoes, to block out everything except her mother, sitting across from her at the kitchen table. Five . . . four . . . three . . . two . . .

"Pancakes, Mother?"

"Not hungry," returned the blonde quickly.

Roxy gave a tight nod to portray Missy's frustration. "Anything you want to do today?"

"Not particularly. I don't see the point."

Roxy gave a bitter laugh. "You know what? Me either." Two steps toward the table. "Why exactly did you bring me home, Mother? Did you think it would be easier to sort through the wreckage if I was manageable? If I was sad to see you like this? Huh? What the hell was it?" In her mind, Roxy replaced the blonde with an older woman. A frail, but stubborn, woman. "You want me to feel guilty, is that it? Should I wear a crown of goddamn thorns on my head and hang myself on a cross to absolve you of the past? It doesn't *work* like that. I don't know how to *feel* anything for you." Roxy picked up an imaginary pill bottle and shook it. She reached deep down inside herself, found a well full of helplessness, and plunged inside. "This doesn't *change* anything. *Nothing. Ever. Changes. Here.*"

It took her a moment to realize the scene had finished. With her pulse racing, she risked a look at the table full of executives. The boredom had fled and had been replaced with interest. Even the blonde who'd read the part of Missy's mother looked a little stunned. Good Lord, she hoped that didn't mean she'd been horrible enough to render them speechless. Please let it be the opposite. She swallowed the knot of unease in her throat and glanced at Johan. At some point during her performance, he'd risen to his feet to stand behind the camera, perhaps to see her live and on screen at the same time.

"Cumberland, do you mind stepping out into the hallway?" Johan asked. "We'll call you back in a minute."

"Sure." All right, that was unusual. Then again, getting *hired* was unusual for her, so this unorthodox procedure could be positive. She hoped. Propelling herself into motion, she stooped down and grabbed her purse before exiting the room. She closed the door behind her and sat in one of the hard plastic waiting room chairs, wishing she could hear the discussion taking place on the other side of the door. The remaining girl who'd obviously come to audition eyed her suspiciously. Another good sign? Or were they already on the phone to the Screen Actors Guild to bar her entry for life?

Five minutes passed before the door opened. All three executives filed out, Bearded Dude even sending her a smile as they left the hallway through the front entrance. Where were they going?

Johan appeared in the doorway, minus his gigantic head-phones. He jerked his head toward the now-empty room behind him. "Follow me, Roxy."

She wanted to ask what was going on, but her throat felt so tight that she worried it might come out sounding like Swahili. Johan led her into the performance area again, although she noted the camera had been switched off. He wheeled out a chair from behind the table and sat, but he didn't offer her a seat, leaving her standing a few feet away. For long, torturous moments, he didn't say anything, simply tilting his head to scrutinize her with a half-smile. A sliver of discomfort worked its way into her stomach at the feeling of being on display, but she refused to break eye contact first. She'd been poked and prodded before. This was no different. If it felt like more than the usual sizing up, maybe she was imagining it.

"You're not what I expected," Johan said finally. "Not at all."

She commanded herself to stop shifting in her high heels. "Likewise."

A laugh burst out of him. "Yes. Definitely unexpected."

A frown marred her forehead. Her performance hadn't been out of the ordinary for her. Why did he seem so surprised? "Do you mind me asking which casting director recommended me? Your assistant never mentioned a name when she called."

He shrugged a vintage-T-shirt-clad shoulder. "Who gives a shit? You've got the part."

White lights blinked behind her eyes. "I—what?"

"You blew us away. Or did you think those three uptight ass-holes go silent for just anyone?"

Roxy's answering laugh sounded a little hysterical. This was really happening. She hadn't misunderstood him. The part of Missy Devlin was hers. She'd be starring in a major production. If she had been having this conversation with anyone else, she would have asked for further proof, someone in a loftier position to speak with. But Johan had written the film and would also be directing. He was the highest on the proverbial food chain. It didn't get any higher.

"Thank you," she managed. "You made the right choice."

Johan looked amused. "I'm going to love working with you." He came to his feet and walked toward her. "And we'll be doing a lot of it. Working together," he said meaningfully.

The unease crept back in. Roxy didn't want to feel it, didn't want some annoying sixth sense to mar this perfect realization of her dream. It stayed anyway, telling her to keep her eyes wide open. "I would hope so," she joked. "You're directing the movie."

"True." He watched her closely. "Our male lead, Marcus Vaughn, will be in Los Angeles for another week. We've been through the script with him several times. When he gets back to town, I'd like you up to speed so we can hit the ground running."

Roxy nodded eagerly "Absolutely. I can take the script home with me today, and—"

"No, no." His smile held just a hint of condescension. She

couldn't help but think *this* might be Johan. Not the friendly, irreverent guy he tried to portray. "You and I are going to need to rehearse a few times. I need you completely ready."

That niggle of unease turned into loud, beeping alarm. She wasn't naïve. Not by a long shot. After two years of waiting in line for auditions and listening to girls swap casting couch stories, she knew the score. While he hadn't come right out and said he wanted something else in exchange for the part, it was there in the fine print. The dream she thought he'd handed her upon walking into the room crumbled just a little, but not all the way. Not yet. If Johan thought she would sleep with him for the part, he had another thing coming. And it wouldn't be him. She just had to stay on her toes and play this right.

"Great. I'm all about rehearsing. The last thing I want is to be behind." She pulled her purse higher on her shoulder, wincing inwardly when she realized she was using it as a type of shield. "Is there paperwork we need to sign?"

Johan's eyebrows dipped. "It's a little early for that. We need to make sure you and Marcus have the right chemistry on screen together. I'm confident you will," he rushed to say. "But we need to make sure you know Missy inside and out before we shoot the screen tests." His hand found its way to her shoulder and lingered. "Why don't we start tomorrow night? Let's meet here around six."

"Six." Roxy moved away subtly until he was forced to remove his hand. "I'll be here."

"Great." His genuine-looking smile was back in place. "Looking forward to it."

She left the office, noticing on the way out that the other girl had apparently given up and left. When she reached the sidewalk, she stopped, feeling at a loss. Conflicted. In a matter of five minutes, she'd gone from a crazy high to a pitiful low. Now she hovered somewhere in the middle. She would find a way to keep this part. She had to. But she wouldn't, under any circumstance, compromise herself for the chance at realizing her dreams. It would only taint them.

Which meant there was every possibility she could lose the part of a lifetime.

Walking toward the subway, she felt exposed. Raw. The idea of going home and sitting in her bedroom, feeling this way until evening fell, seemed like a shitty idea. She'd dwell on the upcoming rehearsal and drive herself insane. She'd binge on the leftovers Honey kept neatly stocked in Tupperware inside the fridge. Hide the remote on herself so she'd have an excuse to watch Lifetime.

No, she needed to feel better. Now. When she thought of what had made her feel happy lately, what made her feel warm and safe . . . she thought of Louis. It didn't sit well, this idea that she needed Louis, a guy, to erase the ickiness Johan had slimed all over her, but the fact remained. Talking to Louis, seeing his face, made her . . . happy.

Instead of taking the uptown 2 train back to Chelsea, she changed direction and headed for the downtown 5. Toward the courthouse.

Chapter 13

*L*ouis winked at one of the kids sitting in the front row of the courtroom, doing his best to radiate confidence, although unlike the kid, he didn't necessarily feel it. The first two rows were filled with members of a local Lower East Side youth community center. Each of them wore a bright green T-shirt to represent the group, an organization that provided after-school programs for public school kids in the city. Unfortunately, they were also at risk of being evicted, thanks to a hefty amount of unpaid back rent. They were working furiously to get the center a government grant to keep their doors open, in addition to pursuing private donations, but time had run out before they could get the full amount together. He'd taken the case, hoping he could get them an extension. Otherwise, all the kids who watched him so seriously from the front row wouldn't have anywhere to go after school. Most of their parents even relied on the center to keep them safe and occupied with positive activities until they got home from work.

The judge indicated he should proceed. He spent the next fifteen minutes giving a detailed outline of everything the community center administrators were doing to make up the rent payments. He presented all the necessary documents, all the while feeling the weight of thirty sets of eyes on his back. He'd gone before this judge a handful of times, and the guy was tough. So when the judge granted the extension, Louis almost asked him if he was sure.

Relief swamped him when a cheer went up behind him. He turned to give the kids high fives, when someone snagged his attention. Roxy? She stood all the way in the back of the courtroom, looking slightly out of place and completely baffled as she watched him. Before he could command his feet to move, he'd already closed half the distance separating them. After a tiny head shake, she met him halfway.

"Rox." He reached out and cupped her cheek. Couldn't help it. She looked so fresh and gorgeous standing in the dusty courthouse full of mostly miserable people. There was something about the way she was looking at him, too. As if she'd just seen him for the first time. Was that a good thing or a bad thing? "What are you doing here? Is everything okay?"

"Everything is fine." She surprised him by turning her face into his hand, brushing his palm with her lips. Part of him wanted to bask in the fact that she'd come to find him at work, instead of waiting until tonight. Not only that, but she seemed . . . *relieved* to see him. It should have had him pounding his chest like some modern version of Tarzan, right? This girl who'd been running him around in circles was standing right here in front him, accepting his touch.

So why was the happiness he felt tempered by worry?

Roxy walked with her shoulders thrown back. The word *walk* really didn't describe it. She glided, with a twist of her hips after each step. Louis knew this because he'd made a study of how she moved, mostly how she looked when moving *away*. Right now, a little bit of that confidence was missing, and he had a good idea why. Dread made itself at home in his stomach. He wanted to kick his own ass for feeling a spark of pleasure that she would come to him after having a bad audition, but it was there, growing by the second. He wanted to make everything better for her. Now.

She cast a glance over his shoulder, back toward the excited voices of the kids. "I didn't know this is what you did." When her eyes found his, they were speculative. Possibly even a little impressed. "That was amazing. You saved their youth center."

"For now." He scratched the back of his neck, wondering why hearing praise from her made him feel so much better about it. Maybe because no one in his family, or his firm, ever brought it up. The only people he ever discussed it with were Ben and Russell. "Still a lot of funds to pull together."

"But you'll help them."

"Yeah." Oh man, it felt way too good to bask in her glow of approval. He had to change the subject, even if it would be an unpleasant one. "How did the audition go?" Louis asked, positive he already knew the answer. Obviously she hadn't gotten the part.

"I'll tell you about it later." She tossed her hair over her shoulder and looked up at him from underneath her eyelashes, full mouth tilted in a smile. He almost did a double take, wondering if he'd imagined the lack of her usual boldness when she'd arrived. It was definitely back in full force now . . . and directed squarely at him. Not many things could get him hot in this setting. Inside the walls of this courthouse, he stayed focused on his job. He took it seriously. There was nothing sexy about paperwork, judges, and shitty coffee.

The second Roxy locked those green eyes on him, he knew what she wanted. Knew why she'd come. His pulse started to hammer, every muscle south of his belt tightening up. *No, no. Not here. Why is she doing this to me?* It felt as though he'd been in a dry spell for eleven months instead of eleven measly days. His mouth had gone dry, his palms were on fire with the need to touch her.

She must have sensed his dawning understanding, because her smile widened. With a single finger, she traced the buckle of his belt. "Is there somewhere we can talk?" When she wet her lower lip, he groaned under his breath. "Please, Louis?"

With a quick look over his shoulder, he made sure no one was within earshot. "You're coming over tonight, Roxy." His voice had deepened so much it was almost unrecognizable. "I was already planning on fucking you into next week. After this, after you coming here and doing this to me, I'm going to make you scream until you lose your voice."

Her cheeks had turned red, but she didn't look embarrassed. She looked turned on. By him. For him. "I can't wait until tonight," she whispered. "I can't."

That need he'd felt to make everything better for her hadn't gone away, it had only shifted. Now it raced out of control. He was standing in the middle of a busy courthouse, his colleagues and professional acquaintances roaming the halls around him, and he saw none of it, none of them. He could only see Roxy with her pleading eyes and parted lips. He'd knelt down on his knees in front of her this morning, and now his body demanded he do it again. *Take care of her.*

In the midst of it all was that aggressive part of him only Roxy seemed to bring to life. He wanted to be mad at her for bringing him to this state. Days' worth of fuck-me kisses and stolen touches had him unable to say no. He couldn't pass up an opportunity to touch her if he tried. No matter where they were standing. And yeah, he kind of *wanted* to be mad at her so he'd have an excuse to give it to her hard. With how he felt, there wouldn't be any other way. This wouldn't be what she deserved, but his body ached, and his ability to think beyond getting her alone had started to fade along with his resolve.

"Louis," she murmured, going up on her toes to lay her mouth over his. "I promise to be quiet, but I need you to fuck me into next week *now.*"

That did it. The mental image of her fighting to contain a scream had Louis grabbing her hand and dragging her into the closest stairwell. As they went down the stairs, he slowed his pace slightly in deference to her high heels, but as soon as they got down two flights and he pulled her out of the stairwell onto a floor populated by administrative offices, his stride picked up speed again. Most of the doors leading to occupied offices were closed, thankfully, since his and Roxy's presence on the floor would be unusual. Not that he could summon the ability to care, with his heart slamming against his ribs like a wrecking ball. It took every ounce of his willpower not to turn and push her up onto the closest surface, right then and there. *Just don't look at her. Not yet.*

Halfway down the hall, he spotted a door with a frosted glass window. Behind the glass, he could see the lights were off, so he went straight for it, Roxy clipping along behind him in those heels that made her legs look a mile long. The heels he'd bought her. God, knowing she wore something he'd bought only made him more desperate to get her on the other side of the door. He turned the knob and pushed it open. His brain only gave him a split second to process they were in a file room before the need to touch her overrode everything else.

He gripped Roxy's hips and pushed her up against the closest file cabinet, hearing the rattle of its drawers as if through a fog. Her breath shuddered out past her lips as his mouth descended. Right before their mouths locked together, he saw her cockiness slip. The same lost expression he'd seen on her face when she'd walked into the courtroom blanketed her pretty features once more, and it revved his need even higher. She'd find herself with him. He could make it all better.

Her mouth moved under his, hot, desperate, perfect. Little sounds vibrated up her throat, ending where their lips worked together furiously. Louis tried to focus on the kiss, on the slide of her tongue against his, but it was too damn much. Lust pumped in his veins, and he needed more. Both of his hands were planted on either side of her on the cabinet, but now they dropped to her thighs, yanking her dress up and over her ass. He hooked his thumbs into the flimsy band of her thong and shoved it down her legs. When she reached down to help him, he groaned into her mouth. She wanted it just as bad.

"I was going to use my mouth on you the first time. How *dare* you take that away from me." He reached between their bodies and palmed her wet heat. *Jesus.* His head spun at the feel of her. With his middle finger, he found her entrance and pushed deep, loving the way her fingernails dug into his shoulders in response. "How dare you drive me so out of my mind that I have to pound you against a fucking file cabinet."

"Stop talking about it and do it, Louis. I can't wait anymore." She removed her hands from his shoulders to work his belt buckle, kissing his neck as she tugged and pushed. When she finally managed to free him, his knees nearly buckled at the relief of no longer being confined to his pants. The relief was short-lived, though, because his boxer briefs were shoved down and her smooth hands were on his dick. Her tight grip moved up and down, twisting at the base, readying him when it was the last thing he needed. The only thing he needed was to get inside her, but Christ, it felt so fucking good.

"Enough of that," he rasped, reaching into his pants pocket to find the condom. He'd put it there this morning before going to see Roxy, just in case. Knowing what she did to him. Such as right now, when he could barely breathe or think past taking her hard and fast and thoroughly. Thoroughly enough that she'd be back for more. Immediately. Tonight.

Louis ripped the condom wrapper open with his teeth, grateful when Roxy did the rest, rolling the latex down his length with shaky fingers. Task completed, she hit him with that look again. That *take me now* look that had landed them downstairs in this dim file room. While those heavy-lidded eyes somehow got him even more worked up, she unhooked the top three buttons on her dress, giving him an eyeful of the black bra underneath, a lacy one that pushed her breasts up like an offering.

His body moved like lightning to pin her hard against the cabinet. "What did I tell you about the next time you wrap those legs around my waist?" He leaned down and kissed each side of her cleavage. "Do you remember?"

She nodded, causing their lips to slip together.

"Is that what you want?"

"Yes," she whispered. "I need it."

He dropped his hands to her ass, running his palms over the rounded flesh and squeezing tight. "Get them up here, then. Right now."

Roxy's arms wrapped around his neck so she could climb his body. Those thighs slipped around his waist with such smooth perfection that he had to bite her shoulder to stop from shouting. Nothing compared, though, to the friction of his dick sliding between her legs, over the spot he'd touched with his hands, dreamed of touching with his mouth. Not one of his fantasies had done justice to the sensation. It drove him past his breaking point. Not taking another second to savor, he gripped himself and drove deep inside her.

Oh, God. So fucking *good. Tight and wet and mine.* Roxy. Roxy. He watched her teeth sink into her bottom lip to prevent a scream from escaping over the feel of *him*. And he fucking lost it. His attention whittled down to one person, one need. Nothing else existed for him. He withdrew slightly, then thrust into her again, harder. Their mutual moans were interrupted by his mouth. Closer. He had to touch all of her, get as close as possible.

Keeping his tongue battling with hers, Louis levered her hips against the cabinet and started to fuck. There was no other way to describe the rough, dirty pace of what he did to her. It only grew more intense when she began moving with him, widening her thighs and circling her hips like she couldn't get enough.

"How dare you make me need to fuck you this bad, Roxy," he growled against her mouth, hips pumping furiously. "How *dare* you."

She fisted his hair and pulled. "Same goes," she gasped. "Don't stop. *Please.*"

"You want it harder, beautiful? Say the word. I'll get it even deeper if you can take it."

"Yes. *Harder.*"

A tide was rising inside him, higher, higher. Dying to be let out. No control . . . he had no control. This lack of restraint never happened to him, and it felt goddamn amazing. He didn't want control if it meant stopping. Roxy's legs tightened around him and started to shake, telling him he wasn't alone. They were in this together. She wanted it harder, and he couldn't think past that. His hips drove her back against the file cabinet with a *slam*, and something wild broke free inside him. He buried his face in Roxy's neck to keep himself grounded as he thrust into her over and over, yanking her thighs up every time they slipped low on his hips.

"*Louis,*" she screamed. Some part of his brain must have still been working, because he covered her mouth with his own to prevent her from making any more noise. He tried to deepen the kiss, but she threw her head back and writhed slowly against him, tightening up where their bodies connected. Pulsing, shuddering. "Oh my *God*."

"You come, baby?" He groaned. "I need to come so bad, Rox. You're squeezing me so tight. Just keep your legs around me a little longer, okay? Just let me fuck you a little longer."

Sweat had started to dot her brow. He loved it. Loved seeing how he affected her. She nodded at him, hooking her ankles together behind his back. "Come on, Louis," she breathed. "Take what you need."

"I need you," he said against her neck. "*You*."

Taking her ass in his hands, he jerked her down onto his hardness in quick hauls. Faster, faster, until his motions blurred. The sexy little surprised sounds she made drove him higher, and he finally let the tide overtake him. He slammed her hips one final time against the cabinet and pushed deep, growling her name into her hair.

"Ah fuck. *Fuck*. Roxy, it's too good. You're so good. Hold on to me."

"I'm here."

He wanted to stay there all day, holding her like this, buried inside her. With her ankles crossed at the small of his back, arms around his neck, they couldn't get any closer. She fit him like a perfect mold. Dammit, he loved the feeling of her clinging to him, the muscles in her body having gone lax. *Needing* him to hold her up. It stirred something in his chest. Something fierce and protective. Now that the urgency had passed, he remembered her reluctance to talk about the audition. That flash of uncertainty he'd seen before she'd hid it. He'd tried to make her happy, help her get the opportunity she deserved, and he'd failed.

Louis pressed his lips to her forehead. "I'm sorry about the audition."

Her body stiffened a little, then relaxed. Green eyes opened to meet his. "Why are you sorry?" A smile tugged at her lips. "I got the part."

"What?" Relief powered through him. "That's amazing. Why didn't you say something?"

"I just did." She untangled her limbs from his waist and stood. If she'd removed her arms from around his neck, he might have panicked. But she didn't. She kept them there. "I believe Strassberg's exact words were *You blew us away.*"

Louis wanted to smile along with her, wanted nothing more than to be happy for her, especially knowing Johan didn't dole out compliments like that unless he meant them. No, he was more the type to receive compliments. Something still ate at him, though. He felt as if he was missing something. Her happiness seemed . . . strained. "Are you sure everything is okay, Rox?"

"I just landed the part of my dreams and an orgasm. All before dinnertime." She brushed a piece of hair out of his face. "'Okay' is a gross understatement."

He leaned down and kissed her slowly, groaning when she opened her mouth for him without hesitation. "I still want to see you tonight," he said against her lips.

"I think that can be arranged."

Chapter 14

*R*oxy used her finger to stir the ice around her glass of Diet Coke. She sat perched on a stool, elbows propped on top of the kitchen island. Somewhere in the apartment, the television buzzed with studio audience applause. Her movements felt lethargic, kind of like when she was in middle school and would sneak into her neighbor's backyard to sit in their Jacuzzi. They'd won it on *The Price Is Right,* making them neighborhood celebrities for the better part of a year, but they'd never *used* the damn thing. She'd watched through the broken fence separating their yards and waited, wondering when they'd light their stupid drugstore-bought tiki torches and sip daiquiris while the hot water swirled around them, like the bikini-clad models had done on the show. Finally she'd gotten fed up and snuck over the fence while they'd been at church, filling it with their own hose and turning on the heater.

That first time she sunk beneath the surface and let the hot water cover her head . . . that's how she felt right now. Boneless, drifting, and without a single worry. In the back of her mind, there was a ticker clicking away until reality intruded again, but for now she was content to sit and enjoy the warm fizziness she'd been walking around with all afternoon.

The front door slammed loudly, jolting her in the stool, making her slosh Diet Coke all over the counter. Abby stomped into the apartment and wrestled with her camel-colored trench to get it off before throwing it into a heap on the floor. She acknowledged Roxy with an unladylike grunt as she made her way to the living room and threw herself onto the couch.

O-kay, apparently not everyone had lucked out with a midday orgasm. *Wait.* In order for Abby to be home, it had to be past five o'clock. How long had she been sitting there? Since coming home from the courthouse, she must have been in a Louis-induced orgasma-coma, because she hadn't even bothered to take off her shoes or jacket. The subway ride back to Chelsea was just a blur of faces and voices now. With a grimace, she remembered trying to get into the wrong apartment, one flight down.

Louis. *Good. God.* She hadn't gone to the courthouse looking to hook up, nor did she get some secret thrill from getting busy in a public place. Although that very well might have changed after this morning, because *holy screaming O.* As she'd watched Louis work, watched him argue on behalf of a pack of ragtag kids and their teachers, she'd been kind of, well, *dazzled.* And Roxy didn't do dazzled. The way those kids had watched him pace the courtroom, he might as well have been wearing a superhero cape instead of a suit. He'd been confident, but not cocky. Even the judge hadn't been able to hide his obvious fondness for Louis.

Before today, when she'd pictured him working, he'd been buried in books, looking for legal loopholes for corporate jerk-offs in suits. She'd never thought to ask him what he actually did at the office, so it had taken her by surprise. Seeing him so passionate and competent had stirred her up with a quickness. Fine, she was also woman enough to admit that listening to him spout legal terminologies with such ease got her motor running.

Unbelievable. She was falling for an Ivy League lawyer.

Not good. Not good at all, a nasal Jersey accent chanted in her head. As much as she wanted to forget, she'd met him the morning after a one-night stand. A one-night stand he'd been totally blasé about, not even remembering the girl's name. Guys like Louis dated around. Why shouldn't he? He had everything going for him. A well-paying job, a ridiculous apartment, looks. Yeah, he might be into her now, might be excited by her refusal to let their association play out his way. What would happen if she stopped leading him on a chase, though? If her past experience with guys served as any indication, he would be onto the next girl in a short skirt so quick she'd be choking on Armani eau pour homme–scented dust.

She hated thinking this way. It was why she hadn't wanted to get involved with him in the first damn place. Now instead of being happy with one steamy session in a file room, she was worrying about more. The *beyond.* The desire for it had snuck up out of nowhere. *Louis* had snuck up out of nowhere. She was leaving herself open to having her heart obliterated, and it made her want to jump ship. Now. Before it got any worse. Then she thought of how it had felt to be filled by him, over and over. How it had felt when he'd shared her excitement over getting the part of Missy.

His asking to see her again, even *after* they'd had sex. When she thought of those things, she didn't want to jump ship. She wanted to snuggle up in the life raft.

"What are you smiling about?" Abby grumbled from the couch.

"Ah, nothing."

"Do you mind turning it down a few notches then?" Her roommate grabbed the remote and stabbed at the buttons impatiently. "It's stressing me out."

Roxy raised an eyebrow. "You want to talk about it?" Jesus, when had she started making offers like that?

"Talk about what?" Honey practically shouted, storming into the room with a bag of Cool Ranch Doritos under her arm. She fell into the couch beside Abby, who was still attacking the remote. "If we're talking about ordering Chinese food, I'm in."

Roxy toed off her new shoes, making sure they landed on the floor gently. "I think I'm meeting up with Louis tonight, so order whatever you guys feel like."

"Oh, fine. Sure."

"That's *great*."

"What is up with you guys?" Roxy asked. "Did I eat your flaxseed tortilla chips or something?"

"Why does something always have to be wrong?" Honey wailed around a mouth of Doritos. "Why are we expected to smile all the time?"

Abby tossed the remote onto the couch with such force that it bounced a foot in the air. "Yes! That is exactly what I'm talking about. Maybe I just want to be upset. *Can't I just be upset?*"

Oh, shit. Roxy backed farther into the kitchen, positioning

herself behind the island. She'd anticipated this happening, but not quite so soon. It was only a matter of time before she got sucked into the vortex that plagues female roommates the world over. She would put it off as long as possible, though. Be the last woman standing.

Her cell phone went off inside her purse and she rummaged for it, continuing to keep an eye on her roommates. "Hello?"

"When can I see you?"

Louis's voice traveled through the phone and punched her in the belly with a silk fist. Dammit, she wanted him standing in front of her. Wanted to touch him, see him, smell him. Why did this have to happen now? "Hey. I'm not sure I can get away tonight. I'm needed at the apartment."

"Don't do this to me, Rox. We didn't even get started this morning."

Her thighs squeezed together all on their own. This guy was going to turn her into a sex-crazed lunatic if she wasn't careful. Even if it would be an amazing descent into padded-walls territory. "Listen, this is probably the last thing you want to hear, but my roommates . . . they've synched up."

A short pause. "You mean their periods?"

"Yeah." She laughed. "You get a gold star for saying that without an accompanying gagging sound."

"Twin sisters," he reminded her grimly. "Why do they need *you* there?"

"I'm afraid they might maim the Chinese food delivery man with a remote control."

Louis sighed loudly. In the background she heard a soft thud, as if he might be banging his head against the wall. "Don't go anywhere, okay? I'll be over as soon as I can."

Roxy straightened from her lean against the island. "Are you sure about that? You might be taking your life into your hands."

"I'm seeing you tonight." Roxy heard the jingling of keys on the other end. "But I'll write out a quick will and testament just in case."

"Can I have your apartment?" She winced inwardly, wishing she could take the words back. He would probably think she was hinting about moving in or something now. Fabulous. "I mean, without you in it. Just me and that big screen."

"If you already want me dead, I'm doing something wrong." A door opened and closed. Locks turned. "If I could get you to stay put in my apartment for longer than a few minutes, we could watch TV together."

"We'll see about that. What's your favorite show?"

"Guess."

"*Law & Order*?" He snorted, so she thought for a moment and tried again. "You're a rerun guy, aren't you? *The X-Files* . . . *The Wire* . . . ?"

"Less aliens. Funnier."

"*Arrested Development.*"

He barked a laugh. "I'm rewatching season two. Watch it with me."

She realized her cheeks were sore from smiling. "I'll think about it."

"She'll think about it," he mumbled. "I'll see you soon, Roxy."

"Okay, Louis."

"Hey." His voice went deeper, creating an answering thrum in her belly. "Even with your roommates around, I'm going to be thinking about fucking you. Wear a skirt for me."

He hung up before she could answer.

BY THE TIME Louis knocked on their door an hour later, Roxy had showered and changed. She'd yanked on a pair of ripped jeans, then cursed and put on the red wraparound skirt she'd been saving for a special occasion. It occurred to her that wearing red around her roommates tonight might be the equivalent of waving the color in front of two bulls, but hey, what was life without risks?

Honey and Abby glared at the door from their positions on the couch, Chinese food cartons scattered around them like little white headstones. RIP Beef Lo Mein.

"Play nice, you two." She slid the chain lock free. "I'm pretty sure you dislocated the delivery guy's collarbone ripping the bag from his hands."

"He was smug," Honey muttered. "Are there any egg rolls left?"

Abby fished through a bag and handed her one. "Finder's fee. I want half."

Roxy smirked at them and turned, bracing herself to open the door. This was ridiculous. How could this guy make her feel nervous and secure at the same time? She wanted to see him, but she also wanted to run back into her room and hide under her bed. A totally unacceptable reaction. Lately, guys tended to be more of a diversion when she had time, but she never grew fascinated with them. The opposite, actually. She walked away from time spent with Louis wishing she had longer. Wanting to know more about him.

She gave herself a silent command to *grow a pair,* then opened the door. Oh man. He looked way too freaking good. Hair still slightly damp from a shower, curling at the ends where he'd probably shoved it back with an impatient hand. Plain white T-shirt untucked over well-worn jeans. Freshly shaven. His mouth immediately kicked into a grin when he saw her, but it dimmed into something darker as he looked her over. She felt her nipples harden underneath her tank top and knew he noticed. There had always been an undercurrent running between them, but after this morning, it seemed to snap and spark, letting off heat in the space separating them. Drawing them closer.

Louis stepped slowly into her personal space before leaning in and kissing the skin beneath her ear. "You thinking about me naked, Rox?"

Her lips curled into a smile. "That's my line."

"Yes, but *you* asking *me* is a waste of time. The answer is almost always yes."

"Almost always?"

He brushed their mouths together. "I'm not going to lie to you. There was about thirty seconds this morning when I was thinking about breakfast."

She pursed her lips. "What kind of breakfast?"

"Waffles. Blueberry."

"All is forgiven."

One strong arm snaked around her waist to pull her close. "Okay, this is a way better greeting than the one I got this morning, but you still haven't kissed me yet. I'm here to charm your crabby roommates. It's the least you could do."

"You haven't soothed the savage beasts yet." She dodged his mouth, even though she wanted to faint in his arms and beg to be ravaged like in a black-and-white movie. "Kisses must be delivered only after the work is completed. You're a lawyer. You understand."

"I could argue that a down payment wouldn't be remiss."

"Stop. No legal talk. I've only recently discovered my weakness for it." Roxy felt herself flush red to her hairline. Admitting weaknesses now? If she kept slipping up around this guy, he was going to run her over like a semitruck.

She tried to bat him away playfully, but he latched onto her wrists and tugged her close. Those brown eyes had gone from amused to intense, forcing her to catch her breath. "I have a weakness for *every* fucking thing about you, so you've still got the advantage. All right?"

Unbelievable. How did he know the exact thoughts swirling around in her head? More than that, how did he know the one thing to say that wouldn't patronize her, the one thing that would make her relax? She started to make some comment unworthy of the moment, one that would get them back to where they'd been when the door had opened, but he kissed her cheek and walked past her into the apartment.

"Oh, are you done mauling our roommate?" Honey asked, waving half an egg roll at him.

"Not even close," Louis answered without missing a beat. For the first time, Roxy noticed he was carrying a plastic grocery bag in his hand. He set it on the kitchen island and reached inside. "Rocky road or butter pecan?"

Her roommates exchanged a look. "Huh?"

"Ice cream." He held up two pints of Häagen-Dazs. "Which flavor?"

"Rocky road," Abby shouted.

Honey made an outraged sound. "Butter pecan, but we switch halfway through."

"Deal."

As Louis tried out a couple of drawers to find the spoons, Roxy realized she was still standing there like a spare tool, with the door open behind her. She quickly closed it, just in time to watch Louis hand each of her roommates a pint of ice cream with a spoon sticking out of the top.

"You want me to microwave them?" he asked. With a straight face.

Abby beamed up at him. "No, it's perfect. Thank you."

Honey gestured toward the kitchen with her spoon. "What else you got in that bag, Mary Poppins?"

Roxy's curiosity got the best of her, so she hopped up on one of the kitchen stools and reached into the bag. "Three . . . no, *four* Snickers bars," she announced. "A bottle of wine. Tylenol. *People* magazine." She peered further into the bag. "And *Bridesmaids* on DVD."

Abby reached out for the bag. "You may continue mauling our roommate now."

"It would appear I can be bought, too," Honey sighed. "Fire up the DVD player."

Louis sauntered back toward Roxy, looking so pleased with himself that she had to laugh. She thought of how he'd calmed his sisters down Saturday night, the way he'd handled the difficult situation with such ease. Even the way he'd talked her down in Fletcher's bedroom after her botched attempt at stripperhood. Who the hell was this guy? The vagina whisperer?

"I suppose you want some kind of reward now?" she said for his ears alone.

He stopped in front of her stool and laid a warm hand on her knee. "Reward? Nah." His touch set off an electric chain reaction, shooting up her thighs and into her belly. His wink told her he knew exactly what he was doing. "But I'll take a beer if you have one."

"Sorry, we're tequila girls." She laid a hand over his and inched it higher. "Abby has some pinot grigio in the fridge, though. I'd say you're her favorite person right now, so she'd definitely share."

He made a face. "If a man drinks pinot grigio, he grows boobs. It's science." Roxy started to laugh again, but he silenced her with his lips, taking her mouth in a slow, drugging kiss. "What about you? Who's your favorite person right now, Roxy?"

"It's a tough call." She wanted to roll her eyes at the breathlessness she heard in her voice. "I'll have to think about it."

"Is that right?" His lips brushed over her jaw, traced a line up to her ear. "You want to show me where you sleep while you think about it?"

"You have all the good ideas." She slid forward off the stool, giving him a challenging look when he refused to move back to give her room. Ignoring the shit-eating grins Abby and Honey threw their way, she led Louis to her bedroom. When they walked inside, she tried to see it through his eyes. There wasn't much to it, especially when compared to the expensively furnished apartment he had all to himself. Her bed was low to the ground, basically a glorified futon. Her clock radio and phone chargers were plugged into the wall and resting on the floor, since she had no nightstand. A chest of drawers she'd found at a flea market sat wedged in the corner, makeup and jewelry scattered across the top. She had two framed posters hanging on the wall, though, which she considered to be her pride and joy. A vintage *King Kong* poster she'd once bartered from a roommate in exchange for her *Sex and the City* box set. And another movie poster for the Tom Hanks classic *Splash*.

She turned, expecting to find him shaking his head over her eclectic taste in movies, but instead found him surveying the room with a concerned look. As soon as he noticed her watching him, it vanished. Only a glimpse and it was gone. Still, that hint of sympathy made her stand up a little bit straighter. Maybe she only had a small room to herself, but she was happy here. She was proud of her space, meager though it might be. She felt the sudden need to regain the upper hand with Louis. The feeling wasn't welcome, she wanted to just let it go. Pretend he didn't look so glaringly out of place in her room, but she couldn't.

Hoping to distract them both from her living quarters while taking a little bit of her pride back, Roxy closed the distance between them. His gaze went darker with every step she took in his direction, and their mouths met in a slow, hungry glide of lips and tongues. Bodies pressed together and molded, curve against muscle. Between them, she let her hands drift to the hem of his shirt before sliding underneath to trace his ridged abdomen with her fingers.

"Rox, hold up." He broke away, shaking his head as if to clear it. "I, uh . . . like your room."

"Thank you." *Liar.* She drew the hem higher to reveal his hard chest and laid an openmouthed kiss on his hot skin. "It would look even better if you took your shirt off."

A groan escaped his lips. "You in a hurry or something?"

Impatience had her gritting her teeth. "Why don't you just take what you came for, Louis?"

He tipped her chin up with a firm hand, all traces of heat gone. "Excuse me?"

She shoved his hand away, knowing she was being insecure and creating conflicts that didn't need to exist, but she was unable to stop it. On top of this underlying worry that she was becoming too attached to a potential player, she didn't like feeling inadequate. He might not throw their economic differences in her face, but they were there. She'd seen it when he'd looked around her sparsely furnished room. "Isn't that what your little show was about? Bringing my roommates ice cream and playing the hero? You said it yourself over the phone that we only got started this morning."

"Yeah. I meant it, too." His eyes snapped with temper. "But I didn't come over here just to 'get my reward,' as you so subtly put it. And I'm sure as hell not fucking you while your roommates listen outside in the hallway."

Two sets of bare feet scurried away from the door, making

Roxy wince. "Too bad. This is where I live. I'm sorry the accommodations aren't good enough."

"Don't do that." He looked disappointed. "Don't give me that shit."

He saw through her so easily. It made her feel restless. She crossed her arms over her chest with a jerky movement. "What *did* you come here for?"

"To *see* you." He shouted the words at the ceiling. "To take you *out*. Why do you keep expecting me to be an asshole, Roxy? I don't get it. It's like you're hoping for it."

Dammit, he was right. He was one hundred percent right. She wanted him to be an asshole so she'd have a reason to *not* give a shit when he stopped calling. Stopped showing up with shoes and ice cream and peanut butter and banana fucking sandwiches. She just wanted it to end now before her feelings got any murkier than they already were. That involved pushing him away *before* he did anything wrong. What she really wanted was to throw herself into his arms and apologize. Unfortunately, she was a little rusty in the apology department. Which came in a close second to admitting she was wrong. So she simply sat there and let him draw his own conclusions.

When a full minute passed without her responding, he gave a resigned nod. "Right." His jaw flexed. "If I have to leave to prove I'm not in this just for sex, I'll go. Enjoy your night."

He slammed the door to her room on the way out, but she could still hear the apartment door slam right through it seconds later. In a surge of anger directed squarely at herself, she grabbed a hairbrush off her chest of drawers and hurled it at King Kong.

Chapter 15

*L*ouis sat at his office desk trying to murder a little blue stress ball with his right hand. He'd been at work for more than an hour and hadn't even bothered firing up his computer yet. Last night had been much the same, minus the stress ball and shitty coffee. He'd paced the floor in his apartment continually talking himself out of going back to Roxy's apartment and shaking some sense into her. *No*, his annoyingly wholesome other half had argued. *This is the right thing to do. She thinks she has you all figured out? Well, fuck that.*

The idea had been to show her she was wrong. To prove he wanted to spend time with her that didn't necessarily end up with her horizontal. Or vertical, depending on file cabinet proximity. Now he wondered if that rash decision to walk out had been a major mistake. Leaving her staring after him, bailing on her in front of her roommates, might not have sent the message he'd been going for. It might have just been the nail in his coffin.

He'd just been so fucking mad. Law school had prepared him for just about every argument he would need to face, but he

couldn't argue with someone who was skeptical about his character. About him as a person. It hadn't been easy to stand there and
take it. At some point last night, roughly around one o'clock in the
morning, he'd realized he might not be able to change her mind.
That revelation had knocked him on his ass. There was a solution
for everything, wasn't there? He always managed to find answers
and repair problems. What if there was no fix for this? Yeah, he
hadn't been looking for a relationship. But now he'd met this girl
who made him feel a thousand different ways at one time, and
he'd already formed an addiction to her. To those overwhelming
feelings. And it might already be over.

This was his punishment, wasn't it? For taking girls home
without knowing their names and not bothering to get phone
numbers. He'd set himself up for Roxy to take one look and peg
him. Christ, maybe she was right. Maybe she was better off without him.

A phone call from his father this morning hadn't helped. He
still hadn't gotten back to Doubleday about signing a new contract minus the pro bono work. Obviously his boss had clued
Louis's father in on the delay, probably wondering what the hell
there was to think about. He wouldn't get another job like this. If
he voluntarily left a job at one of the top firms in New York City,
potential employers would probably assume he had a screw loose.
He thought of Roxy, the way she seemed to tackle everything on
her own. What would she do in this situation? A smile ghosted
his lips. She'd give them the finger and never look back.

Kind of like *he'd* done yesterday. The stress ball in Louis's hand
squeaked in protest. Yeah, he'd told her he didn't play games, but

maybe this wasn't a game. Maybe it really *was* a genius plan. She would come around. *Have faith, old boy.* He snatched up his cell phone and grimaced at the blank screen. Apparently he'd reached the stage of Roxy-induced grief where he started deluding himself. He thought of her in the short red skirt, the way her mouth had felt moving on his skin . . . and he dropped his forehead onto the desk with a groan. Why hadn't he just walked her backward to the bed, thrown her down, and banged her ever-loving brains out? So what if her roommates had been listening? He'd probably done worse somewhere along the line.

He knew why he hadn't done it, though. This was Roxy. She was different for him. He felt it, felt *her*, everywhere. Moving around in his head and chest, ruining him for anyone else. *God, please let this be the right thing.*

Someone knocked on his office door, dragging him from a fantasy involving Roxy's belly and melted rocky road ice cream. "Come in," he shouted, grimacing at the misery in his voice.

His misery took a backseat to surprise when his future brother-in-law walked in. Louis was almost grateful for the distraction, until he remember Fletcher had almost gotten a lap dance from Roxy, which just sent him back to Miseryville on a one-way ticket, with a layover in I-Want-To-Punch-Him-In-The-Nuts Town. Still, why the impromptu visit? Fletcher had never come to see him in his office before, and as far as Louis knew, he wasn't in need of legal counsel. Unless, of course, Lena had committed a crime, which was not outside the realm of possibility.

Louis stood up behind his desk and shook the man's hand, trying his best not to squeeze hard enough to break fingers. "What's up, Fletch?"

"Hey, man." Fletched dropped into a chair and tugged at his tie. "Your sister sent me over. She's making dinner tomorrow night and wants you there."

"My sister is cooking?" Louis swallowed heavily. "Like . . . with fire and knives?"

"Yeah."

They both shuddered.

Louis didn't have to think about whether or not he had plans tomorrow night. Nope. His calendar this week was painfully empty, thanks to a certain stubborn, green-eyed actress. "Fine. I'll come early just in case we need to reattach limbs or—"

"Order pizzas."

Louis half-smiled. "Why'd you come all the way over here? You could have just called."

"You're right. I could have." Fletcher shifted in his seat. "Listen, I wanted to thank you in person for not telling your sister about the stripper. She would have cut off my nuts."

Louis forced himself not to jump down Fletcher's throat for referring to Roxy as *the stripper*. Fletcher's tone of voice made him feel sick, as if they were coconspirators. He wanted to get the guy out of his office as fast as possible, so he shrugged off the apology. "No worries. Nothing happened anyway."

"You sure about that?" Fletcher tilted his head and gave him a sly smile, obviously not picking up on Louis's hint to drop the subject. "You two looked pretty cozy. You hitting that?"

Blood rushed to Louis's head, darkening his vision. When pain shot up his arms, he realized he was gripping the edge of the desk so hard it creaked. "*That*? Am I hitting *that*?"

Fletcher must have been trying to beat the record for world's most oblivious man, because his sickening grin only widened. He still hadn't picked up on Louis's growing desire to launch himself across the desk and wipe the smile off his face with both fists. "Hey man, I don't blame you. I'm thinking about ringing the agency back and getting a private show, maybe at the office. Did you see her ass? *Jesus*. You think she'd charge extra to let me slap it a few times?"

"*Get out.*"

Finally, awareness dawned on the other man's face. He rose to his feet with an uncomfortable laugh. "I was making a joke, man. Take it easy."

If Louis had to spend another minute in this asshole's presence, he was going to need his own lawyer. A criminal one. Louis rounded the desk and opened the door. "Don't tell me to take it easy. I said get the *fuck* out." When Fletcher only looked incredulous, Louis grabbed him by the collar and jerked him toward the exit. "I swear to God, if you ever speak about her again, or call that agency for *anything*, Lena will be the last person you have to worry about. I will make you so goddamn sorry."

Fletcher threw up his hands, dislodging Louis's grip in the process. His movements were confident, but his expression was far from it. He'd gone pale. "See you at dinner?"

Louis slammed the door in his face.

Everything in his office was bathed in red. He paced to one end and back toward the other, breathing deeply against the urge to grab the signed Derek Jeter baseball bat off his wall and smash everything in sight. His skin felt itchy, crawling underneath his dress shirt, so he yanked off his tie and threw it in the garbage. He wanted to go back five minutes in time and un-hear every- thing his sister's fiancé had said, but that was impossible, so it replayed over and over until he knew he'd never forget it.

Remembering the way he'd been fantasizing about Roxy's body before Fletcher had walked in, he wanted to kick himself. When it came right down to it, he was no better than Lena's fiancé, was he? Roxy had met him the morning after a one-night stand, for chrissakes. He'd never made it a secret that he wanted to sleep with her. Hell, he'd broadcasted it to her friends before their first date. That was why. Why her knee-jerk reaction was to believe the worst of him. She wasn't stubborn, she was just smart. It would take her a little longer than a couple weeks to trust him. So what? He liked that about her. He liked the fact that she made him work harder to earn it. Yet he shouted at her and walked out like an idiot? Dammit. *Dammit.* All he wanted to do at that moment was look at her face, smell her hair, and apologize. Not just for himself, but for every other prick in the world who had made her so wary.

A knock on his door did nothing to calm him down; it only made him angrier. Fletcher had probably come back to beg him not to tell his sister what he'd said. To give him some bullshit apology that should have been directed at Roxy. Not him. Louis surged to his feet and strode to the door. "I told you to get the fuck out."

He threw the door open.

Roxy stood on the other side with her hand raised midknock. Based on her wide-eyed look, she'd heard what he'd said. "Bad time?"

His heart started knocking against his ribs at one hundred miles an hour. He didn't even want to question *why* she was there, it only mattered that she *was* there. After all the ugliness he'd just gone swimming in, the sight of her felt like the first breath when you breach the surface. Something about her appearance struck him as different, but he couldn't look away from her face long enough to check. She looked tired, though, probably reflecting the exhaustion on his own face. He really didn't like seeing her so tired. Hated knowing he was at least partially responsible.

"Um." She gave a sideways glance down the hallway. "You're kind of leaving me hanging here. Is there no room at the inn or something?"

The hint of insecurity in her voice snapped Louis out of his trance. "Get in here," he growled, snagging her wrist and hauling her up against him. He kicked the door shut and wrapped her tightly in his arms, letting the scent of cherry blossoms clear away the remaining ugliness. "I just didn't expect to see you here."

Her body gradually relaxed. "I didn't plan on coming here. I kind of just ended up outside." She put a hand on his chest and pushed him away gently. He took that opportunity to figure out what was different about her, or he would drive himself crazy trying to figure out why she didn't want to be held. If she'd come here to officially break things off. Louis took a bracing breath and studied her. Clothes. Her clothes were different. The high heels he'd never seen her without had been replaced by a pair of white Converse. She wore snug black pants and a thin, cream-colored sweater. Sexy as all get-out, but conservative compared to her usual attire.

"I'm glad you ended up outside." He tucked her hair behind her ear. "If you hadn't come to me, I was going to you."

She scrutinized his face, as if trying to decide whether or not to believe him. "I'm here to say I'm sorry about last night. You brought my hormonal roommates ice cream and then I acted like a jerk." He started to tell her it was okay, but she clapped a hand over his mouth. "If you haven't decided yet that I'm too much trouble, I want to take you out tonight to make up for it. On a date-date."

Louis's lips spread into a slow smile against her palm. When was this girl going to stop catching him off guard? He hoped the answer was never. Ten minutes ago, he'd been ready to beat his head against the wall. Unbelievable how quickly things had changed. He couldn't be more thankful at the moment not to have a self-induced concussion. Roxy had just asked him out. Would she take back the invitation if he did the running man?

Slowly, she removed her hand from his mouth. "So. How about it, McNally?"

"We're down to just one name now?" She studied her nails, looking bored, which only made his smile widen. "Where are you taking me on this date-date?"

"Not telling." She shoved his shoulder. "Is that a yes?"

"That's a hell yes." *Don't reach for her. Don't do it. Make it through the date.* "What time should I pick you up?"

"I'm picking *you* up. This is my show."

Louis's old-fashioned instincts gave a collective grunt of disapproval, but he shot them the mental middle finger to shut them up. No way was he rocking the boat when he'd finally gotten her to come around. *Don't kiss her, even though she's tossing her hair around now like she wants it. Don't. Do. It.* "Okay, Rox. What time should I have my hair washed by?"

"Funny. I have rehearsal later, so I'll be at your place around eight."

"Rehearsal," he repeated. "Already?"

Why wouldn't she look at him? "Yeah. Johan just wants to help me get comfortable with the script." She tossed her hair one final time and waited, but he didn't take the bait. Even though it churned his insides up not to touch her like she clearly wanted. "Fine. If that's how we're playing it. . . ." She backed toward the door, a mischievous smile playing around her mouth. "See you tonight, Louis."

"Shit," he muttered when the door clicked shut. He had a feeling he'd just issued a challenge he didn't have the willpower to face. He couldn't wait to get started.

Chapter 16

Roxy stepped off the elevator in Louis's building. The marble hallway and picture windows looking out onto Stanton Street already felt familiar, even though she'd only been there twice. She needed that right now. Familiarity. She'd almost called the whole night off but had somehow forced herself onto the subway and down to the Lower East Side. This date had been her idea, her peace offering, and she couldn't blow it off, even if she wanted to crawl into bed and blast music inside her headphones as loud as it could go.

Her rehearsal with Johan had started off okay. There had been a full half hour when she'd convinced herself she'd been wrong about him. They'd shared a couple laughs, he'd bought her a Diet Coke from the vending machine. *So he was overly flirtatious at the audition,* she'd thought. *Big deal.* It wouldn't be the first time she'd come across a touchy-feely dude in this industry. As the rehearsal had gone on, however, those friendly touches had started to linger just a little too long. On her waist, her shoulders. He'd started closing in on her when the scene hadn't called for it, making her start all over when she'd grown too uncomfortable to get her lines right. She'd managed to complete the rehearsal without dodging a blatant come-on, but it was only a matter of time. Tomorrow they were meeting again, and it would be make or break.

She felt a little too exposed, too agitated to enjoy a date right now. Just like this morning, though, she found herself walking in Louis's direction. Wanting to see him, yet not fully understanding the assurance that he would make everything seem better. Last night, she'd planted herself between her two menstruating roommates and eaten enough ice cream to sink the Staten Island Ferry, but it had only made things worse. With every bite she'd taken, she'd remembered how adorable he'd looked humoring Honey and Abby. How genuine he'd sounded when trying to convince her he'd come to spend time with her, not just between her scratchy sheets. She'd thought of him watching *Arrested Development* all by himself and had wanted to crawl onto his lap and laugh at the Bluths right along with him.

The second he'd pulled her into his office and held her this morning, her frayed threads had stitched themselves back together. While she recognized the danger of that, of relying on a guy to feel better, she couldn't seem to help herself. She'd fallen prey to the Louis Effect.

She wanted to see him again after tonight, so she would set aside her unsettled mood for now. *Think about Johan and his sticky fingers tomorrow. Stop worrying about Louis's dating habits. Keep it casual. Avoidance is your friend.*

Roxy braced herself in front of Louis's door and knocked. And waited. When Louis didn't answer for a full minute, she frowned and checked her cell phone clock. Crap. Half an hour early . . . rehearsals must have gone by much quicker than they'd felt. Maybe he wasn't home yet? She started to call him, but the door swung open to reveal Louis before her thumb hit the button.

His appearance brought her up short. He looked . . . odd. Shirtless and barefoot, his upper lip was dotted with sweat, and the top button of his jeans was undone. His breath came faster than usual pants, as if he'd just run a mile. She would have guessed he'd been working out if he hadn't looked so distinctly uncomfortable. Shifting on the balls of his feet, he wouldn't even look her directly in the eye. A pit formed and yawned wide in her stomach. Oh, God. Had she caught him in the middle of entertaining a girl? He'd told her that day in his office that he didn't do relationships. Had her early arrival screwed up his plans for a double header?

She wanted to roundhouse him in the nuts, but what right did she have to do that? They weren't exclusive. He had every right to date around, same as she did. So why did she feel like wailing obscenities at the sky and beating her fists against his chest? Before she could embarrass herself by doing just that, Roxy turned and jogged for the elevator. Good. *It's over now and you're escaping with minimal damage.*

Sweet. Even her inner monologue sounded skeptical.

"*Hey.*" His heavy tread pounded after her. "Where the hell are you going?"

Louis gripped her wrist before she could punch the elevator button. "Sorry to interrupt. You can get back to what you were doing now."

"How do you know what I was doing?" he asked quickly. Too quickly.

She yanked at her wrist, but he wouldn't let it go. "Dude, you look like you just narrowly escaped death by orgy. I'm not joining whatever party you have going on in there."

"What—?" His question was cut off by the elevator door sliding open and an elderly woman disembarking with her leashed poodle. Her perfectly plucked eyebrows raised at the sight of a shirtless Louis standing in the hallway, but her sophisticated New Yorker status kept her walking past without comment. Roxy took advantage of the distraction and dove into the elevator, but Louis followed right on her heels. His arms wrapped around her from behind, and he hugged her close despite her struggles. "Okay, I'm starting to catch up now. You think there is an orgy in my apartment because I'm sweaty."

She elbowed him in the ribs, but he held on tight. "You looked guilty when you opened the door. Which is stupid because I'm not your girlfriend. But it turns out I'm also not kosher with being second in the batting order."

"Oh, sure. Make a baseball reference and get even cuter than you already are." His forehead came to rest on her shoulder. "There's no one in my apartment, Rox."

Hope inflated in her chest, but she stuck a pin in it. "What were you doing?"

He groaned. "Don't make me tell you. It's goddamn embarrassing."

The elevator started to descend toward the first floor. Knowing someone would join them in the small space when it reached its destination, she tried once more unsuccessfully to break free of his hold. "Tell me or I walk."

"Had a feeling you would say that." She started to turn in his arms, but he prevented her by tightening them. "No, this'll be much easier if you're not looking at me." A long sigh ruffled the hair beside her ear. "I'm attracted to you, Roxy. Painfully fucking attracted. I was trying to relieve some pressure before you came over on the off chance I might make it ten minutes tonight without wanting to tear your clothes off and throw you on the floor. So. That about sums it up."

It took her a beat to understand. Relief only had a split second to calm her before it was replaced with amusement. "You were—"

The elevator came to a stop. A man climbed in wearing a business suit.

"Don't say it," Louis warned against her neck.

Her lips twitched. "Self-lovin'? Polishing the family jewels?"

A discreet cough behind them sent Roxy into a laughing fit. She tried to keep silent, but as soon as the suited man climbed off on the floor beneath Louis's, she doubled over and gave in to the urge. Louis punched the button for his floor and shoved his hands into his pockets. "I'm glad you think it's funny. I didn't quite . . . polish the jewels . . . as much as I needed to. The situation is *not* under control."

His terse tone almost set her off again, but he looked so uncomfortable that she found a way to contain herself. "Do you want me to wait outside while you finish?"

He looked at her like she'd sprouted horns. "No way I'm letting you out of my sight. I'm good."

"You're so not."

His head fell back on his shoulders. "I'm *so* not."

The elevator door opened to reveal his floor and he indicated she should lead the way, even looking slightly suspicious that she might try and take off again. As she bypassed him into the hallway, she noticed him holding his breath, staring determinedly at a spot over her head. His neck flushed red the closer she came. Wow. The guy was in pain. Over her. It kind of turned her on.

No, it *really* turned her on. Close on the heels of that budding awareness came the realization that she hadn't thought about her shitty rehearsal in the past five minutes. She didn't feel restless and semi-ill anymore. She felt hot and desirable, knowing he wanted her so bad he had to touch himself before they even spent time together. He'd done it so he'd be in the condition to prove a point. That he wanted more than physical contact with her. It made her like him even more than she already did. It made her want to take the pain away. After the intimate conversation they'd just had, the images it had projected across her mind, she also felt like being a little . . . bad.

When they reached the door to his apartment, she very deliberately brushed against him on the way inside, letting her breasts drag across the tops of his abs. His eyelids drooped and he cursed. "Please, Roxy. If my balls get any bluer, this date is going to take place in the emergency room."

"What were you thinking about?" She reached behind him and pushed the apartment door shut, letting their bodies glide together. Letting her mouth drag slowly, *slowly* against his neck. "When you were . . . polishing."

"I can't say." He spoke through gritted teeth. "A man's spank bank is sacred."

"Is that so?" Roxy trailed a finger down the center of his stomach, tucking it just beneath the waistband of his jeans. "I might be willing to help if you tell me."

The back of his head hit the door. "Somebody up there either hates me or loves me." He took a deep breath. "Roxy, I meant what I said last night. I want more than this from you."

Something deep inside her chest responded to the frustration in his voice. She kissed his mouth softly and looked him in the eye. "I know that, Louis. I'm convinced, okay?" Their next kiss lingered, but seeing that his eyes were squeezed shut, she pulled back before he could deepen it. "Tell me what you thought about."

He growled low in his throat. "You. I thought of you in the stupid cheerleader uniform. I hate the damn thing, but I cannot fucking stop thinking about it. You were . . ." His teeth sunk into his bottom lip. "Touching yourself."

Heat settled low and heavy in her midsection. With anyone else, this kind of confession would bother her. It didn't with Louis. Misery laced with honesty in his voice, making her feel safe. Sympathetic. Turned on. So many different emotions that she didn't know where to direct them. So she went with what felt right. And it felt right to help ease his suffering.

"Well, I don't have the uniform with me." She flicked open the button on her jeans and drew down the zipper. "But I can touch myself for you, Louis."

His bare chest shuddered. "No?"

She tilted her head. "Was that a question?"

"I don't know?"

Oh, Jesus. I really like this guy. A lot. Roxy let her eyes drift shut and slipped her fingers inside her panties. When her fingers met the most sensitive part of her, she gasped and Louis groaned. His hands shook as he reached out and unbuttoned the top three buttons of her shirt, then shoved the material wide. Those dark eyes devoured the sight of her breasts, his mouth working as if he could already taste them.

"Tell me what you want, Rox."

"I want to finish what you started."

She watched the debate take place inside his head, but when his eyes glazed over, she knew need had won out. He worked the fly of his jeans quickly, wincing as he took himself out. His hand worked his hard flesh as he watched her, appearing riveted by the sight of her hand moving inside her jeans. He looked fucking gorgeous, teeth torturing his bottom lips, arm and stomach muscles flexing with every smooth, practiced movement. The entryway light picked up the sheen of sweat on his chest, making his skin glow. She needed this relief just as bad as he did, she just hadn't realized it.

"Tell me what it feels like to you."

A sob tripped over her lips. "Warm. Soft. It feels like me."

"I already know how you feel. Don't I? Did you like my hand up your skirt that night?"

"*Yes.*"

How often had he done this while thinking of her? Was today the first time? She didn't have the capacity to ask, because she felt the oncoming release tightening her muscles. So soon? She leaned close and licked at the seam of his mouth until he opened up. He kissed her wildly as their hands moved between them. The hungry moan that erupted from his throat finished her. She shook as pleasure flooded her system. Relief, surprise . . . she felt overwhelmed by the combination. He still hadn't reached the end, and she suddenly wanted him there with her so desperately that she found herself dropping to her knees.

"*Roxy*." His breathing grew even harsher. He clearly wanted what she was offering, but he still attempted to draw her back to her feet. "Fuck. I can't say no right now. I can't."

"So don't." She gripped him at the base of his thick arousal and brought him to her lips. He felt so full inside her mouth, his hands so good in her hair, that she lost herself to the moment. Every stroke of her tongue, nip of her teeth, and pump of her fist drew a reaction from him. His words blurred together above her as she worked him with her mouth, up and down, taking him deep and sucking her way back up. She'd never enjoyed doing this much before, but it felt right with Louis. It felt great. Perfect.

"Stand up, baby. Please. I can't. Don't do . . . yes, *fuck* yes. Grip it tighter." His free hand formed a fist in her hair. "I'm there . . . I'm there, Rox. Jesus, get up here. Let me kiss you while I come."

She heard him begging but didn't want to obey. The choice was taken away from her when Louis yanked her, one-handed, to her feet and stamped his mouth over hers, hot and frantic, matching the pace of his strokes. The loud groan he released into her mouth moved through her, shivering its way into her belly and spreading. She could actually *feel* the strength of his release.

His movements slowed and he sagged back against the door,

taking her with him. Together, they slid down the wood and ended up on the ground, her sitting on his lap. He pulled her close but was careful not to touch her with his right hand. She suspected he'd need to get up soon to find a washcloth. Funny how the idea of that didn't embarrass her at all. After what they'd just shared, she wasn't sure anything between them would ever be embarrassing. It made her feel free. Light. So of course, her other half, the half that felt uncomfortable with light and easy, chimed in and told her to be cautious. To look out for dropping shoes.

Louis blew out a long breath and kissed her forehead. "I don't go on a lot of dates, but I'm almost positive blow jobs are reserved for after dinner."

"Are you complaining?"

"As God is my witness, I'll never complain about anything ever again."

Their quiet laughter filled the apartment.

Maybe she could stop waiting for the other shoe to drop. Just for tonight.

Chapter 17

*A*t least one question had been answered tonight. Somebody up there definitely loved him.

Louis threw his arm around Roxy's shoulder as they weaved through pedestrian traffic on Grand Street. He tried not to smile like a jackass when she leaned into him. Fine, the evening had definitely not started as he'd planned, with her knocking on his door as he'd performed the holiest of acts, but damn. How *beautiful* were the stars tonight? He'd never really noticed before!

What *had* gone according to plan so far with this girl? Oh, that's right. Nothing. Not being able to pin her down had driven him crazy in the beginning. It still did. But he'd just started to realize Roxy couldn't be situated or handled. She handled herself and decided when and how she wanted to include him. He hoped that would change as she got to know him better, but for tonight, he was pretty damn content to hold her close as they walked down the street. If he had to struggle not to look at her mouth every time she spoke to him, well, he was only a man. And this man had just had his world rocked.

It was more than the amazing things she'd done to him, *for* him. Amazing didn't even begin to cover it, actually. It was the way she'd been afterward. He'd expected her to clam up, make an excuse to leave. He thought he'd truly fucked up letting himself get carried away with her, when he'd gone to such lengths to convince her of his good intentions. Then she'd smiled up at him without a hint of remorse on her face, and he'd kind of fallen half in love with her. *Stop kidding yourself, you're more than halfway there.* Louis didn't know exactly where he fell on the love time line; he only knew that the cautious happiness he'd watched transform her since they'd left the apartment was having a direct effect on his own. It made him feel like a fucking rock star, and he wanted her to *stay* happy. To be the *reason* she stayed that way.

For now, though, he needed to get himself in check before he scared her back to Chelsea. He knew he shouldn't make plans, should just let everything happen naturally, but he couldn't help it. He'd always been a planner, and his job only exacerbated the trait. Tonight he wanted to find out more about her. Everything, if possible. He wanted to make her laugh more . . . and Jesus Christ, he wanted her to spend the night in his arms. No interruptions or impromptu popcorn parties. His sisters were at a dinner party in Brooklyn tonight. He'd triple-checked.

"You're thinking awfully hard about something, McNally."

Relax, idiot. You're being too obvious. "I'm trying to figure out where you're taking me."

"Scared?" She tugged him down a side street, throwing him a smile over her shoulder that made him want to pick her up and squeeze her against his chest. "I'm going to feed you the best meal you've ever eaten. I'm going to do it for free, too."

"A free meal in Manhattan?"

"That's right." Her hair lifted off her shoulders in the breeze. "How are your acting skills?"

"You're assuming I have some."

"Right." Excitement danced in her eyes. "I guess this is going to be a one-woman show."

She reached down and twined their fingers together before pulling him to a stop at the corner of the block. The action temporarily distracted him until he realized they'd stopped moving. He looked around for a restaurant but didn't see any for another block. Roxy appeared to be scoping something out on the adjacent side street, so he followed her line of vision and saw two food trucks. They were on opposite sides of the road, a scattering of college students eating on the curbs beside them. Both trucks had giant signs on their roofs boasting The BEST Falafel in New York City.

"Follow my lead," she instructed before strolling down the center of the block. Louis immediately wanted to pull her back to the safety of the curb, until he realized the street was closed down for foot traffic only. He watched curiously as she stopped in the middle of the street, an equal distance between the two food trucks. She tapped a finger against her lips, looking from one truck to the other. "I've heard only one of them has the *best* falafel," she stage-whispered. "But I can't remember which one. Do you know, honey?"

Louis bit back his smile. *Crafty girl.* God, she was full of surprises. "I don't know." He did his best to appear torn. "Maybe we should try that dumpling truck I saw on the way over. I don't want to get a bad falafel if we pick the wrong one."

A hint of surprise made its way into her expression, but she hid it just as quick. "You're right. We should g—"

"Hold on now," a man called from the truck to their left. "I'm the best truck. You come to me."

"Bullshit." A man poked his head out the window of the opposite truck. "You wouldn't know a good falafel if it grew legs and danced in front of you. I am the best falafel in this city."

"You cook something in that truck. It is not falafel, brother."

"They're brothers?" Louis whispered in Roxy's ear.

She nodded, nuzzling her cheek against his mouth. "They used to work the same truck, but they had a fight. Both of them refuse to give up the block."

"How do you know this?"

"The starving actress newsletter."

He half-smiled at the joke even though he didn't find the idea of her hungry funny. At all. It made him feel impatient . . . twitchy. While his mind headed down that path, it occurred to him that she'd just blown his mind *and* was now in charge of getting them fed. It kind of killed him a little, knowing he hadn't returned the favor—*yet*—or was allowed to buy her a decent meal. If he didn't think she'd dig in her heels, he'd give her the choice of any restaurant in town. He'd sit there, watch her eat, and feel like he'd . . . earned her. Christ. Apparently he wasn't as enlightened as he'd thought, something he'd only realized since meeting Roxy and being blindsided by the urge to take care of her. She could take care of herself, he knew that. It didn't stop him from wanting the job.

Roxy's voice lured him back to the present. "There's only one way to settle this, gentlemen. One falafel from each truck." She pursed her lips. "Whose should we try first?"

"Mine."

"Right this way."

Roxy bit her lip, splitting a conflicted look between the two men. "I-I can't decide. If I eat the bad one first, it might ruin falafel for me forever."

"Here!" The man to their left tossed a Styrofoam container onto the metal perch beneath his window. "I'm so sure you'll pick mine as the best, I give it for free."

"Oh, no, you don't." The other man briefly disappeared into his truck. "Mine is free, too."

"Bingo," Roxy said out of the side of her mouth before swaggering toward the first truck. "Well . . . if you insist . . ."

They sat on the curb, a few yards away from the rowdy college students, and ate falafel. Since the truck owners were watching them anxiously from their windows, they switched once in a while and pretended to be in a deep discussion concerning the merits of each meal.

"And you claim to have no acting ability." She eyed him suspiciously. "You were a regular Leonardo DiCaprio out there."

"I might have picked up a few things in law school."

"How to put on a show for the jury? That kind of thing?"

Louis popped a falafel into his mouth and nodded. Here they were, talking about him again. It was like she had some kind of mental block when it came to talking about herself. "What about you? Who taught you how to act?"

She stabbed at her food with the fork but didn't eat it. "Uh . . . no one, I guess. Just me." Louis waited, hoping she would say more. "There was a drama teacher in high school that gave me a chance, but there were so many other students. He couldn't really guide me."

"What about acting classes?"

He laid a hand on her knee when it started bouncing, earning him a cautious look. "I took a couple when I moved to Manhattan. Before that, no. My parents . . . they don't think wanting to be an actress is practical. Or realistic." She laughed a little. "They're probably right."

This is where he should stop asking questions. The witness had given up as much information as he would get. But he wanted to know more. "What did they want you to do instead?"

She didn't talk for a while, abandoning her container of food on the sidewalk next to her. When she finally spoke, he realized he'd been holding his breath. "They didn't care. They *don't* care, Louis." Their gazes met. "The only reason they said acting is impractical was so they wouldn't have to dip into their beer money for my acting classes. I haven't talked to them since Christmas. They genuinely don't give a shit."

"I don't believe that. How could anyone not give a shit about you?"

"I was an accident." She looked shocked to have said the words out loud. Words that carved right into his gut. "My father got my mother pregnant at their high school prom. I think being the product of a cliché is what hurts the most." Her laughter was forced. He could tell she was trying to disguise the hurt, but he didn't want her to. Even if he hated seeing it, he wanted this piece of her. "They went to IHOP afterward. I wish I didn't know that, but I do. They had unprotected hotel room sex and went to a fucking IHOP in Newark. I overheard that while they were fighting one night."

He'd been expecting something bad because of the ten-foot-high wall she usually had up to protect her, but that didn't make it any easier to hear. Her parents not caring or encouraging her to pursue her goals made him angry on her behalf. She was dynamic, smart, and talented. She deserved better than that. His family might be bat shit crazy, but they supported one another. In their own annoying, often long-distance way.

He started to tell her he was sorry. That he wished her parents appreciated her, saw her for the amazing girl she was, but she shook her head at him. "Talk to me about something else for a while, okay?"

She seemed uncomfortable with what she'd revealed, so he took the focus off her. For now. "My firm doesn't want me to do any more pro bono work." As soon as he said the words, he realized he'd been wanting all along to talk to her about it. "Cases like the youth center . . . they think it's a waste of their resources. Also known as me."

Her expression turned serious, eclipsing the gratefulness he'd seen when he'd changed the subject. "But it's so important to you," she said.

"Yeah, but—" *Back up.* He shook his head. "I never told you that."

"It was obvious. You care about those kids. They need you." She pushed her falafel around with her fork. "Who's going to help them if you're not around?"

He blew out a breath, when her words echoed the ones that had been circling his own mind. "I don't know. Another lawyer. Maybe no one."

Roxy stayed silent a moment. "I'm not going to pretend I understand the world you work in. It's nothing like mine. But it seems to me . . ." She pushed her hair back over her shoulder. "If they know it means a lot to you and don't care . . . you can do better."

"Maybe they think they can do better, too." The concern he hadn't even allowed himself to voice slipped out before he could stop it. "Better than me."

"No," she said decisively. "I saw you work, Louis. I didn't understand a crap load of it . . ." They shared a laugh. "But I know if they let you leave, they'd be letting one of the good guys go. I know that."

Shit. His throat hurt a little. He wondered if she'd push him off or hold him closer if he tackled her onto the sidewalk. "Thanks."

They passed a few minutes in comfortable silence before Roxy spoke again. "What I said before made it sound like I'm bitter. About my parents, everything. I'm not," she continued. "I've had to work harder to do it on my own. I *want* to succeed on my own, without any help. And I'm going to."

Fear trickled through his veins. He'd never seen her look so determined. Succeeding on her own was important to her. Possibly the *most* important thing to her. He'd taken that away from her with one phone call. He'd given his help without asking, thinking she might turn it down if he was up-front about it. Now he knew for certain she would have turned it down. But it was too late to take it back.

"I'm sorry."

"Why are *you* sorry?"

For being a selfish, presumptuous prick, he wanted to say, but the flippant way she posed the question told him she needed a distraction from the topic. He wanted to give it to her. Wanted to give her *anything* she wanted. Not to mention, he sorely needed one himself. "I'm sorry you've got the job of informing truck number one his falafel came in second place."

Her mouth lifted at the edges. "I concur. Overcooked."

He took their containers and stood before tossing them into a nearby garbage can. When he saw that the truck owners were distracted, he winked at Roxy. "Maybe we should just make a run for it."

Without missing a beat, she took his hand and started jogging. "I like your style, McNally."

Chapter 18

Roxy's nerves buzzed as she and Louis stepped into his apartment. Unbelievable. She was actually nervous. Only a couple of hours ago, she'd done things to him that should have wiped her clean of any anxiety, but somehow the time they'd spent together tonight had only heightened it. She'd opened up to him, let him see a part of her she rarely exposed to anyone. That was why she suddenly felt like bolting. Now he knew exactly who he'd be touching, kissing. Hiding didn't appear to be an option anymore, and that scared the hell out of her.

What scared her even more? It seemed as if her opening up had only served to interest him more. He hadn't stopped touching her since they'd left their spots behind on the curb. His touches hadn't all been sexual, though. A brush of his thumb across her bottom lip, a soft kiss at the nape of her neck . . . those weren't touches she was used to. From Louis or anyone. She loved them a little too much, was starting to crave and expect them a little too soon.

Dammit, she hated this. Sex should be a spontaneous thing

that doesn't give either party time to stress out and overthink everything. Courthouse sex against a file cabinet, that was more her style. Not this perfect date bullshit followed by some preplanned lovemaking. Too many high expectations. *Right, as if sex with Louis would be anything less than amazing.* Still. The ritual of it made her jumpy.

Louis threw the dead bolt on his apartment door and came up behind her. Before he'd even touched her, an insistent pounding started in her chest. Her skin started to tingle. Where would he touch her first? She didn't have a preference, as long as she could feel his hands on her body.

Her eyes popped open to find him standing in front of her, looking half concerned, half amused. "What's going on in that head?" he asked.

"You don't want to know."

"I disagree."

Roxy blew out a breath. She'd already been honest with him once tonight, and it had gone okay, right? Might as well go for broke. At least it would stall until she got her stupid nerves under control. Or scare him off so she could go back to worrying only about herself. Which suddenly sounded terrible. Still . . . "Here's my nightmare. You making some tired joke while opening a bottle of merlot. Us both drinking a glass, pretending like we care what the other person is saying when really we're just killing time until the main event. You making some practiced move in order to kiss me. Cut to five minutes later, we're doing it in the missionary position."

Louis frowned. "Would you prefer a cabernet?"

A laugh escaped, sounding more like a groan. "That better be a joke."

One of his eyebrows lifted. "I could say the same to you."

He sounded . . . mad? She hadn't expected that. At the end of her speech, she'd fully expected him to brush her hair back and say something reassuring. Tell her they would never be those people she'd just described. Instead, he looked as if he wanted to shake her. "I didn't mean to offend you, I just—"

"You just what?" He closed the distance between them and kept right on coming, until she had to back up or get run over. She'd only taken two backward steps when her bottom hit the kitchen table. Louis planted his fists on either side of her, forcing her to lean back. "You thought I'd give you some shitty wine and a boring fuck?"

"No, I—"

"No? That's what it sounded like." He removed one hand from the table to unbutton her jeans before yanking down the zipper. Roxy's breath started to race in and out, joining her quickening pulse. Oh, God. What was going on here? She should be alarmed at his obvious anger, but her body was responding to his aggression like crazy. *More.* "I don't drink wine, I don't need an excuse or some lame-ass move to kiss you." He shucked her shoes, ripped her jeans down her legs, and tossed them over his shoulder in one movement. "And, baby, I'd still get you off screaming in the missionary position. Too bad that's not what you're going to get tonight, huh?"

She started to say yes, or maybe it was no. The answer leaked out of her head when he picked her up by the waist and set her on the table. "Can you please repeat the question?"

Louis didn't answer. His gaze swept her instead, traveling up her legs and ending between her thighs. She now wore only her light blouse and a turquoise thong. That perusal made her so anxiously hot that she found herself letting her knees fall further apart so he could see her better. His fingers dragged down the sensitive inside of her thigh before tracing over the turquoise material gently. "It's only been one day since I was deep inside here, but it's been too long." Unexpectedly, he gave her a rough squeeze through her panties. "I know ways to get it deeper."

Roxy's back arched on a moan. *Ohmygodohmygod.* "Louis . . ."

"Louis, what?" He didn't give her a chance to answer as he tugged the panties down her legs and dropped them onto the table. A hungry sound hummed in his throat as he looked her over. "You look like you're going to be sweet, Rox."

Heat rocked her, making her dizzy. That dizziness, that escape from reality, gave her the excuse to be a little wild. To live in the now. She reached for the hem of her shirt and drew it over her head. When she started to remove her bra, Louis stayed her hand and did it himself, leaving her completely naked. And him still fully clothed. Knowing the gorgeous body he was hiding, that felt like sacrilege.

She reached out with the intention of unbuttoning his pants, but he caught her wrist. "Not yet. If you touch me, I'm going to need to get inside you."

"Sounds good."

Humor only momentarily eclipsed the hunger in his eyes, before it came back even stronger than before. "You don't like plans or traditional shit. I get that." He pushed her legs wide and licked, long and slow, down the inside of her right thigh. "But I do like plans. I've been planning all week on going down on you. So lay back and deal with it."

Roxy collapsed back onto the table at the first touch of his mouth. His energy changed almost immediately. His tongue dragged over her flesh with devastating thoroughness, slow, *slooooow*. Until something inside him seemed to break and cost him his discipline. The hands holding her thighs apart grew rougher, his throaty growls vibrating her center sent shock waves through her body she swore would kill her. His tongue curled around the part of her that needed the most attention, then worried it quickly.

"Faster, faster." She plowed her fingers into his hair. He made an appreciative noise, letting her know he liked that, so she pulled on the strands harder. "*Oh, God. So good.*"

Already her muscles had started to tighten, all the way up to her throat. Her breasts heaved, blocking her view of anything but Louis's broad back and her spread thighs on either side of him. The sight pushed her a little closer, she just needed—

Louis slid two big fingers inside her, sucking her clitoris into his mouth at the same time. A scream launched all the way from her midsection as she came. It happened without warning, like being hit by a tidal wave, and all she could do was sink down, down. Louis yanked her back to the surface, though, dragging her from the table before she could refill her lungs with oxygen. She held on to the table and watched him through bleary eyes as he freed himself from his pants and rolled on a condom. As it had earlier that night, seeing his hand wrapped around his length sent a bolt of electricity to her core. Already her body wanted more. More of everything he could give.

She gasped when he spun her around to face the table. A firm hand at the center of her back pressed her forward, bending her at the waist. Her pulse kicked back up into its earlier erratic rhythm at the realization he was going to take her this way. *Yes.* This is what she wanted. What she'd been dying for. The rush. The urgency. No planning or pretense required.

Louis jerked her hips higher, forcing her to bow her back. The confidence in his touch made everything inside her twist with need. She flipped her hair over her shoulder and looked back at him, wanting to remember everything about this moment later.

"Fuck, Rox." He slipped the head of his erection between her legs. "Do you have any idea how you're looking at me right now?"

"How is that?" she asked, voice unrecognizable.

"Like you'd beg for it if I asked."

Roxy felt drugged, hot. Outside of herself but still wildly attuned to her body. "Is that what you want?" She worked her hips in a slow circle. An answer wasn't needed; his groan told her everything she needed to know. The power it gave her was heady. "*Please,* Louis. Please?"

"*Jesus,* stop. I can't take any more," he grated, before thrusting into her hard. A harsh sob fell from her lips at the sudden, perfect fullness. Relief at finally being joined faded quickly, and he started to move. Tight, quick thrusts forced her to plant her hands more securely on the table. "You think I need a reason to want you any more? When it's already so goddamn much?"

She moaned. "I don't know, just don't stop."

He settled a hand at the small of her back and pushed down, creating a different angle, one that allowed him to hit the spot inside her that had never been reached before. Every upward thrust of his hips drove her closer to release. *Too fast. Too fast.* She wanted to hold on longer, but he only sped up until she was facedown and clinging to the table's edge. Was that *her* screaming at him to go harder? She wasn't entirely conscious of anything but the pressure building inside her, threatening to swallow her up. Her belly was pressed against the table, her legs spread wide. She had no way of relieving the unbelievable ache—she could only rely on him to do it for her.

"*Louis.* I need it. Please."

"You *would* come fast. Of course you would. Just another thing to drive me fucking crazy." She felt his hand smooth over her thigh before slipping between her legs, circling his middle finger right where she needed it. "Go ahead, baby. I need you a little longer."

Something about the gravel in his voice pushed her that final step to release. She cried out as it rolled through her, but it was muffled by the table, her voice vibrating with the force of Louis's drives. He felt rock hard inside of her, unyielding. All she could do was hold on as his rhythm grew erratic, then sped up. Beneath her, the table scraped on the floor and wedged against the wall.

"Fuck, I'm coming, Rox. You good?"

"Yes," she managed.

His fingers dug into the flesh of her hips, hard, as he started hammering into her, so fast it rattled her teeth. An image of them together at the courthouse flashed through her mind. Of his hips moving so fast they blurred . . . she knew that's what he looked like now even though she couldn't see him. Could envision the look of intensity on his face. Louis McNally came like a fucking freight train, and she loved that. Loved being the one to draw it out of him. Behind her, he pushed deep one final time and fell forward onto her back, shaking against her.

"So good, feels so *fucking* good." His mouth moved, hot and open, over her back. "No one else does this to me. I already want you again. *Fuck.*"

Roxy opened her mouth to beg for a break—there's a first time for everything—but he pulled her upright, back against his chest. His lips traced the side of her neck and kissed her ear. Her limbs felt weak and liquefied, like she would melt without his arms around her. He chuckled into her hair, telling her he sensed what she was going through. One of his arms looped under her knees and he lifted her, carrying her toward the back of the apartment.

"Come on." He kissed her forehead. "You get into bed and I'll get us both a nice glass of cabernet."

"Smart-ass."

Chapter 19

*L*ouis watched Roxy take a lap around his room and drop onto the edge of his bed. Oh, boy. His heart tried to pound its way out of his chest. Moment of truth. A hint of self-consciousness had crept into her expression, and he knew why. His room was massive. It could probably fit ten of her bedrooms inside it and still have enough space for his treadmill. He'd never really given a thought to it before. Born and raised in Manhattan, he knew square footage came at a premium, but family money, then his own income, had always allowed him to be more than comfortable. Since he was pretty sure his first fight with Roxy had been sparked over her lack of personal space, it felt like he was walking over a field of land mines. He wanted her there, though. Frequently. So this had to happen sooner or later.

When she ran her hands up her arms to grip her elbows, she looked so much smaller than her personality, her presence. Going on instinct, he crossed to his dresser and found a T-shirt for her to wear, worried that if she left the bedroom to get her own clothes, she'd keep right on walking out the door. If that happened, he might just embarrass himself by grabbing hold of her leg and telling her she'd have to drag him down the hallway in order to leave. At the same time, he didn't like seeing Roxy on a bed he'd spent time in with other girls. He kind of wanted to set it on fire and buy a new one tonight. Jesus, apparently Lena was rubbing off on him.

Okay, so he'd been with a healthy amount of partners. After all, he was a certified nine, right? But something different happened when he was with Roxy. Inside her . . . buried all the way to the back with just enough room to move. Louis almost groaned out loud at the memory of it. She fit him perfectly, and still there was so much *more* happening when they were connected in that way. The buildup of feelings burning through him would have scared him if he hadn't felt her right there with him, feeling the same goddamn thing. He *knew* she did . . . could sense it. They moved together in a way he didn't think was a simple matter of chemistry, though God knew, they fucking had that covered. Back in the kitchen, he'd gone somewhere else . . . somewhere he'd been able to only see her, see them. She'd become an on-the-spot addiction he didn't want to kick.

First things first, bro. If he had any hope of feeding his Roxy addiction, he needed to make her okay with them. With their differences. Those differences didn't mean a damn thing, when every minute they spent together felt special. Like it mattered.

He stopped in front of her and tugged the T-shirt over her head, smiling over the way it messed up her hair. She pushed the dark wave out of her face, looked down, and read the front with a grimace. "Winston and Doubleday company softball game 2014? Don't you have a Guns N' Roses T-shirt in there?"

"We can turn it inside out if you want."

She eyed him. "You just want to see my rack again."

"Guilty." He stepped back slightly so he could unbutton his shirt and kick off his jeans. "Someday maybe I'll actually get my clothes off first, huh?"

"Oh, I don't know." She reclined back on her elbows, and his pulse sped up. *In my bed. She's in my bed and showing no signs of leaving.* "I kind of like knowing you can't wait another second."

He swallowed heavily. "I couldn't. I can't."

The smile on her face slowly faded. She looked as if she wanted to say something, but changed her mind and sat up again, fidgeting with the hem of his T-shirt. "So what happens at company softball games? Does everyone let the boss win at the risk of losing their job?"

"My boss would see right through that." Louis walked to the other side of the bed and got in, counting the seconds until he would reach for her. "Someone usually gets too competitive and makes the whole thing brutally awkward. Sometimes it's me."

Her laugh made it impossible to wait any longer to touch her, so he looped an arm around her waist and pulled her across the bed. A sigh blew across his shoulder when their bodies met, almost as if she'd been bracing herself. Tension leaked out of her almost immediately, her back molding to his chest, her bottom fitting against his lap. The smell of her hair had his eyes drifting shut, his body relaxing. Or as relaxed as it could get with Roxy mostly naked up against him. There had been a strain racking his muscles since they'd met, but it eased now, little by little, as if she'd cured him just by being there. Finally, a night where he didn't have to wonder where she was. What she was doing. She was sleeping with *him*, that's what the hell she was doing.

"Oh my God." She yawned. "This is the most comfortable bed in the world."

"That's because I'm in it."

The hum in her throat traveled up his arm. "You and those approachable abs."

His head came off the pillow. "What was that now?" She shook her head, indicating she wouldn't answer, so he tickled her ribs, making her squirm. "Explain what you said."

"Fine," she gasped. "Just stop tickling me."

He gave her one final squeeze before stopping.

She tilted her head back on his shoulder. "The first time you answered the door without your shirt on, I thought your abs were approachable. Like you do sit-ups when you feel like it, but not so many that you're trying too hard."

Louis processed that with a frown. "I can't tell if I should be happy about that."

"You should." He must have been projecting his skepticism, because she turned to look at him. "I also thought your happy trail should be called a rapture path. Does that help?"

"Fucking right it helps." Oh Lord, her sleepy giggle made his throat hurt. Especially knowing he'd been the one to make her do it. *Rapture path . . . nice.* "Know what I thought about you?"

"Why is this chick dressed up like a rabbit?"

"After that." He tucked her head under his chin. "Before you took the mask off, your voice reminded me of someone I'd met before. It bothered me after you left. If I'd met you before, I would definitely remember, so it didn't make any sense." *Am I saying too much? Probably.* "When I finally tracked you down, I realized I didn't know you from anywhere. I just knew *you*. Does that make sense? You were familiar to me even though I'd never met you."

She stayed silent for a long time, her breathing deep and even. His nature demanded he roll her over to try and decipher her expression. Demand she say something. Just when he thought they were destined to fall asleep with his TMI moment hanging over their heads, she kissed the inside of his arm. "You win, Louis. I'll stick around."

Relief blanketed him. He pulled her close and fell into the deepest sleep he could remember.

HE WOKE UP moaning. Someone was licking his dick like a Popsicle, and it felt in-*credible.*

Popsicles. Roxy. Roxy's mouth.

Louis's eyes flew open. There were no more someones. There was only Roxy now. She'd stayed the night and . . . *ohhh God.* His hands flew to the mass of dark hair laying on his stomach and thighs, snagging it with his fingers. She was trying to kill him, when he'd only had the opportunity to sleep beside her one time? He was so hard that he couldn't catch his breath. The room was still half dark in the early morning light, and he struggled to see her more clearly through blurred vision. When she came into sharp focus, he almost wished he'd kept his eyes closed. At the sight of her, his stomach muscles screamed into tight coils and he almost came.

She was naked, his softball shirt long gone, knelt down between his outstretched legs. Her breasts swayed with every movement of her mouth, every long lick of her tongue. Both of her eyes were closed up tight, soft, pleasurable sounds purring past her lips. As if she sensed him watching her, those gorgeous eyes opened under heavy eyelids. Keeping their gazes locked, she licked him bottom to top, pausing at the top to lap at the head.

Louis's hips came off the bed on a curse. "For chrissake, get up here so I can fuck you."

She gently teased the inside of his thigh with her fingernails. "I'm not done."

He jackknifed into a sitting position and gripped her above the elbows. She made a sound of protest as he dragged her warm, sexy body onto his lap. Until they came face-to-face, he didn't realize she still looked drowsy from sleep. Soft. Her lips, hair . . . eyes. She looked so beautiful and soft. But he couldn't control the lust she'd sparked long enough to enjoy it. Or the fact that she'd obviously slept so well in his bed, his arms. No, he needed her too bad. He reached between them to stroke his dick once, run it through the flesh at the juncture of her legs to test whether or not she was ready. *Christ*, of course she was ready. So slick and ready.

"You get that way sucking me off?" Reaching toward his bedside table blindly for a condom, he bit her bottom lip and tugged. "Wet as fuck."

"Yes." The single word came out sounding like a shudder. She hummed in her throat as he rolled the condom on, as if she couldn't wait another second. Good, he couldn't, either. "You were saying my name in your sleep, so I—"

He cut her off by driving deep inside her on a hard upward thrust, savoring, his eyes shut, the scream she let loose. *Heaven. I never want to leave here. Now. This morning with her.* "Now you know, huh? Now you know I can't stop thinking about you even when I'm asleep."

She gasped as he rolled his hips. "I think about you, too."

"Not like I think about you. Impossible." He gripped her ass, molding it with his hands, remembering the promise he'd made her the night of the bachelor party. *The first time you ride me, I'm going to grip your ass just like this. I'm going to move you where I want you. How fast. How slow. It'll all be up to me and this grip.* He remembered his promise word for word because he'd been fantasizing about it ever since his subconscious had created the image. Now, he fell back onto the bed and pumped his hips into her twice. "You'll be thinking about me a lot more after this, won't you? *Move.*"

Eyes lit up with challenge, she braced her hands on his shoulders. She lifted, lifted until he was only partially buried inside her, then she came down on him *hard*.

"*Fuck*," he grated. With her thighs spread wide on either side of him, she worked him up and down, breathy whimpers filling the air between them. The look on her face summed up how he felt. In disbelief that something could feel this good and right. His need for more took over then. He'd woken up to this and hadn't had time to anticipate the avalanche of lust she always shot him full of. Slow and sweet wouldn't be happening this morning. Maybe never where he and Roxy were concerned.

He urged her to move faster, up and back. She liked that, he could tell by the way her breath caught, the way her eyes squeezed shut. It rubbed her against him, stroked that spot he'd used to set her off earlier with his fingers. But he knew her, he knew she liked hard and fast. Same as him. He tightened his hold on her ass and let her bounce a few times, while thrusting up to meet her.

She sobbed loudly. "Yes. *More,* Louis. Faster."

God, he loved those words coming from her mouth. He'd never get tired of them. "How fast, baby?" He kept her elevated above his hips and drove up into her hard and quick, over and over, the sound of smacking flesh making him even harder. "How's that feel? You want it faster?"

It was too late, though. She clenched up around him, her thighs shaking and flexing as she cried out. "Oh God, oh God, oh *God.*"

Unable to give her even a second to recover, he flipped her onto her back. His blood raced through his veins; a roaring took up residence in his ears. *Need her. I fucking need her.* He locked their hands together and pinned them over her head, burying himself deeper inside her on a growl. "Just you and me from now on, Rox. No one else. Ever. Just each other, okay?"

She looked up at him through cloudy eyes, or maybe his own were cloudy. He was too far gone to tell. Only knew she was every-thing, this moment was everything, and he couldn't be without her. No fucking way. She locked her ankles at the small of his back and nodded. "You and me, Louis."

He buried his face against her neck and gave himself over to relief, chanting her name as he went off inside her. With her arms wrapped around his back, thighs squeezing his waist, he'd never

felt so powerful, while at the same time feeling completely helpless. Without her, he'd never have felt this. He *required* her. Another person. He'd never expected to feel that way in his life.

They lay that way, bodies fused together, for what felt like
hours, but it still went too quickly. Sunlight slowly filled the room
as he focused on her breathing, perfectly content to let her trail
her fingers up and down his back for the rest of his life if she
would agree to it. He finally threw a resentful glance at his bedside clock, sickened when he realized he only had half an hour to
shower and get to work. Roxy must have interpreted his sigh correctly, because she slapped his ass and rolled out from under him.

"Get moving, McNally. Someone has to save the world, and it's
not going to be me."

You save my *world.* "I think I'm coming down with a cold." He
gave a fake cough and shivered. "I'd hate to get everyone in the
office sick."

"I take back what I said about your acting skills."

She smiled at him over her shoulder, and it pummeled him in
the gut. Sunlight lit her eyes up so they were almost translucent . . .
made the skin of her bare back glow. He wondered if she had
any idea how beautiful she was. Especially this morning, when
the barrier he'd always sensed in her seemed to have fallen. She
seemed lighter, more open. It made his chest ache. "What are you
doing today?"

Was it his imagination, or did her spine stiffen? "I've got some
practicing to do before my rehearsal tonight. I need to know the
lines backwards and forwards." His lawyer's sense was dinging,
telling him he was missing something. He didn't have the chance

to ask before she continued. "I can come over and watch *Arrested Development* with you later, though."

Louis started to respond with *hell yes* before remembering Lena was cooking tonight. "Shit. I can't tonight. I have a family dinner thing." This is where he would invite his girlfriend to join. That realization blinked on in his head like a lightbulb, although he had no idea why, since he'd never dated anyone exclusively. At least not since middle school. His instincts were telling him this is what boyfriends did when they were serious about a girl. They introduced said girl to their family. Even now, he could kind of sense a question in Roxy's silence. This would be his chance to make her feel secure, to prove he wanted the real thing.

But he couldn't. Not yet.

He flat-out *refused* to bring her around Fletcher after what he'd said. If that prick looked at her the wrong way, Louis would lose his ever-loving mind. Worse, it would make Roxy uncomfortable, seeing Fletcher again, remembering she'd almost given him a lap dance. He didn't want to blow his first time bringing her home, and this would only end badly. Lena would know something was up the second Fletcher and Roxy stood in the same room. His sister might have a screw loose, but she sniffed out drama like a bloodhound. No, the first time he introduced Roxy to his family, he didn't want to leave any room for failure. He wouldn't fail when it came to her.

"I, uh . . ." He swiped a hand through his hair, knowing he'd let the silence go on too long. How had she gotten dressed so quickly? How long had he just been sitting there? "Maybe you can come next time?"

Her smile looked like it might crack. Dammit, he'd fucked up. He'd already fucked up. "We'll see. Family dinners aren't really my thing. I'm going to go . . . there's a crosstown bus leaving in . . ."

She didn't even bother to finish her sentence before she sailed from the room. Louis sat there stunned for a moment before taking off after her. "*Rox.*"

"What?"

She paused with her hand on the doorknob. This was it. He needed to tell her the truth, but he dreaded the outcome too much. On their first date, she'd been horrified when he'd told her Fletcher was engaged to his sister. She'd thought seeing Louis past that night was pointless, when his future family member knew her as a stripper. If he told her he didn't want her around Fletcher, he'd only be justifying her worry. No way would he tell her what Fletcher had said, either. He wouldn't upset her with that garbage. He had to take care of this situation before he brought her around his family. And he would. It *would* happen.

"What is it, Louis?"

A knot formed in his throat. "I'll call you."

The door clicked shut on his final word.

Chapter 20

*R*oxy took the final sip of her coffee and tossed it into the trash can. Five minutes until she was scheduled to meet Johan for rehearsal, and she didn't want to be a second early. She hated this. Hated the jittery feeling, the pit in her stomach. This was wrong. She shouldn't feel this way. It would end tonight, one way or the other. That was what she continued to tell herself, over and over. It was the only thing that had convinced her to put on her high heels and leave the apartment.

She leaned back against the outside of the coffee shop and watched traffic zoom past. Her body felt tired, weighed down. Anxiety was making her muscles sore. There was a buzzing in her head that wouldn't go away. Yesterday, she'd gone into the rehearsal confident. She'd known what the fucker was about and she'd still walked in with her shoulders back, her chin up. Today, she didn't feel that way. It made her beyond pissed off, because she knew what it stemmed from.

Stupid. She'd been so fucking *stupid*. For one night she'd let her guard down, and now she'd pay for it. Louis's behavior had been almost comical this morning. She hadn't been expecting an invitation to dinner. But a tiny part of her had hoped. He'd still wanted her to stay over that night his sisters had shown up, right? Meeting the rest of his family wasn't that far-fetched. Even if it scared her. Even if she'd never had the experience of meeting a guy's parents before, she'd be okay meeting Louis's family, as long as he was with her.

The way he'd clammed up, stammering his way through some way to avoid seeing her or bringing her around his family . . . it told her everything she needed to know. Either he'd gotten what he wanted and didn't want to bother with her anymore, or— maybe even worse—he was ashamed to bring a struggling actress who slept on a futon around his wealthy family. Either way hurt. She didn't need this hurt right now. It dog-piled on top of her Johan-induced nerves and flattened her to the floor. Normally she would get right back up, but today she felt like curling up and staying there.

Dammit. She'd liked him. So much. It felt like she'd left a part of herself behind with him.

Her lack of determination scared her, because she'd never been without it. She didn't want to walk into this inevitable confrontation with Johan with anything less than one hundred percent confidence. She needed it in order to turn down the role of a lifetime, because it wasn't going to be easy. If last night and this morning had proven anything, it was that sex was just that. Sex. Maybe it hadn't felt that way with Louis. Maybe it had been incredible . . . ruining her for a good long while. At the end of the day, though, it had been a means to an end. Louis had wanted her, so he'd done what he'd needed to do to *get* her. The chase was over now, though. Just like every other guy she'd been with, her giving in had been his curtain call.

This mindset was a dangerous thing when one was presented with a major choice. Was turning down the role worth avoiding one unpleasant encounter? If all it meant was another meaningless night? Her self-respect was on the line here, but so was her career. She could walk out of rehearsal with her pride intact, but she'd find her ass back in New Jersey working retail fast enough to make her head spin. Where was the pride in that?

God, there might have been a tiny part of her that wanted to give in to Johan, just to prove a stupid point to herself. That she didn't need Louis or his perfect touch or sweet words. He hadn't meant those words. They'd been said in the heat of the moment, but they didn't hold water now.

No, she wouldn't let this be about making a point. She wouldn't give Louis any more power over her mind than he already had. If she found it impossible to abandon the role of Missy, a role she'd become seriously attached to, she would look at it as a business transaction. Nothing else.

You can't really be considering this. Johan makes your skin crawl. Maybe she wasn't considering it. Perhaps it was simply the pain talking. Pain that had been driven home with a clichéd *I'll call you* as she'd walked out Louis's door this morning. She'd blocked his phone number before the elevator had reached the lobby. Not once would she check her phone, hoping to see his number. Not going to happen.

Roxy looked at her cell phone screen. One minute to go. She

crossed the street toward the studio's offices and went in the front entrance. The hallway was empty and silent as she made her way toward the back, where she and Johan had rehearsed the night before. He sat cross-legged on the floor reading a magazine, so deceptively laid-back she almost laughed. She could easily excuse herself for having the wrong impression of him. The image he projected to the media screamed fun-loving genius, when in reality he was a man who got what he wanted the wrong way. He was nothing more than a spoiled, overgrown dickhead.

She rapped on the open door once to alert him to her presence. His predatory smile when he looked up made her feel nauseous, but she breathed through it. Even though her purse felt like a safety net, she took it off her shoulder and set it on the table. "Hey."

"Hey, hey. Come on in." He came to his feet. "You look gorgeous."

"Thank you." She'd worn pants and a long-sleeved, button-down shirt to send him a message. Apparently it had been intercepted at the door by his ego. "I've been running through the lines all day. I'm feeling a lot more comfortable with the driving scene."

He nodded, looking distracted. "Let's start with the scene where you got tripped up yesterday. The, uh . . ." His smile widened. "Bar scene where Missy and Luke dance together."

Zero points for subtlety. "That's not the scene where I got tripped up."

"No?" He snatched his beaten-up script off the table and flipped through a couple pages. "Well, let's start there anyway. It's an important scene, and you need to get the timing down."

"There's not a lot of dialogue in that scene." *Back off. Please, back off.* "I don't think I'll have any problem with it. I'd rather work on something else."

He scratched the back of his head, the face she'd once thought handsome transforming with amusement. "Last time I checked, I wrote the screenplay." His gaze pegged her. "And I'm casting the film."

There it was. A thinly veiled ultimatum. Her heart jumped into her throat when he moved closer. She wanted to turn and run out the door, but she felt rooted to the spot. Goose bumps broke out along her skin, cold ones that made her want to wrap her arms around herself for heat. When she thought he would stop in front of her, he circled around behind her instead.

"I like you, Roxy. I think you're perfect for this role." He brushed her hair behind her shoulder. A move that reminded her of Louis so much that she wanted to cry. This wasn't Louis. He wasn't anything like Louis . . . or the Louis she'd thought she knew. "I want you to be comfortable with me. This role is so important to the film. *We* need to connect before we can bring Missy to life. *Together.*"

Oh, God. Gross. She would have turned around and laughed in his face if she hadn't wanted to bawl like a baby. He must have done this before to have lines like that one locked and loaded. How many actresses had he done this to? She didn't want to be another victim who had to keep the secret or risk being shamed. She *loathed* the idea of it. "Johan, Missy is important to me. I'll bring her to life. I will."

He circled back around to stand in front of her, giving her a considering look. "Then let's start with the dancing scene, shall we?"

Knowing it was mistake, she nodded once. Johan tossed his script back onto the table, looking like a toddler who'd just been handed a shiny new toy. He didn't waste any time stepping into her personal space and settling a hand on her right hip. Her posture stayed rigid as he tugged her close. She squeezed her eyes shut against the unwanted sensation of his breath against her ear. They started to sway, but she couldn't relax, couldn't force her muscles to loosen.

Don't do this. Wrong. So wrong. Get the hell out of here.

And do what, Roxy? Go back to singing telegrams? Stripping? Go home and admit failure to your parents? They would love it. They would grin and tell you life's a bitch, *then go back to drinking Budweiser on their shitty couch.*

Grief slammed her. Self-pity that she'd never let herself feel before swarmed down on her, making up for lost time. What did any of this matter? Who cared about her pride besides herself? No one. No one gave it a thought. No one cared. Why should she?

Louis's smiling face appeared in her head, and she couldn't stop the tears from tracking down her cheeks.

Johan's hand slipped further down her back.

LOUIS KNOCKED A little too loudly on Lena's apartment door. He really wanted to put his fist through something, anything. Needed an outlet for this anxious frustration he'd been living with since this morning. Roxy had blocked his number. Unbelievable. He'd had no idea what he would have said if she'd answered, but he could at least have done better than *I'll call you.* What the fuck kind of idiot was he, anyway? I'll call you? She was right to walk out without looking back. It made him nauseous thinking of how many times he'd said that to a girl and not meant it. How dare he say it to Roxy? Jesus, he deserved every minute of this suffering. As soon as he straightened out this headache with his sister, he was going to find Roxy and beg until his face turned blue.

He'd replayed the scene this morning a dozen times, trying to see it from her perspective. Yeah, she definitely thought he'd been giving her the brush-off. He'd done nothing to convince her otherwise. As fragile as her trust in him was, he'd snapped it like a twig.

Goddammit, he missed her already. It baffled him that she could second-guess him when he felt like this about her. Wasn't it visible? He didn't think he was capable of hiding something this big, something that felt like it was continually pouring from his chest.

A lock turned in the door, and Lena suddenly stood in front of him. She held a spatula in one hand and a fire extinguisher in the other. "What up, bro ham? I hope you brought your appetite. Or an extra fire extinguisher."

He skirted past her into the apartment. "What did you set on fire?"

"Ketchup."

Louis decided not to ask. "Listen, I came early so we could talk. Is anyone else here?"

"Nope." She picked a glass of wine off the counter and took a healthy sip. Great, she was drinking. *This* was going to go well. "Just me. Celeste will be here in ten, though, so spit it out."

"Thanks," he returned dryly, going to the fridge for a much-needed beer. Possibly his last beer, ever, if this conversation took a turn for the worse. He downed half the bottle and set it down on the counter. "Remember the other night, when I told you there were no strippers at Fletcher's bachelor party?"

Lena reached over and picked up a butcher knife from the kitchen counter. "Yeah."

"It wasn't a lie." He thought of Roxy. Thought of the way she'd absorbed all the sunshine in his room. Where was she now? What was she doing? "The girl who showed up to take her clothes off wasn't a stripper. She's my girlfriend." He watched the knife closely. "She needed the money because she was going through a rough patch, but the only person in that room she's ever taken her clothes off for is me. And it's going to stay that way."

His sister watched him through narrowed eyes. "But Fletcher knew she was coming?"

"Yeah." He sighed into his beer. "For what it's worth, Lena, that kind of thing happens at a lot of bachelor parties. This was pretty tame compared to some of the ones I've been to."

"He promised." She buried the tip of the knife into a wooden cutting board, twisted it. "Is that the kind of girl you should be dating?"

His jaw flexed. "If you mean a beautiful, intelligent girl that makes me insanely happy every time I'm with her, then yes. That kind of girl. She's stubborn and driven and brave. She's every-thing. And she's mine. So you need to get okay with that. With her. I don't care what she did."

Lena stuck out her bottom lip. "You don't have to be nasty about it."

Louis swallowed his knee-jerk apology. He wouldn't apologize when he'd meant every word. "I'm just telling it like it is. If I have my way, she'll be around more often. I want her to feel comfort-able."

"If she's so important to you, where is she tonight?" Lena let the knife clatter onto the counter and crossed her arms. "I made enough paella to feed Manhattan."

He hid his smile. That had been his sister's way of saying, *if she's important to you, she's important to us.* "She's at a rehearsal," he hedged. "Not that I even invited her. Because I'm a moron."

Lena neither agreed nor disagreed with his self-assessment. "Hmm. You can bring her some on your way home. A man shows up with Tupperware, he gets a pass." She picked up the knife again and brought it down hard on an unsuspecting shrimp. "Ex-cept for lying. That's inexcusable."

"Right." He drained the rest of his beer. "There's another rea-son I came early."

Obviously picking up on the serious note in his voice, she looked up at him warily. "Shoot."

Louis blew out a breath. "You're my sister and I love you. Hon-estly, you're also more than a little crazy upstairs, but I think you already knew that."

She bobbed her head once. "Continue."

"As crazy as you are, Lena . . ." He laid a comforting hand on her arm. "You're not crazy enough to marry Fletcher. Strippers and lying aside, he's not good enough for you. Not even close."

"I know. Celeste has been saying the same thing, but I didn't want to listen." Tears filled her eyes. "There's not a lot of guys who'll put up with my shit."

"You're going to do a hell of a lot better than him." He opened his arms just in time to catch her when she propelled herself across the kitchen. Just managing to hold his ground, he hugged her close. "In the meantime, we'll have popcorn parties at my place. Okay?"

" 'Kay."

She stepped back, wiping her eyes, cheeks red with embarrassment. "So, uh . . . what is Roxy rehearsing for? Anything I know?"

He leaned against the counter, grateful she'd changed the subject but depressed by the reminder of his deception in getting Roxy the audition. "Probably. It's Johan's new movie."

"Johan Strassberg? The squirrelly dude who used to follow us around with a camera?" She snorted. "His parents threw those obnoxious lawn parties in the Hamptons. Everyone had to wear white. Remember?"

"Oh, yeah."

Lena shivered. "That guy always skeeved me. I don't know why." She popped a single finger into the air. "Oh, I remember. Celeste and I caught him filming us in the outdoor shower once at a pool party. He wasn't even ashamed to get caught. Big shit-eating grin on him."

Unease weighed heavily in his stomach. "Why didn't you tell me?"

"We did. Kind of." She winced. "Remember when we drove to his house and slashed his tires? It wasn't because he came in first in the summer camp talent show. Even we aren't that vindictive. It was for filming us showering and letting everyone watch it on a projector screen."

"That was Johan's car?" His words sounded far away. That night had been so long ago that he barely remembered it, half-asleep as he'd been in the backseat. Obviously his memory of it had been pieced together, like parts of a dream.

Lena seemed to misinterpret his silence. "Don't make a big deal out of it. Everyone sees me naked sooner or later." She smirked to let him know she was joking. "Either way, he always creeped me out. There was a rumor going around that same summer that his father paid quite a bit of cash to get him clear of some charges. Never found out the reason." A timer went off on the stove, and she reached over to turn it off. "I always thought it had to do with a girl. Just a feeling."

Louis straightened away from the counter, feeling slightly dizzy. It seemed as if a golf ball had lodged itself inside his throat, which didn't help when his breaths had started coming faster. The apartment tilted around him when he thought of Roxy's reluctance to discuss the rehearsals with Johan. Her stiffness every time he'd brought it up. The lost expression on her face the day in the courthouse . . . immediately following the audition. An audition he'd arranged for her. A shout worked its way up his chest, but he managed to strangle it at the last second.

Lena watched him with concern that slowly turned into recognition. "Go."

Chapter 21

I don't want to do this. I don't want to do this.

Had anyone who'd ended up on the casting couch ever really wanted to do this, though? What made her any different from them? The day she'd dropped out of school and come home to collect her things, her mother had told her. Told her she was just another girl with dreams too big for her capabilities. Had she been right? Maybe this was all she had. Maybe she'd been headed straight here ever since that day, and all the auditions had been a complete waste of time.

Johan's hand grazed her backside, settling there more firmly when the words that would reject his touch stuck in her throat. Her stomach pitched violently. It would be over in twenty minutes, tops. Right? Then she could go home and scrub him away in the shower, bury herself under the covers until the sun came up. She'd been with losers before. She could just close her eyes and pretend it wasn't happening. No one would know.

I'd know. I'm better than this.

The little voice she'd been ignoring broke through the fog bank of self-pity. She'd come to New York to survive on her own. If she slept with Johan and retained the part, it wouldn't be as a result of honest work or a reflection of her talent. It would be a cheap win. He'd be handing her the role in exchange for her dignity. Nothing was worth that.

And *dammit*, she couldn't let another man touch her when she could still feel Louis's hands on her skin, his breath in her ear. It might make her pathetic, but she wanted—*needed*—to savor those memories, hold them to her, as long as she could.

"You can take your hand off my ass now."

He laughed near the top of her head, his hot breath on her forehead making her cringe. But he didn't remove his hand. Instead, he yanked her closer. She could feel his arousal against her belly, and it made her panic. "No time for this whole playing-hard-to-get act, Roxy, I have another meeting after this."

She pushed against his chest. "Let go."

Finally his touch left her backside, but only so he could grip her forearm. She flinched as his fingers dug into her bicep. "What, you like it rough? No problem."

When he leaned in to kiss her, Roxy's balled-up fist connected with his nose, creating an extremely satisfying crunching noise. He stumbled back with a high-pitched yelp, blood already beginning to pour from his nostrils.

"Ah! What the fuck?"

She shook her hand out, wincing at the resulting pain. She'd swung Jersey-style, which meant *hard*. *God*, it had felt good. Not just to take out her frustration and anger on the person who'd caused it; she'd also gotten herself back in that moment. She might have had some weak thoughts, some temporary confusion, but when it had come down to it, she'd been better than this. Better than him.

Part of her wanted to stand there and watch him stumble around in pain a while longer, but she needed to get the hell out of there. He hadn't backed off when she'd asked him to, and that scared her. She'd thought he was just another sleazebag using his status to get her onto the casting couch, but she'd been wrong. He was potentially much worse than that. She wasn't going to stick around and find out.

First, though, a parting shot was in order. "Hey, asshole." She waited until he looked at her through squinted eyes. "There isn't a role on this planet worth your disgusting hands on me. You can take it with you straight to hell. Have fun continuing to rip off Wes Anderson, you second-rate piece of garbage."

She only caught a glimpse of Johan bristling over the insult as she exited the room and strode down the hallway. When she heard his footsteps pounding after her, she started to jog, heart beating out of control in her chest. A few more feet and she'd be outside on the busy sidewalk.

Before she could reach the door, he grabbed her arm. "If you tell anyone about this, you'll be laughed at. Just another actress making shit up to get on camera the easy way."

"Let go of me," she demanded, twisting free. He grabbed for her again and managed to snag her shirt, ripping several buttons free and tearing the material. Even he looked a little stunned over what he'd done, and she used his distracted state to yank the door open, stumbling out onto the sidewalk.

Right into Louis.

The events of that morning flew right out of her head, and relief swamped her. He looked so perfectly familiar and solid, standing there in his work clothes. She didn't think twice about throwing her arms around his neck and holding tight, inhaling his scent greedily. His body felt rigid, though. So unlike him. He took hold of her wrists and tugged her away, his gaze tracking down her body with what appeared to be leashed rage. Slowly, he extended his hand and traced the edge of her ripped shirt before his attention locked on Johan, still standing behind her in the doorway.

"I'm going to kill you," Louis growled, his body vibrating against her.

Johan's voice sounded muffled, as if he was still holding his bleeding nose, but his voice was mocking. "Whatever, man. Rehearsal's over. Just take her and go."

Louis moved like lightning to get past her, landing a punch in Johan's face before she'd even fully turned around. Johan stumbled back into the office through the doorway, and Louis followed, hands clenched at his sides. "What did you do to her?"

Johan stomped a foot. "Dammit. My nose is definitely fucking broken."

"Answer me."

"*Nothing.* She hits harder than *you* do. Calm down."

"Calm. *Down?*" Louis twisted the front of Johan's shirt in his fist. "I'm going to break more than your nose if you touched her."

Johan actually looked bored by the line of questioning. This definitely wasn't the first time he'd been on the receiving end of a right hook. Disgust snapped Roxy out of her stupor. She put her hands on Louis's shoulder and tried to stop him from entering the building, but he wouldn't come. Behind her on the sidewalk, people were stopping to check out the commotion. She had to get Louis out of there before someone alerted a cop. "Louis, let it go. He's not worth it. Nothing happened."

He turned, looking at her as if he wasn't really seeing her, eyes bright with temper. "How did your shirt get ripped, then?"

She didn't want to lie to him, only wanted to get as far away from Johan as possible, but that hesitation gave Louis what he needed. He balled his fist and gave Johan another two shots to the face.

In a burst of energy, Johan managed to get free, falling back a step when Louis lost his grip. "You called *me*, Louis. I could have hired any actress in this fucking town. This was a *favor*."

Louis stiffened. His hands fell to his sides as if a string had been cut. Roxy's mind raced, trying to decode what Johan had said. A favor? How . . . how did Johan even know Louis's name? The answer hit her with the force of a battering ram. *Oh, Jesus, no.*

"What did you do?" she whispered.

Louis didn't turn around. "I can't have this discussion with you right now, Roxy. I'm too fucking mad."

"We're having it anyway." She stepped to the side so she could see Johan. "Did he call you? Did he . . . ask for a favor to get me this part?"

Johan gave an exaggerated smirk. "No good deed goes unpunished, I guess."

A sob rushed past her lips. "Dammit. *Dammit*, Louis." Misery rolled through her in a wave as the last couple of weeks played through her head in slow motion. A casting assistant calling her on a Saturday night, giving her the opportunity she'd always dreamed of. An opportunity she'd thought she'd earned but *hadn't*. How naïve could she be? This whole time she'd been secretly proud of herself, assuming she'd done something right somewhere down the line, impressed the right people. Gotten noticed on her own merit. When in reality, it had been handed to her by the guy who'd wanted to sleep with her. It enraged her. It made her heart squeeze so tight that she thought it might rupture in her chest. No. She couldn't handle any more. Since this morning, she'd been pulled through an emotional wringer, and it was her fault. She'd left herself wide open for it. The pride she'd carried out of Johan's office after her audition was now littered across the sidewalk like yesterday's trash.

Louis turned around slowly, wincing at whatever he saw on her face. "I only got you the audition," he said, pulling her further down the sidewalk, out of Johan's earshot. "You earned the part. It was just a matter of getting you in the door."

"Bullshit. I don't believe you." She smacked her forehead when she remembered being only one of three actresses auditioning that day. It had seemed so odd, but she'd ignored it. "You must have been laughing at me when I got that phone call. You must have thought I was so *stupid*."

"You could never look stupid to me. Never."

"I thought you understood . . ." She swallowed hard. "I told you how important it was to do this on my own, and I thought you understood that. Me. You took that goal away from me."

He swiped his hair back impatiently, knuckles dotted with

blood. "Yeah? Well, that's not how the world works. People hire their friends, they make phone calls and repay favors. It's ugly, but it's true. I know you wanted to do this on your own, but your way wasn't working."

She flinched as his words stabbed her in the belly.

"God, I'm sorry. That came out wrong." He made a frustrated noise. "I can't talk about this now. Not when all I can see is you standing there with a ripped shirt, looking like you've been crying."

No. She wouldn't let him get to her. Wouldn't feel sorry for him. "You can't just make decisions without consulting the people involved."

"You would have turned down the help. I had no choice."

"Why didn't you have a choice?" The answer dawned, making her queasy. "You needed to date someone worthy, is that it? If you were going to date an actress, she better be a successful one. *Right?* Not one who needed to strip to make rent."

"No." He pinched the bridge of his nose. "I just wanted you happy."

Knowing it wasn't fair at all but wanting to take a strip of flesh with her, she gestured to Johan where he sat bleeding on the ground. "Well, you failed. I guess he didn't mention sleeping with him was part of the deal. Nice job."

Louis's body deflated right before her eyes. She hated herself in that moment. Hated *him* for making her feel so goddamn lousy and important at the same time. *I've got to get out of here.*

"Good-bye, Louis."

She made it to the street corner before the tears fell.

Chapter 22

Roxy opened one eye, saw Honey and Abby perched on the edge of her bed, and promptly closed the eye. Maybe if she stayed completely still, they would think she'd fallen back asleep and they'd go back to watching *Bridesmaids* or baking shit. Or whatever the living did outside of their bedrooms, out in the open. Anything but force her to acknowledge that she'd been in bed for two full days, still wearing a ripped shirt.

She wanted to take it off, but she'd forced herself to keep it on. It was silly, and yeah, kind of unhygienic. But *she* felt ripped in half, and having a visible representation of that allowed her to wallow with impunity, didn't it? She had no intention of un-wallowing anytime soon, so she wanted her two pain-in-the-ass roommates to bail, pronto. Even if she knew the moment she closed her eyes, she'd have to deal with memories of Louis. It was better than *not* dealing with his memory, though, as she'd be doing for the rest of her life. She'd lost him. Or he'd lost her. Who the fuck cared? They weren't *together*, but as long as she stayed in this bed, at least she'd have the heartache he'd given her. Right now, it felt like she didn't have anything else.

Someone, probably Honey, nudged her elbow.

"What," Roxy said through clenched teeth, "do you want?"

"Another delivery of falafel came for you," Abby said.

"We ate it," Honey added. "You ignored the last two, and where I come from, we don't let food go to waste. It was amazing. Thinking of coming up with my own recipe."

Roxy's chest hurt from hearing Louis had sent another round of falafel. Why wouldn't he *stop*? Too much had happened, too many of the wrong words exchanged. He'd stolen her independence. It might make her stubborn, but even if she weren't pissed at him, she didn't think she could ever look him in the eye again. He'd seen her at too many low points. The *lowest* points of her life. Every time she looked at him, that's what she'd see. She'd wonder if he was imagining her stripping or singing in a costume or running from a man she'd *known* was bad news from the beginning but had ignored the warning signs.

"Next time, don't answer the door. Please. I don't want him to think I'm accepting it."

Honey crossed her arms. "You going to tell us what happened? I need some incentive if I'm going to turn down free food."

"I have an idea." Abby clasped her hands together and split an anxious look between them. "We'll tell you our worst breakup stories first. Maybe that will make it easier."

"It won't."

"I'll go first," Honey said, neatly ignoring Roxy's protest. "Elmer Boggs was my high school sweetheart. Just a big old lug, linebacker for the football team. Sweet as pie and slow as molasses." She tilted her head and smiled. "If he had his way, I would have been barefoot and pregnant before the ink dried on our high school diplomas, but I shared no such notions."

"What about college?" Abby whispered, as if she couldn't imagine a world where everyone didn't earn a degree. "Didn't he want to go?"

"Well, that's where we differed. Elmer was more than happy to take a job selling cars at his father's dealership. I wanted something more." Honey paused for a moment. "I broke up with him the day I was accepted at Columbia. Let's just say he didn't take it well. Showed up outside my house, drunk as a skunk at two in the morning. He held a giant boombox over his head, just like in that movie *Say Anything*. But instead of Peter Gabriel, he was blasting 'The Devil Went Down the Georgia.'"

Roxy quirked an eyebrow. "Was that your couple's song or something?"

"No." Honey shook her head. "I think he just liked it."

"Huh."

After a minute, Abby broke the thoughtful silence. "When I was seventeen, I dated Vince Vaughn for one whole week."

"Wait." Roxy massaged her forehead. She so wasn't equipped for this conversation right now. "Vince Vaughn the actor?"

"No, no. Different Vince Vaughn." Abby smoothed her hair, suddenly looking self-conscious. "It was Halloween night, and we'd planned on dressing as M&M's. I was going to be green, and he—aptly—chose yellow. But when I got there, he wasn't in his

M&M costume, he was dressed as Popeye and his *new* girlfriend came as skanky Olive Oyl."

"Ouch."

Abby acknowledged Honey's comment with a severe nod. "I stormed out of the party dressed like a giant piece of candy." She blew out a breath. "Half a block away, my high heel broke, and I fell facedown on a neighbor's lawn. Of course, I couldn't get up because the costume was so damn *awkward*. I had to scream for the owners of the house to come out and help me up."

Roxy and Honey stared at her a moment in stunned silence before bursting into laughter. There was no way to avoid it, the image of her struggling to stand was too funny. Abby's cheeks colored, but she took it in stride, even chuckling along with them. At first, it felt great to laugh. To have any emotion at all besides regret and sadness. But it busted open the dam Roxy had constructed inside her, letting everything else out, too. Her laughter subsided, to be replaced with tears. Hot, noisy tears, the likes of which she hadn't cried since she was a child.

"Dammit." Roxy pressed the heels of her hands over her eyes. "I shouldn't have let things with him go on so long. If I'd ended it when I should have, this wouldn't hurt so bad."

"Why did it have to end at all?" Abby asked softly.

She told them. The whole sordid story about Johan, straight through to Louis's involvement in getting her the part, his reluctance to introduce her to his family. Honey and Abby listened without saying a word, which was exactly what she needed to get the words out. "He needed to feel better about me. Or himself. I'm not sure." She swiped at her damp eyes. "I just know he wasn't happy with who I am, and he tried to change it. If he tried to change me after a couple weeks, he'd do it again. And again. I won't lose myself. I'm all I've got."

Honey exchanged a look with Abby. "What are we, yesterday's trash?"

Roxy gave a watery laugh, even though the simple effort of it hurt. "I guess I'm stuck with your asses now, too."

ROXY FLOPPED DOWN onto the stoop and kicked off her high heels. Her old, worn-in high heels. The ones Louis had given her were stuffed in the back of her closet underneath winter clothes, where she couldn't see them. She would just sit here for a while and watch Ninth Avenue sprint by in a flash of colors and white noise. Just until she pulled herself together enough to face her roommates, who'd been freakishly nice to her for the past week. At first, she'd put on a brave face and let them fuss over her. She'd let them make her plates of leftovers, and she'd indulged them in watching a slew of Molly Ringwald movies. But as the week had worn on, she'd started hiding from them more and more, wishing they would just go away and let her cope.

She wasn't coping, though. After the two days she'd spent in bed, she'd somehow pulled herself together enough to leave the apartment, needing to disappear into her familiar routine. She'd been going on auditions nonstop, grinding her sleep-deprived self into the ground. All because she missed the gorgeous fucker like crazy. Even though she hadn't heard a word from him since that day, apart from the deliveries that had finally started to ebb, he hadn't left her alone for a second. She woke up to his laugh and fell asleep to his heartbeat. How in the hell was that possible, when they'd only spent one night together? Had she contracted some kind of illness as she'd slept in his bed, which was ruining her for life?

Johan had called and apologized, although since the call had been made with his publicist on the line feeding him the sullen apology, it hadn't technically counted. She'd filed a complaint with the studio in an effort to make sure girls weren't put in that position anymore, and they'd promised to take the complaint seriously. Knowing it was bullshit, she'd taken it one step further by filing a complaint with the police, only to be referred to an officer who'd recorded an existing complaint, filed by Louis. The cop explained he knew Louis from the courthouse. He'd anticipated her concern about media attention and assured her there would be none, thanks to a favor called in by Louis. She couldn't even summon the energy to be angry at Louis for calling the police without consulting her. Instead, it only reminded her how outraged he'd been on her behalf outside Johan's office. How his arms had felt like the safest place in the universe.

God, not one minute passed where she didn't wonder about him. Thinking of his tortured face when he'd arrived on the scene with Johan. Hearing his words playing on repeat until she had to do a mental scream to drown them out. She wanted him to be wrong. He *had* been wrong to go behind her back and omit the truth. But his actions had been done in consideration of her, and that was where she got tripped up. Her anger over what he'd done was tempered with an annoying sprinkle of gratefulness. He cared. He'd done it because he cared. And now he was gone.

Roxy pressed her fingers to her forehead and massaged the sudden ache. So tired. She was just so damn tired. It hurt to be back at square one, just another face in a sea of actresses. Yes, her optimism over the part in Johan's movie had been cautious, but she'd let herself hope just a little too much. Part of her wanted to give up, but then she'd have time to think. About Louis. About how long she'd been pounding the pavement with no success. She just had to push through. This empty feeling would eventually pass. Right?

Irritated with her defeated attitude, Roxy snatched up her high heels and rose to enter the building.

"Hey, you."

A rough Queens accent halted her in her tracks. She turned on the top step to find two young guys looking up at her. They were both good-looking in vastly different ways. One was tall and muscular, head shaved, jeans threadbare. The other, dark-haired one looked like he was hiding a whole lot behind his glasses and white dress shirt. No mistaking it, they were both pissed as hell.

"Are you Roxy?" Shaved Head called up to her.

Oh, she so wasn't in the mood for this. Whatever *this* was. "Who the fuck wants to know?"

"That's her, all right," Glasses said dryly.

She split a glare between them. "Mind telling me how you know my name and what this little ambush is about?"

"I'll tell you what it's about. We want our friend back." Shaved Head rolled his shoulders uncomfortably. "I just got used to him, all right? I liked having him around."

Glasses muttered something to Shaved Head that sounded like

Simmer down, but he was looking at her as if taking her measure. His gaze was so intelligent and discerning that she felt a little exposed being on the receiving end of it. "We just wanted to talk. It's not like Louis to be this messed up." He shifted on his feet. "He did what he did because he couldn't help it, Roxy."

Roxy's attention had snagged on the words *messed up.* Her heart twisted painfully. She didn't like hearing that. Not at all. Out of necessity, she put it aside and focused on what else Glasses had said. "Of course he could have helped it. He made a decision. No one forced him."

Shaved Head snorted, looking ultra-disappointed in her. Which really pissed her off, since they didn't even know her. Nor did she know them. They didn't have any right to come here and throw kerosene on her brittle emotions, then set them on fire. Her feet wouldn't move, though. She hadn't heard Louis's name spoken anywhere outside her head in a week, and hearing it now, hearing about *him,* was like a drug feeding into her veins. Calming her down. It didn't make any sense.

"Who are you two, anyway? His fan club?"

Glasses jerked a thumb toward Shaved Head. "This is Russell and I'm Ben. Nice to meet you." He ignored Roxy's frown and continued. "Look, you spent enough time with Louis to know that—"

"Too much time," Russell interjected. "Valuable bullshitting and beer drinking time."

Ben sighed. "Louis doesn't know how to leave things unfixed. He saw you were having a problem, he knew how to fix it. So he did."

"If you ask me, you're ungrateful." When her mouth dropped open, Russell shrugged belligerently. "I call it like I see it."

"Then you need glasses more than he does." They both laughed, but they sobered immediately, as if they'd been caught off guard and resented her sense of humor. "I didn't *want* Louis's help. Anyone's help. He knew that, and he ignored me."

"It's not a reason to punish him," Russell said seriously.

"I'm not punishing him," she burst out. "I haven't even seen him."

Ben pointed in the direction of downtown. "*We* have. And it's not pretty." He paused. "Look, whatever happened, he's blaming himself for more than just going behind your back. He sent you to that guy, and he's going through hell knowing what he subjected you to—"

"Please." She held up a hand, not wanting to hear any more. Her throat felt dry and scratchy with the need to cry, her skin paper-thin. "What do you want from me?"

Russell threw up his hands impatiently. "Go fix him. We want you to go *fix* him."

Footsteps pounded behind her in the building foyer. "Hey!" *Oh shit*. It was Abby, and she sounded livid. "You can't just come here and yell at her like this. You didn't even call ahead, like decent people. I should call Mark the super to handle this."

"Rodrigo, you mean."

"Dammit," Abby whispered for Roxy's ears alone. "Either way, he'll make you leave."

Ben looked unconcerned about being threatened.

Russell looked like the heavens had just opened up and spat out an angel. His lips moved, no sound escaping, but Roxy thought she read the words *Pretty, so pretty*.

She laid a hand on Abby's arm. "It's fine, mother hen. They were just leaving."

"Yeah, we'll leave." Ben noticed Russell's Abby-induced stupor and shoved his friend's shoulder hard. The dude barely budged. "Just think about going to see him, okay? The guilt is killing him. He hasn't left his apartment in a week."

Russell finally shook his way free of his trance. "Yeah. Then maybe we could all hang out sometime. Like . . . all five of us—"

Ben made an impatient noise and dragged his friend away from the stoop.

Roxy said nothing. She couldn't manage a single word. An entire week without leaving his apartment? It didn't seem possible, until she remembered her instinct had been to lay down in bed and stay there, too. If she'd been weighed down with the guilt she'd heaped on top of Louis, she would have done it. Absolutely. Might even still be there.

She closed her eyes and tried to find the anger. The resentment she'd felt when her independence had been taken away. When she'd found out he'd been lying to her, letting her believe she'd finally gotten her big break. She searched and searched for the anger. But she couldn't find it anymore.

LOUIS SWITCHED ON the lamp beside his couch so he could examine the Cheeto in the light. Unbelievable. The little orange snack looked exactly like Elvis. Forget the potato shaped like the Virgin

Mary. In his hand, he held *the* Elvis Cheeto. He would be famous as soon as the media got a hold of this.

He tossed it into his mouth, crunching it between his teeth. Without looking, he reached over and switched the lamp back off, bathing the apartment in darkness once more. He'd finally, clearly, gone around the bend. There had been a moment yesterday when he'd challenged himself to an arm wrestling contest that he thought signaled the change, but no. Seeing The King's face in a bag of Cheetos was definitely the beginning of the end.

Nine days. He'd been inside these walls for nine long days. Immediately following the scene with Roxy outside Johan's office, he'd put in a phone call to his boss, Doubleday. Even in the midst of the horrifying realization that he'd lost Roxy, he'd had a moment of clarity afterward. The words he'd said to her, sounding so like his father, had come back to him. *That's not how the world works. People hire their friends, they make phone calls and repay favors. It's ugly, but it's true.* If he'd started to believe that, to *rely* on that, he'd failed himself. So he'd quit.

At some point, he would need to get up. Shave his face, maybe put on a clean T-shirt. He would need to leave his apartment and walk to the store for food, like a normal human being. He'd need to start sending out resumes to firms that would let him continue his pro bono work, even if it meant starting at the bottom of the ladder. But first he needed to *get up*. Otherwise, the coroner would find him with a stomach full of stale Cheetos and flat ginger ale. Not exactly what he would have chosen as his last meal. What would he have chosen as his last meal?

Falafel. Definitely falafel.

He pitched sideways on the couch, his face landing in a throw pillow. How long had he been sitting here? He had a brief recollection of Ben and Russell coming in and trying to drag him to the Longshoreman for a beer. Had he really socked Russell in the face? His sore knuckles told him the answer was yes. It had been satisfying at the time, but like everything else—finding the Elvis Cheeto or beating himself in an arm wrestling contest—the shiny satisfaction dimmed almost immediately, replacing itself with absolute fucking misery.

Every time he closed his eyes, he thought of Roxy. Sometimes a good memory would come to mind. How her face had lit up when she'd seen the elephants. Their first kiss, right over by his front door, before he'd even known her name. Most of the time, though, he thought of her tear-stained face outside Johan's office. How she'd leapt into his arms, her body shaking like a leaf. When he thought of that horrifying moment, he set himself back another hour, until his misery-sabbatical had stretched to a week.

This was what happened when you lied. People got hurt. People you cared about so damn much that it hurt to be away from them. But he didn't have a choice. Why would she ever want to see him again? He'd been responsible for every shitty thing that had happened to her in the last few weeks. Why had she been dressed as a giant pink rabbit? His one-night stand. Why had she been booked as a stripper? His one-night stand's wrath. Why had she been propositioned in exchange for a role? Him and his ill-advised attempt to help. He'd done nothing but screw up since she'd knocked on his door that first day.

His knee-jerk reaction had been to repair the damage. Apologize to Roxy like mankind depended on her forgiving him and win her back. It had almost been a compulsion. *Go to her. Hold her.* He'd never thrown in the towel before, especially when something this important was on the line. Forcing himself to leave her alone might go down in history as his greatest accomplishment. If he wanted her to be happy, though, did he have a choice?

A knock on his door.

Louis didn't move. If he just stayed perfectly still, they would go away. He didn't want to see anyone or hear them say words like *You'll get over her, give it time, porn cleanse* . . . blah blah blah. For the moment, he didn't want to get over her. If he did that, he wouldn't be able to think about her, and he wanted to hold on to every minute they'd spent together as long as possible. So whoever was at the door could fuck off.

"Louis?"

He groaned into the throw pillow. Great. Now he was hearing her voice? He'd been right about going around the bend. Goddammit, he missed her so much. How did he fuck this up so bad?

"McNally, I really need you to open the door."

"Go away, voice. I already ate the Elvis Cheeto."

A long stretch of silence passed. Louis jerked into a sitting position. Maybe he didn't want the voice to leave. Maybe he wanted it to stay. Oh yeah. Definitely, stay. "Are you still there?" he called.

"Yes. Although now I'm nervous about what I'm going to find in there."

Louis looked around the apartment, feeling as though he was seeing it for the first time. Food containers, beer bottles, clothes that apparently hadn't made it to the hamper were strewn about his living room. Perfect. On top of ruining people's lives, he was also a slob.

"You *should* be nervous. It's not pretty in here."

"That's okay. I'm not a judgmental rabbit."

Louis's head snapped up. Was it possible . . . ?

His feet had carried him to the door before the hopeful thought had finished processing. He looked through the peephole and felt as though hands were squeezing his throat, cutting off his oxygen.

A giant pink bunny stood on the other side.

"Rox?"

"You know anyone else who dresses like this?" He turned the lock quickly and opened the door. *Please don't let this be a freaky hallucination.* His hands itched to tug the mask off her face, but she beat him to it. The hand holding it dropped to her side. He watched the mask hit the floor out of the corner of his eyes, because he couldn't stop looking at her face. Every detail had been catalogued in a matter of seconds, from her exhausted eyes to the lips he missed kissing so bad it caused him physical pain. "Oh no, Louis," the lips said.

She sounded so sad that he took a step forward. "What?"

"You look like shit."

His face broke into a smile for the first time in a week. It felt so good to be standing near her, listening to her talk, inhaling the smell of cherry blossoms. "I've been avoiding mirrors." He swallowed hard, barely resisting the urge to reach for her. "Why did you come?"

Roxy sucked in a slow breath. "I'm sorry I blamed you for what happened. That was horrible of me." He was mesmerized by her green eyes, glassy with tears. Tried to focus on them so her words wouldn't open a dam inside his chest. "One of the things I love about you is this responsibility you feel to help people. I can't love that part of you and be mad when you turn it on me. It makes me a hypocrite."

"No. I'm the one who's sorry, Rox—"

"Wait. Let me finish." She appeared to steel herself. "This acting thing . . . I *am* going to do it on my own. It's important to me. But I don't want to *be* on my own. Not now. I know what it's like to be with you, and it's a really amazing place to be." A tear leaked out, tracking down her cheek. "I miss you so much," she ended on a whisper. "Be with me again? Please?"

So light. He felt so *light,* as if he might float to the ceiling if she wasn't there to anchor him. Not willing to be without her in his arms another second, he lunged across the threshold and dragged her up against his body. The sob she released into his neck sounded relieved, leaving him utterly baffled. Had she actually thought he would say no to this? To her?

"Roxy, I was never without you, believe me. Not for a single second." He wrapped her hair in his fist and brought it to his nose, inhaling deeply. "The real thing is a lot better, though. Please don't go away again. I start seeing dead rock stars in my snack foods."

"I won't. That's crazy, but I won't." She pulled back slightly and kissed his mouth. It sent a final bolt of relief, bliss, straight through him. "I'm fucked up over you, Louis."

"I'm fucked up over you, too, Rox."

Her laugh was a half sob. "Good. Let's go inside. You take a shower while I get out of this bunny suit."

"Did I mention you're a genius?"

He lifted her into his arms and strode inside, kicking the door shut behind him.

Just a man and his bunny.

Don't miss the other books in the
Broke and Beautiful series . . .

Need Me and Make Me

The full series is available now wherever books are sold.

And keep an eye out for the next book from
#1 *New York Times* bestselling author Tessa Bailey . . .

Wreck the Halls

Coming October 2023
Read on for a sneak peek at this fun,
spicy holiday rom-com!

Prologue

The second Beat Dawkins entered the television studio, it stopped raining outside.

Sunshine tumbled in through the open door, wreathing him in a halo of glory, pedestrians retracting their umbrellas and tipping their hats in gratitude.

Across the room, Melody witnessed Beat's arrival the way an astronomer might observe a once-in-a-millennium asteroid streaking across the sky. Her hormones activated, testing the forgiveness of her powder-fresh-scented Lady Speed Stick. She'd only gotten braces two days earlier. Now those metal wires felt like train tracks in her mouth. Especially while watching Beat breeze with such effortless grace into the downtown studio where they would be shooting interviews for the documentary.

At age sixteen, Melody was in the middle of an awkward phase—to put it mildly. Sweat was an uncontrollable entity. She didn't know how to smile anymore without looking like a constipated gargoyle. Her milk chocolate mane had been carefully styled for this afternoon, but her hair couldn't be tricked into forgetting about the humidity currently plaguing New York, and now it was frizzing to really *accentuate* the rubber bands connecting her incisors.

Then there was Beat.

Utterly, effortlessly gorgeous.

His chestnut-colored hair was damp from the rain, his light blue eyes sparkling with mirth. Someone handed him a towel as soon as he crossed the threshold and he took it without looking, rubbing it over his locks and leaving them wild, standing on end, amusing everyone in the room. A woman in a headset ran a lint brush down the arm of his indigo suit and he gave her a grateful, winning smile, visibly flustering her.

How could she herself and this boy possibly be the same age?

Not only that, but they'd also been named by their mothers as perfect complements to each other. Beat and Melody. They were the offspring of America's most legendary female rock duo, Steel Birds. Since the band had already broken up by the time Beat and Melody were born, their names were bestowed quite by accident, without the members consulting each other. Decidedly *not* the happiest of coincidences. Not to mention, children of legends with significant names were supposed to be interesting. Remarkable.

Obviously, Beat was the only one who was meeting expectations.

Unless you counted the fact that she'd chosen teal rubber bands.

Which had seemed a lot more daring in the sterility of the orthodontist's office.

"Melody," someone called to her right. The simple act of having her name shouted across the busy room caused Mel to be *bathed in fire*, but okay. Now the backs of her knees were sweating—and oh God, *Beat was looking at her*.

Time froze.

They'd never actually met before.

Every article about their mothers and the highly publicized band breakup in 1993 mentioned Beat and Melody in the same breath, but they were locking eyes for the very first time IRL. She needed to think of something interesting to say.

I was going to go with clear rubber bands, but teal felt more punk rock.

Sure. Maybe she could cap that statement off with some finger guns and really drive home the fact that he'd gotten all the cool rock royalty genes. Oh God, her feet were sweating now. Her sandals were going to squeak when she walked.

"Melody!" called the voice again.

She tore her attention off the godlike vision that was Beat Dawkins to find the producer waving her into one of the cordoned-off interview suites. Just inside the door was a camera, a giant boom mic, a director's chair. The interview about her mother's career hadn't even started yet and she already knew the questions she would be answering. Maybe she could just pop in very quickly, recite her usual responses, and save everyone some time?

No, I can't sing like my mother.

We don't talk about the band breakup.

Yes, my mother is currently a nudist and yes, I've seen her naked a startling number of times.

Of course, it would be amazing for fans if Steel Birds reunited.

No, it will never happen. Not in a million, trillion years. Sorry.

"We're ready for you," sang the producer, tapping her wrist.

Melody nodded, flushing hotter at the suggestion she was holding things up. "Coming."

She snuck one final glance at Beat and walked in the direction of her interview room. That was it, she guessed. She'd probably never see him in person again—

"Wait!"

One word from Beat and the humming studio quieted, ground to a halt.

The prince had spoken.

Melody stopped with one foot poised in the air, turning her head slowly. *Please let him be talking to me*, otherwise the fact that she'd stopped at his command would be a pitiful mistake. Also, *please let him be talking to someone else.* The train tracks in her mouth were approximately four hundred pounds per inch, the teal dress she'd worn—oh God—to match her rubber bands, didn't fit right in the boob region. Other girls her age managed to look normal. *Good*, even.

What was it *TMZ* had said about her?

Melody Gallard: always a before picture, never an after.

Beat *was* talking to her, however.

Not only that, but he was also jogging over in this athletic, effortless way, the way a celebrity might approach the mound at a baseball game to throw out the ceremonial first pitch, the crowd cheering him on. His hair had arranged itself back to a perfect coif, no evidence of the rain she could see, his mouth in a bemused half smile.

Beat slowed to a stop in front of her, rubbing at the back of his neck and glancing around at their rapt audience, as if he'd acted without thinking and was now bashful about it. And the fact that he could be shy or self-conscious with charisma pouring out of his eyeballs was astounding. Who *was* this creature? How could they possibly share a connection?

"Hey," he breathed, coming in closer than Melody expected, that one move making them coconspirators. He wasn't overly tall, maybe five eleven, but her eyes were level with his chin. His sculpted, clean-shaven chin. Wow, he smelled so good. Like a freshly laundered blanket with some fireplace smoke clinging to it. Maybe she should switch from powder fresh Speed Stick to something a little more mature. Like ocean surf. "Hey, Mel. Can I call you that?"

No one had ever shortened her name before. Not her mother, classmates, or any of the nannies she'd had over the years. A nickname was something that should be attained over time, after a long acquaintance with someone, but Beat calling her Mel somehow seemed totally normal. Their names were counterparts, after all. They'd been named as a pair, whether it had been intentional or not.

"Sure," she whispered, trying not to stare at his throat. Or inhale him. "You can call me Mel."

Was this her first crush? Was it supposed to happen this fast? She usually found members of a different sex sort of . . .

uninspiring. They didn't make her pulse race, the way this one did. *Say something else before you bore him to death.*

"You stopped the rain," she blurted.

His eyebrows shot up. "What?"

I'm dissolving. I'm being absorbed by the floor. "When you walked in, the rain just . . . stopped." She snapped her fingers. "Like you'd turned it off with a switch."

When Melody was positive that he would cringe and make an excuse to walk away, Beat smiled instead. That lopsided one that made her feel funny *everywhere*. "I should have thought of switching it off before walking two blocks in a downpour." He laughed and exhaled at the same time, studying her face. "It's . . . crazy, right? Finally meeting?"

"Yeah." The word burst out of Melody and quite unexpectedly, her chest started to swell. "It's definitely crazy."

He nodded slowly, never taking his eyes off her face.

She'd heard of people like him.

People who could make you feel like you were the only one in the room. The world. She'd believed in the existence of such unicorns, she just never in her wildest dreams expected to be given the undivided attention of one. It was like bathing in the brightest of sunlight.

"If things had been different with our mothers, we probably would have grown up together," he said, blue eyes twinkling. "We might even be best friends."

"Oh," she said with a knowing look. "I don't think so."

His amusement only spread. "No?"

"I don't mean that to be offensive," Melody rushed to say. "I just . . . I tend to keep to myself, and you seem more . . ."

"Extroverted." He shrugged a single shoulder. "Yeah. I am." He waved a hand to indicate the room, the crew who were still captivated by the first—maybe only—meeting of Beat Dawkins and Melody Gallard. "You might think I'd be into this. Talking, being on camera." He lowered his voice to a whisper. "But it's always the same questions. Can you sing, too? Does your mother ever talk about the breakup?"

"Will there ever be a reunion?" Melody chimed in.

"Nope," they said at the same exact time—and laughed.

Beat eventually turned serious. "Look, I hope this isn't out of line, but I notice the way the tabloids treat you. Online and off. It's . . . different from how they treat me." Fire scaled the sides of her neck and gripped her ears. Of course he'd seen the cringe-inducing critiques of Melody. They were usually included in articles that profiled him, as well. The most recent one had whittled her entire existence down to the line, *In the case of Trina Gallard's daughter, the apple didn't just fall far from the tree, it's more of a lemon.* "I always wonder if it bothers you. Or if you're able to blow that bullshit off."

"Oh, I mean . . ." She laughed, too loudly, waved a hand on a floppy fist. "It's fine. People expect those gossip sites to be snarky. They're just doing their job."

He said nothing. Just watched her with a little wrinkle between his brows.

"I'm lying," she whisper-blurted. "It bothers me."

His perfect head tilted ever so slightly to one side. "Okay." He nodded, as if he'd made an important decision about something. "Okay."

"Okay what?"

"Nothing." His gaze ran a lap around her face. "You're not a lemon, by the way. Not even close." He squinted, but not enough to fully hide the twinkle. "More of a peach."

She swallowed the dreamy sigh that tried to escape. "Maybe so. Peaches do have pretty thin skin."

"Yeah, but they have a tough center."

Something grew and grew inside of Melody. Something she'd never felt before. A kinship, a bond, a connection. She couldn't come up with a word for it. Only knew that it seemed almost cosmic or preordained. And in that moment, for the first time in her life, she was angry with her mother for her part in breaking up the band. She could have known this boy sooner? Felt . . . *understood* sooner?

Someone in a headset approached Beat and tapped his shoulder. "We'd like to get the interview started, if you're ready?"

Unbelievably, he was still looking at Melody. "Yeah, sure."

Did he sound disappointed?

"I better go, too," Melody said, holding out her hand for a shake.

Beat studied her hand for several seconds, then gave her a narrow-eyed look—as if to say, *don't be silly*—and pulled her into the hug of a lifetime. The hug. Of a lifetime. In a millisecond, she was warm in the most pleasant, sweat-free way. All the way down to the soles of her feet. Light-headedness swept in. She'd not only been granted the honor of smelling this boy's perfect neck, he was encouraging her with a palm to the back of her head. He squeezed her close, before brushing his hand down the back of her hair. Just once. But it was the most beautiful sign of affection she'd ever been offered, and it wrote itself messily all over her heart.

"Hey." He pulled back with a serious expression, taking Melody by the shoulders. "Listen to me, Mel. You live here in New York, I live in LA. I don't know when I'll see you again, but . . . I guess it just feels important, like I need to tell you . . ." He frowned over his own discomposure, which she assumed was rarer than a solar eclipse. "What happened between our mothers has nothing to do with us. Okay? Nothing. If you ever need anything, or maybe you've been asked the same question forty million times and can't take it anymore, just remember that I understand." He shook his head. "We've got this big thing in common, you and me. We have a . . ."

"Bond?" she said breathlessly.

"*Yeah.*"

She could have wept all over him.

"We *do*," he continued, kissing her on the forehead hard and pulling Melody back into the second hug of a lifetime. "I'll find a way to get you my number, Peach. If you ever need anything, call me, okay?"

"Okay," she whispered, heart and hormones in a frenzy. He'd given her a *nickname*. She wrapped her arms around him and held tight, giving herself a full five seconds, before forcing herself to release Beat and step back. "Same for you." She struggled to keep her breathing at a normal pace. "Call me if you ever need someone who understands." The next part wouldn't stay tucked inside of her. "We can pretend we've been best friends all along."

To her relief, that lopsided smile was back. "It wouldn't be so hard, Mel."

A bell rang somewhere on the set, breaking the spell. Everyone flurried into motion around them. Beat was swept in one direction, Melody in the other. But her pulse didn't stop pounding for hours after their encounter.

True to his word, Beat found a way to provide her with his number, through an assistant at the end of her interview. She could never find the courage to use it, though. Not even on her most difficult days. And he never called her, either.

That was the beginning and the end of her fairy-tale association with Beat Dawkins.

Or so she thought.

Chapter 1

December 1
Present Day

Beat stood shivering on the sidewalk outside of his thirtieth birthday party.

At least, he assumed a party was waiting for him inside the restaurant. His friends had been acting mysterious for weeks. If he could only move his legs, he would walk inside and act surprised. He'd hug each of them in turn, like they deserved. Make them explain every step of the planning process and praise them for being so crafty. He'd be the ultimate friend.

And the ultimate fraud.

When the phone started vibrating again in his hand, his stomach gave an unholy churn, so intense he had to concentrate hard on breathing through it. A couple passed him on the sidewalk, shooting him some curious side-eye. He smiled at them in reassurance, but it felt weak, and they only walked faster. He looked down at his phone, already knowing an unknown caller would be displayed on the screen. Same as last time. And the time before.

Over a year and a half had passed since the last time his blackmailer had contacted him. He'd given the man the largest sum of money yet to go away and assumed the harassment was over. Beat was just beginning to feel normal again. Until the message he'd received tonight on the way to his own birthday party.

I'm feeling talkative, Beat. Like I need to get some things off my chest.

It was the same pattern as last time. The blackmailer contacted him out of the blue, no warning, and then immediately became persistent. His demands came on like a blitz, a symphony beginning in the middle of its crescendo. They left no room for negotiation, either. Or reasoning. It was a matter of giving this man what he wanted or having a secret exposed that could rock the very foundation of his family's world.

No big deal.

He took a deep breath, paced a short distance in the opposite direction of the restaurant. Then he hit call and lifted the phone to his ear.

His blackmailer answered on the first ring.

"Hello again, Beat."

A red-hot iron dropped in Beat's stomach.

Did the man's voice sound more on edge than previous years? Almost agitated?

"We agreed this was over," Beat said, his grip tight around the phone. "I was never supposed to hear from you again."

A raspy sigh filled the line. "The thing about the truth is, it never really goes away."

With those ominous words echoing in his ear, a sort of surreal calmness settled over Beat. It was one of those moments where he looked around and wondered what in the hell had led him to this time and place. Was he even standing here at all? Or was he trapped in an endless dream? Suddenly the familiar sights of Greenwich Street, only a few blocks from his office, looked like a movie set. Christmas lights in the shapes of bells and Santa heads and holly leaves hung from streetlights, and an early December cold snap that turned his breath to frostbitten mist in front of his face.

He was in Tribeca, close enough to the Financial District to see coworkers sharing sneaky cigarettes on the sidewalk after too much to drink, still dressed in their office attire at eight P.M. A rogue elf traipsed down the street yelling into his phone. A cab drove by slowly, wheels traveling over wet sludge from the brief afternoon snowfall, "Have a Holly Jolly Christmas" drifting out through the window.

"Beat." The voice in his ear brought him back to reality. "I'm going to need double the amount as last time."

Nausea lifted all the way to his throat, making his head feel light. "I can't do that. I don't personally have that kind of liquid cash and I will not touch the foundation money. This needs to be *over*."

"Like I said—"

"The truth never goes away. I heard you."

Silence was heavy on the line. "I'm not sure I appreciate the way you're speaking to me, Beat. I have a story to tell. If you're not going to pay me to keep it to myself, I'll get what I need from *20/20* or *People* magazine. They'd love every salacious word."

And his parents would be ruined.

The truth would devastate his father.

His mother's sterling reputation would be blown to smithereens.

The public perception of Octavia Dawkins would nose-dive, and thirty years of the charitable work she'd done would mean nothing. There would only be the story.

There would only be the damning truth.

"Don't do that." Beat massaged the throbbing sensation between his eyes. "My parents don't deserve it."

"Oh, yeah? Well, I didn't deserve to be thrown out of the band, either." The man snorted. "Don't talk about shit you don't know, kid. You weren't there. Are you going to help me out or should I start making calls? You know, I've had this reality show producer contact me twice. Maybe she would be a good place to start."

The night air turned sharper in his lungs. "What producer? What's her name?"

Was it the same woman who'd been emailing and calling Beat for the last six months? Offering him an obscene sum of money to participate in a reality show about reuniting Steel Birds? He hadn't bothered returning any of the correspondence because he'd gotten so many similar offers over the years. The public demand for a reunion hadn't waned one iota since the nineties and now, thanks to one of the band's hits going viral decades after its release, the demand was suddenly more relevant than ever.

"Danielle something," said his blackmailer. "It doesn't matter. She's only one of my options."

"Right."

How much had she offered Beat? He didn't remember the

exact amount. Only that she'd dangled a lot of money. Possibly seven figures.

"How do we make this stop once and for all?" Beat asked, feeling and sounding like a broken record. "How can I guarantee this is the last time?"

"You'll have to take my word for it."

Beat was already shaking his head. "I need something in writing."

"Not happening. It's my word or nothing. How long do you need to pull the money together?"

Goddammit. This was real. This was happening. *Again.*

The last year and a half had been nothing but a reprieve. Deep down, he'd known that, right? "I need some time. Until February, at least."

"You have until Christmas."

The jagged edge of panic slid into his chest. "That's less than a month away."

A humorless laugh crackled down the line. "If you can make your selfish cow of a mother look like a saint to the public, you can get me eight hundred thousand by the twenty-fifth."

"No, I can't," Beat said through his teeth. "It's impossible—"

"Do it or I talk."

The line went dead.

Beat stared down at the silent device for several seconds, trying to pull himself together. Text messages from his friends were piling up on the screen, asking him where he was. Why he was late for dinner. He should have been used to pretending everything was normal by now. He'd been doing it for five years, since the first time the blackmailer made contact. Smile. Listen intently. Be grateful. Be grateful at all times for what he had.

How much longer could he pull this off?

A couple of minutes later, he walked into a pitch-black party room.

The lights came on and a sea of smiling faces appeared, shouting, "*Surprise!*"

And even though his skin was as cold as ice beneath his suit, he staggered back with a dazed grin, laughing the way everyone would expect. Accepting hugs, backslaps, handshakes, and kisses on the cheeks.

Nothing is wrong.

I have it all under control.

Beat struggled through the inundation of stress and attempted to appreciate the good around him. The room full of people who had gathered in his honor. He owed them that after all the effort they'd clearly put in. One of the benefits of being born in December was Christmas-themed birthdays, and his friends had laid it on thick. White twinkling lights were wrapped around fresh garland and hanging from the rafters of the restaurant's banquet room. Poinsettias sprung from glowing vases. The scent of cinnamon and pine was heavy in the air and a fireplace roared in the far corner of the space. His friends, colleagues, and a smattering of cousins wore Santa hats.

As far as themes went, Christmas was the clear winner, and he couldn't complain. As far back as he could remember, it had been his favorite holiday. The time of year when he could sit still and wear pajamas all day and let his head clear. His family always kept it about the three of them, no outsiders, so he didn't have to be *on*. He could just be.

One of Beat's college buddies from NYU wrestled him into a playful headlock and he endured it, knowing the guy meant well. God, they all did. His friends weren't aware of the kind of strain he was under. If they did, they would probably try to help. But he couldn't allow that. Couldn't allow a single person to know the delicate reason why he was being blackmailed.

Or who was behind it.

Beat noticed everyone around him was laughing and he joined in, pretending he'd heard the joke, but his brain was working through furious rounds of math. Presenting and discarding solutions. Eight hundred thousand dollars. Double what he'd paid this man last time. Where would he come up with it? And what about next time? Would they venture into the millions?

"You didn't think we'd let your thirtieth pass without an obnoxious celebration, did you?" Vance said, elbowing him in the ribs. "You know us better than that."

"You're damn right I do." A glass of champagne appeared in Beat's hand. "What time is the clown arriving to make balloon animals?"

The group erupted into a disbelieving roar. "How the hell—"

"You ruined the surprise!"

"Like you said"—Beat saluted them, smiling until they all dropped the indignation and grinned back—"I know you."

They don't know you, *though. Do they?*

His smile faltered slightly, but he covered it up with a gulp of champagne, setting the empty glass down on the closest table, noting the peppermints strewn among the confetti. The paper pieces were in the shape of little B's. Pictures of Beat dotted the refreshment table in plastic holders. One of him jumping off a cliff in Costa Rica. Another one of him graduating in a cap and gown from business school. Yet another photo depicted him on-stage introducing his mother, world-famous Octavia Dawkins at a charity dinner he'd organized recently for her foundation. He was smiling in every single picture.

It was like looking at a stranger. He didn't even know that guy.

When he jumped off that cliff in Central America, he'd been in the middle of procuring funds to pay off the blackmailer the first time. Back when he could manage the sum. Fifty thousand here or there. Sure, it meant a little shuffling of his assets, but nothing he couldn't handle in the name of keeping his parents' names from being dragged through the mud.

He couldn't manage this much of a payoff alone. The foundation had more than enough money in its coffers, but it would be a cold day in hell before he stole from the charity he'd built with his mother. Not happening. That cash went to worthy causes. Well-deserved scholarships for performing arts students who couldn't afford the costs associated with training, education, and living expenses. That money did not go to blackmail.

So where would he get the funds?

Maybe a quick call to his accountant would calm his nerves. He'd invested in a few start-ups last year. Maybe he could pull those investments now? There had to be something.

There isn't, whispered a voice in the back of his head.

Feeling even more chilled than before, Beat forced a casual expression onto his face. "Excuse me for a few minutes, I just need to make a phone call."

"To whom?" Vance asked. "Everyone you know is in this room."

That was not true.

His parents weren't here.

But that's not who his mind immediately landed on—and it was ridiculous that he should still be thinking about Melody Gallard fourteen years after meeting her *one time*. He could still recall that afternoon so vividly, though. Her smile, the way she whisper-talked, as if she wasn't all that used to talking at all. The way she couldn't seem to look him in the eye, then all of a sudden she couldn't seem to look anywhere else. Neither had he.

And he'd hugged thousands of people in his life, but she was the only one he could still feel in his arms. They were meant to be friends. Unfortunately, he'd never called. She'd never used his number, either. Now it was too late. Still, when Vance said, *Everyone you know is in this room,* Beat thought of her right away.

It *felt* like he knew Melody—and she wasn't here.

She might know him the best out of everyone if he'd kept in touch.

"Maybe he needs to call a woman," someone sang from the other side of the group. "We know how Beat likes to keep his relationships private."

"When I find a woman who can survive my friends, I'll bring her around."

"Oh, come on."

"We'd be on our best behavior."

Beat raised a skeptical brow. "You don't have a best behavior."

Someone picked up a handful of B confetti and threw it at him. He flicked a piece off his shoulder without missing a beat, satisfied that he'd once again diverted their interest in his love life. He kept that private for good reason. "One phone call and I'll be back. Don't start the balloon animals without me. I'm going to see if the artist can create me a sense of privacy." He gave them all a grin to let them know he was joking. "It means a lot that you organized this party for me. Thank you. It's . . . everything a guy could hope for."

That sappy moment earned him a chorus of boos and several more tosses of confetti until he had to duck and cover his way out of the room. But as soon as he was outside, his smile slid away. Back on the sidewalk like before, he stood for a full minute looking down at the phone in his hand. He could call his accountant. It would be a waste, though. After five years of having the blackmailer on his back like a parasite, he'd wrung himself dry. There simply wasn't eight hundred thousand dollars to spare.

You know, I've had this reality show producer contact me twice. Maybe she would be a good place to start.

His blackmailer's words came back to him. Danielle something. She'd contacted Beat, too. Had a popular network behind her, if Beat recalled correctly. His assistant usually dealt with inquiries pertaining to Steel Birds, but he'd forwarded this particular request to Beat because of the size of the offer and the producer's clout.

Instead of calling his accountant, he searched his inbox for the name Danielle—and he found the email after a little scrolling.

Dear Mr. Dawkins,

Allow me to introduce myself. I'm your ticket to becoming a household name.

Since Steel Birds broke up in ninety-three, the public has been desperate for a reunion of the women who not only cowrote some of the world's most beloved ballads, but inspired a movement. Empowered little girls to get out there, find a microphone, and express their discontent, no matter who it pissed off. I was one of those little girls.

You're a busy man, so let me be brief. I want to give the public the reunion we've been dreaming about since ninety-three. There are no better catalysts than the children of these legendary women to make this happen. It is my profound wish for you, Mr. Dawkins, and Melody Gallard to join forces to bring your parents back together.

The Applause Network is prepared to offer each of you a million dollars.

Sincerely,
Danielle Doolin

Beat dropped the phone to his thigh. Had he seriously only skimmed an email that passionate? He hadn't even made it to the middle the first time he'd seen the correspondence. That much was obvious, because he would have remembered the part about Melody. Every time someone mentioned her, he got a firm sock to the gut.

He was getting one now.

Beat had zero desire to be a household name. Never had, never would. He liked working behind the scenes at his mother's foundation. Giving the occasional speech or social media interview was necessary. Ever since "Rattle the Cage" had gone viral, the requests had been coming in by the mother lode, but remaining out of the limelight was preferable to him.

However.

A million dollars would solve his problem.

He needed to solve it. *Fast.*

And if—and it was a *huge* if—Beat agreed to the reality show, he'd need to talk to Melody first. They might have grown up in the same weird celebrity offspring limelight, but they'd gotten vastly different treatment from the press. He'd been praised as some kind of golden boy, while every single one of Melody's physical attributes had been dissected through paparazzi lenses—all when she was still a *minor.* He'd watched it from afar, horrified.

So much so that the first and only time they'd met, he'd been rocked by protectiveness so deep, he still felt it to this very day.

Was there any way to avoid bringing her back into the spotlight if he attempted to reunite Steel Birds? Or would she be dragged into the story, simply because of her connection to the band?

God, he didn't know. But there was no way in hell Beat would agree to anything unless Melody was okay with him stirring up this hornet's nest. He'd have to meet with her. In person. See her face and be positive she didn't have reservations.

Beat's pulse kicked into a gallop.

Fourteen years had passed and he'd thought of her . . . a weird amount. Wondering what she was doing, if she'd seen whatever latest television special was playing about their mothers, if she was happy. That last one plagued him the most. Was Melody happy? Was he?

Would everything be different if he'd just called her?

Beat pulled up the contact number for his accountant, but never hit call. Instead, he reopened the email from Danielle Doolin and tapped the cell number in her email signature, with no idea the kind of magic he was setting into motion.

Chapter 2

Melody stood at the top of the bocce ball court, the red wooden ball in hand.

This throw would determine whether her team won or lost.

How? How had the onus of demise or victory landed on her birdlike shoulders? Who'd overseen the lineup tonight? She was their weakest player. They usually buried her somewhere in the middle. Her heartbeat boomed so loudly, she could barely hear the *Elf* soundtrack pumping through the bar speakers, Zooey Deschanel's usually angelic voice hitting her ears more like a witch's cackle.

Her team stood at the sides of the lane, hands clasped together like it was the final point at Wimbledon or something, instead of the bocce bar league. This was low stakes, right? Her boss and best friend, Savelina, had *assured* her this was low stakes. Otherwise, Melody wouldn't have joined the team and put their success at high risk. She'd be at home watching some holiday baking championship on the Food Network in an adult onesie where she belonged.

"You can do it, Mel," Savelina shouted, followed by several cheers and whistles from her coworkers at the bookstore. She hadn't known them well in the beginning of the season, considering she worked in the basement restoring young adult books and almost never looked up from her task. But thanks to this semitorturous bocce league, she'd gotten to know them a lot better. She *liked* them.

Oh, please God, grant me enough skill not to let them down.

Ha. If she didn't screw this up, it would be a miracle.

"Do you need a time-out?" asked her boss.

"What made you think that?" Melody shouted. "The fact that I'm frozen in fear?"

The sprinkle of laughter boosted her confidence a little, but not by much. And then she made the mistake of glancing backward over her shoulder and finding the entire Park Slope bar watching the final throw with bated breath. It was the equivalent of looking down at the ground while walking on a tightrope. Not that she'd ever experienced such a thing. The craziest risk she'd taken lately was hoop earrings. *Hoops!*

Now she was breathing so hard, her glasses were fogging up.

Was everyone looking at her butt?

They had to be. She looked at everyone's butts, even when she tried not to. What would make this crowd any different? Did they think her floor-length pleated skirt was a weird choice for bocce? Because it totally was.

"Mel!" Savelina gestured to the bocce lane with her pint of

beer. "We're going to run out of time. Just get the ball as close to the jack as possible. Slice of cake."

Easy for Savelina to say. She owned a bookstore and dressed like a stoned bohemian artist. She could pull off gladiator sandals and had a favorite brand of oolong tea. Of course she thought bocce was simple.

The crowd started cheering behind Melody in encouragement, which was honestly very nice. Brooklynites got a bad rap, but they were actually quite friendly as long as they were being offered drink specials and strangers regularly complimented their dogs.

"Okay! Okay, I'm going to do it."

Melody took a deep breath and rolled the red wooden ball across the hard-packed sand. It came to a stop at the farthest position possible from the jack. It wasn't even remotely close.

Their opponents cheered and clinked pint glasses, the home team bar heaving a collective sigh of disappointment. They probably thought an underdog-to-hero story was unfolding right in front of their eyes, but no. Not with Melody in the starring role.

Savelina approached with a sympathetic expression on her face, squeezing Mel's shoulder with an elegant hand. "We'll win the next one."

"We haven't won a game all season."

"Victory isn't always the point," her boss suggested. "It's trying in the first place."

"Thanks, Mom."

Savelina's tight, brown curls shook with laughter. "Two weeks from now, we have the final game of the season and I have a good feeling about it. We're going to head into Christmas fresh from a win and you're going to be a part of it."

Mel didn't hide her skepticism.

"Let me clarify," Savelina said. "You *must* be a part of it. We only have enough players if you show up. You're not taking off early to visit family or anything, are you?"

As a rare book restoration expert, Mel's work schedule was loose. She could take a project home with her, if needed, and her presence in the store largely depended on whether or not there was even a book that currently required tender loving care. "Uh, no." Mel forced a smile onto her face, even though a little dent formed in her heart. "No, I don't have any plans. My mother is . . . you know. She's doing her thing. I'm doing mine. But I'll see her in February on my birthday," she rushed to add.

"That's right. She always comes to New York for your birthday."

"Right."

Mel did the tight smile/nodding thing she always did when the conversation turned to her mother. Even the most well-intentioned people couldn't help but be openly curious about Trina Gallard. She was an international icon, after all. Savelina was more conscientious than most when it came to giving Mel privacy, but the thirst for knowledge about the rock star inevitably bled through. Mel understood. She did.

She just didn't know enough about her mother to give anyone what they wanted.

That was the sad truth. Trina love-bombed her daughter once a year and once a year only. Like a one-night sold-out show at the

Garden that left her with a hangover and really expensive merch she never wore again.

Melody could see Savelina was losing the battle with the need to ask deeper questions about Trina, probably because it was the end of the night and she'd had six beers. So Mel grabbed her kelly green peacoat from where it hung on the closest stool, tugged it on around her shoulders, and looked for a way to excuse herself. "I'm going to settle my tab at the bar." She leaned in and planted a quick kiss on Savelina's expertly highlighted brown cheek. "I'll see you during the week?"

"Yeah!" Savelina said too quickly, hiding her obvious disappointment. "See you soon."

Briefly, Mel battled the urge to give her friend something, anything. Even Trina's favorite brand of cereal—Lucky Charms—but the information faltered on her tongue. It always did. Speaking with any kind of authority on her mother felt false when most days, it felt as though she barely knew the woman.

"Okay." Mel nodded, turned, and wove through some Friday night revelers toward the bar, apologizing to a few customers who'd witnessed her anticlimactic underdog story. Before she could reach the bar, she made sure Savelina wasn't watching, then veered toward the exit instead—because she didn't really have a bar tab to settle. Customers who recognized her as Trina Gallard's daughter had been sending her drinks all night. She'd had so many Shirley Temples she was going to be peeing grenadine for a week.

Cold winter air chilled her cheeks as soon as she stepped out onto the sidewalk.

The cheerful holiday music and energetic conversations grew muffled behind her as soon as the door snicked shut. Why did it always feel so good to leave somewhere?

Guilt poked holes in her gut. Didn't she *want* to have friends? Who didn't?

And why did she feel alone whether she was with people or not?

She turned around and looked back through the frosty glass, surveying the bargoers, the merry revelers, the quiet ones huddled in darkened nooks. So many kinds of people and they all seemed to have one thing in common. They enjoyed company. None of them appeared to be holding their breath until they could leave. They didn't seem to be pretending to be comfortable when in reality, they were stressing about every word out of their mouth and how they looked, whether or not people *liked* them. And if they did, was it because they were a celebrity's daughter, rather than because of their actual personality? Because of who Melody was?

Melody turned from the lively scene with a lump in her throat and started to walk up the incline of Union Street toward her apartment. Before she made it two steps, however, a woman shifted into the light several feet ahead of her. Melody stopped in her tracks. The stranger was so striking, her smile so confident, it was impossible to move forward without acknowledging her. She had dark blond hair that fell in perfect waves onto the shoulders of a very expensive looking overcoat. One that had tiny gold chains in weird places that served no function, just for the sake of fashion. Simply put, she was radiant and she didn't belong outside of a casual neighborhood bar.

"Miss Gallard?"

The woman knew her name? Had she been lying in wait for her? Not totally surprising, but it had been a long while since she'd encountered this kind of brazenness from a reporter.

"Excuse me," Melody said, hustling past her. "I'm not answering any questions about my mother—"

"I'm Danielle Doolin. You might recall some emails I sent you earlier this year? I'm a producer with the Applause Network."

Melody kept walking. "I get a lot of emails."

"Yes, I'm sure you do," said Danielle, falling into step beside her. Keeping pace, even though she was wearing three-inch heels, her footwear a stark contrast to Melody's flat ankle boots. "The public has a vested interest in you and your family."

"You realize I was never really given a choice about that."

"I do. During my brief phone call with Beat Dawkins, he expressed the same."

Melody's feet basically stopped working. The air inside of her lungs evaporated and she had no choice but to slow to a stop in the middle of the sidewalk. Beat Dawkins. She heard that name in her sleep, which was utterly ridiculous. The fact that she should still be fascinated by the man when they hadn't been in the same room in fourteen years made her cringe . . . but that was the *only* thing about Beat that made her cringe. The rest of her reactions to him could best be described as breathless, dreamlike, whimsical, and . . . sexual.

In her entire thirty-year existence, she'd never experienced attraction like she had to Beat Dawkins at age sixteen when she spent a mere five minutes in his presence. Since then her hormones could only be defined as lazy. Floating on a pool raft with a mai tai, rather than competing in a triathlon. She had the yoga pants of hormones. They were fine, they definitely *counted* as hormones, but they weren't worthy of a runway strut. Her lack of romantic aspirations was yet another reason she felt unmotivated to go out and make human connections. To be in big, social crowds where someone might show interest in her.

It was going to take something special to make her set down the mai tai and get off this raft—and so far, no one had been especially . . . rousing. A fourteen-year-old memory, though? Oh mama. It had the power to make her temperature peak. At one time it had, anyway. The recollection of her one and only encounter with Beat was growing grainy around the edges. Fading, much to her distress.

"Well." Danielle regarded Melody with open interest. "His name certainly got your attention, didn't it?"

Melody tried not to stumble over her words and failed, thanks to her tongue turning as useless as her feet. "I'm sorry, y-you'll have to refresh my memory. The emails you sent me were about . . . ?"

"Reuniting Steel Birds."

A laugh tumbled out of Melody, stirring the air with white vapor. "Wait. Beat took a phone call about *this*?" Baffled, she shook her head. "As far as I know, both of us have always maintained that a reunion is impossible. Like, on par with an Elvis comeback tour."

Danielle lifted an elegant shoulder and let it drop. "Stranger things have happened. Even Pink Floyd set aside their differences for Live 8 in 2005 and no one believed it was doable. A lot of time has passed since Steel Birds broke up. Hearts soften. Age gives a different perspective. Maybe Beat believes a reunion wouldn't be such an impossible feat after all."

It was humiliating how hard her heart was pounding in her chest. "Did . . . did he say that?"

Danielle blew air into one cheek. "He didn't *not* say it. But the fact that he contacted me about the reunion speaks for itself, right?"

Odd that Melody should feel a tad betrayed that he'd changed his position without consulting her. Why would he do that? He didn't owe her anything. Not a phone call. Nothing. "Wow." Melody cleared her throat. "You've caught me off guard."

"I apologize for that. You're very difficult to get in contact with. I had to dig quite a bit to find out where you worked. Then I saw a picture of your bocce team on the bookstore's Instagram. Thank goodness for location tags." Danielle gestured with a brisk, gloved hand to the general area. "I assure you, I wouldn't have ventured into Brooklyn in twenty-degree weather unless I had a potentially viable project on the table. One that, if done correctly, could be a cultural phenomenon. And it *would* be done correctly, because I would be overseeing production personally."

What was it like to be so confident? "I'm afraid to ask what this project entails."

"That's why I'm not going to tell you until we're in my nice, warm office with espresso and a selection of beignets in front of us."

Melody's stomach growled reluctantly. "Beignets, huh?"

"They piqued Beat's interest, as well."

"They did?" Melody's breathless tone hit her ears, cluing her in to what was happening. The tactic that was being employed. "You keep bringing him up on purpose."

Danielle studied her face closely. "He seems to be my biggest selling point. Even more than the money the network is willing to pay, I'm guessing," she murmured. "If I hadn't mentioned his name, you never would have stopped walking. Surprising, since the two of you haven't maintained any sort of contact. According to him."

"No, I know," Melody rushed to blurt, heat clinging to her face and the sides of her neck. "We don't even know each other."

And that was the God's honest truth.

Fourteen years had passed.

However. Beat was a good person. He'd proven that to her—and he couldn't have changed so drastically. The kind of character it took to do what he'd done . . .

About a month after they'd met in that humid television studio, she'd passed through the gates of her Manhattan private school, expecting to walk to class alone, as usual. But she'd been surrounded by buzzing girls that morning. Had she seen Beat Dawkins on *TMZ*?

Considering she avoided that program like the plague, she'd shaken her head. They'd cagily informed her that Beat had mentioned her during a paparazzi ambush and she might want to watch the footage. Getting through first period without exploding was nearly impossible, but she'd made it. Then she'd rushed to the bathroom and pulled up the clip on her phone. There was Beat, holding a grocery bag, a Dodgers ball cap pulled down low on his forehead, being pursued by a cameraman.

Normally, he was the type to stop and suffer through their silly questions with a golden grin. But this time, he didn't. He halted abruptly on the sidewalk and, to this day, she could still remember what came out of his mouth, word for word.

I'm done talking. You won't get another word out of me. Not until you—and all the similar outlets—stop exploiting girls for clicks. Especially my friend Melody Gallard. You praise me for nothing and disparage her no matter how hard she tries. You can fuck right off. Like I said, I'm done talking.

That day, Melody hadn't come out of the bathroom until third period, she'd been so frozen in shock and gratitude. Just to be seen. Just to have someone speak up on her behalf. That clip had been shared all over social media. For weeks. It had started a conversation about how teenage girls were being portrayed by celebrity news outlets.

Of course, their treatment of her didn't change overnight. But it slowly shifted. It lightened in degrees. Bad headlines started getting called out. Shamed.

And shockingly, her experience with the press got better.

Melody was so lost in the memory, it took her a moment to notice the smile flirting with the corners of Danielle's glossy mouth. "He's coming to my office on Monday morning for a meeting. I've come all the way here to invite you, as well." She paused, seemed to consider her next words carefully. "Beat won't agree to the reunion project unless *you* are comfortable with it moving forward. He made your approval a condition."

Melody hated the way her soul left her body at Danielle's words. It was pathetic in so many ways.

Beat Dawkins was eons and galaxies out of her league. Not only was he blindingly gorgeous, but he had *presence*. He commanded rooms full of people to give speeches for his mother's foundation. She'd seen the pictures, the occasional Instagram reel. His grid was brimming with nonstop adventures. Equally glamorous friends were pouring out of his ears. He was loved and lusted after and . . . perfect.

Beat Dawkins was perfectly perfect.

And he'd taken her into consideration.

He'd thought of her.

This whole Steel Birds reunion idea would never fly—the feelings of betrayal between their mothers ran deeper than the Atlantic Ocean—but the fact that Beat had said her name out loud to this woman basically ensured another fourteen years of infatuation. *Sad, sad girl.*

"You mentioned money," Melody said offhandedly, mostly so it wouldn't seem her entire interest was Beat-related. "How much? Just out of curiosity."

"I'll tell you at the meeting." She smiled slyly. "It's a lot, Melody. Perhaps even by the standards of a famous rock star's daughter."

A lot of money. Even to her.

Despite her trepidation, Melody couldn't help but wonder . . . was it enough cash to make her financially independent? She'd been born into comfort. A nice town house, wonderful nannies, any material item she wanted, which had mainly turned out to be books and acne medication. Her mother's love and attention remained out of reach, however. Always had—and it was beginning to feel as though it always would.

Melody's brownstone apartment was paid in full. She had an annual allowance. Lately, though, accepting her mother's generosity didn't feel right. Or good. Not when they lacked the healthy mother-daughter relationship she would gladly take instead.

Could this be her chance to stand on her own two feet?

No. Facilitating a reunion? There had to be an easier way.

"At least take the meeting," Danielle said, smiling like the cat who'd caught the canary.

The woman had her and she knew it.

To be in the same room with Beat Dawkins again . . .

She wasn't strong enough to pass up the chance.

Melody shifted in her boots and tried not to sound too eager. "What time?"

About the Author

#1 *New York Times* bestselling author TESSA BAILEY can solve all problems except for her own, so she focuses those efforts on stubborn, fictional blue-collar men and loyal, lovable heroines. She lives on Long Island, avoiding the sun and social interactions, then wonders why no one has called. Dubbed the "Michelangelo of dirty talk" by *Entertainment Weekly*, Tessa writes with spice, spirit, swoon, and a guaranteed happily ever after. Catch her on TikTok @authortessabailey or check out tessabailey.com for a complete list of her books.